MW00464343

Chaos Comes to Longbourn

A Pride and Prejudice Variation

Victoria Kincaid

This is a work of fiction. Names, characters, places, and incidents are products of the author's imagination or are used fictitiously. Any resemblance to actual events or persons, living or dead, is entirely coincidental.

Copyright © 2016 by Victoria Kincaid

All Rights Reserved

No part of this book may be used or reproduced in any manner whatsoever without written permission, except in the case of brief quotations embodied in critical articles or reviews.

Please do not participate in or encourage the piracy of copyrighted materials in violation of the author's rights. Purchase only authorized editions.

ISBN: 978-0-9975530-2-4

This book is dedicated to the wonderful Jane Austen Fan Fiction readers and authors I have encountered during my journey as a writer. Thank you all for your support. I could not do it without you!

Chapter One

Why do I wish to dance with Elizabeth Bennet?

This must have been the fiftieth time Darcy had asked himself that question. As he had seen her speaking with her sisters, the impulse to request her hand for the dance had been so strong that Darcy had only resisted by quitting the Netherfield ballroom altogether. He strode away from the room as fast as was socially acceptable, ignoring a few quizzical glances as he fought the impulse to return.

It was true that Miss Elizabeth's eyes were fine, especially when she smiled. They sparkled as if she knew some wonderful secret to happiness. And her figure was light and pleasing, particularly draped in the ivory silk gown she wore tonight. She was an accomplished dancer; he could discern her superior abilities even though she had been partnered with that oaf, the pastor who was her cousin. And her hair...all those dark curls. If Darcy could only sink his fingers into—

No! Darcy paused in the middle of the corridor, resisting the impulse to bang his head against the wall. *I must not think about her. Dancing with her is out of the question.* Her station in life was decidedly beneath his, and many members of her family ignored proper social decorum. Even friendship was out of the question. Given how much she occupied his thoughts, he should not even speak with her. Just spying her across the room wreaked havoc with his equilibrium.

Determined to leave this strange obsession behind, Darcy resumed striding along Netherfield's back hallway. He would sequester himself in the library, where he could safely pass the time until these unbidden and unnecessary sensations had passed.

He scrutinized the line of closed doors before him. Which one led to the library again? A volume of history or one of Shakespeare's plays should serve as a sufficient distraction until he recovered his wits and could once more trust himself in Elizabeth Bennet's presence.

***

"Oh…Wickham!" Lydia sighed as the man traced a line of kisses from her ear to her shoulder. Truthfully it tickled, but she stifled her giggles; the man in the dashing red coat wanted to hear noises of pleasure from her.

"Lydia," Wickham whispered. "You are the prettiest girl I ever beheld."

Oh, he was so romantic! Lydia could not suppress a delighted giggle this time. To be sure, no one had ever uttered similar words to any of her sisters. She was the first! Well, perhaps Mr. Bingley had said something similar to Jane but not while he kissed her neck.

Lydia could barely see Wickham. His form was silhouetted by the moonlight streaming in through the window, but his face was in shadow. Not that she needed to see him when she could feel him; his hands on her back, her shoulders—even her bottom—felt deliciously illicit.

"Remember that we must not tell anyone about this…little tryst," Wickham murmured. His warm breath ghosted over her bare neck.

"I will remember."

Wickham's mouth once again latched onto her neck.

Idly, Lydia wondered which room they had slipped into. After she had consumed all those cups of wine punch, Wickham had escorted her outside to the gardens behind Netherfield, but she had objected vociferously to the cold, so he had found an unlocked door which admitted them to a dark, unoccupied room at the back of the house. They had not found a candle to light the room, but from the sound of the echoes, it must be fairly large. The floor also seemed somewhat uneven, but that might have been the effect of the wine punch.

Wickham's fingers stole inside the edges of her neckline, and Lydia gasped. *What a wicked place to touch her!* He paused for a moment, observing her closely, but after she smiled, he continued his exploration.

Wickham's hand slipped further into Lydia's bodice, caressing her shoulder; he showered her mouth with sloppy, open-mouthed kisses. She moaned with a completely inauthentic enthusiasm. Denny was a far superior kisser, but he was too "proper" to do something as fun as stealing away from a dance for some laughs. Wickham was just as handsome and wore a red coat, too—and he was far more fun.

Why was it so "wicked" to be alone with a man? She was supposed to attract male attention; after all, it was the whole object of a dance. Most girls her age only attracted boys, not real men like Wickham. And the way Wickham touched her was not unpleasant—for the most part. Lydia just knew that if she gave these soldiers what they wanted from her, one of them would propose marriage. Then she would be the first Bennet sister to be married—and she, the youngest of them all! As Wickham kissed her neck, Lydia stared into the darkness and smiled at that vision.

However, an unwelcome thought struck her. What if Mr. Bingley proposed to Jane, and Lydia was still unwed? That would not do! She must redouble her efforts to capture Wickham's attention.

Lydia arched her back, pushing her breasts against Wickham's chest. Men seemed to like that, and Wickham was no exception. He groaned huskily, and his hands moved to massage her back.

A loosening at the back of her gown told her that Wickham had untied the laces that held her dress together. "Oh!" she exclaimed. This was a new experience but not necessarily unwelcome. Perhaps Wickham would propose if she allowed him this liberty.

Her dress slid off one shoulder, baring her breast to the cool air. Lydia could not prevent a shiver. In the next moment, Wickham's hand held her breast, mashing it most unpleasantly. But Lydia did not flinch. Perhaps this was the method for winning a proposal, although she had trouble imagining Mr. Bingley doing this with Jane.

Fortunately, the act was not too uncomfortable, and Lydia wanted Wickham to like her, so she would not complain. She stared into the surrounding darkness and made the little moaning noises men seemed to like. *I wonder what room we are in...?*

***

"Mama?" Elizabeth dared to interrupt her mother in mid-gossip with Mrs. Long. "Where is Lydia?"

Standing near the ballroom's windows, Elizabeth's mother could not have looked more annoyed. "Oh, I do not know!" Her hands fluttered about. "Off dancing with one of the officers, no doubt, which is what you had best be doing. They are a handsome lot!"

Elizabeth caught her mother's arm before she could rejoin the chattering ladies. "She is not dancing. I have not seen her this past half hour. Even Kitty does not know her whereabouts."

Mama shrugged carelessly. "Perhaps she is with that handsome Mr. Wickham getting some punch."

"Mr. Wickham?" Elizabeth asked. "I thought he had avoided the ball because of Mr. Darcy."

"Well, of course, Mr. Wickham wished Mr. Darcy to believe that!" Mrs. Bennet waved around her closed fan. "Mr. Darcy has such a handsome…fortune. What a shame he does not have a better character."

Elizabeth tended to agree; the man was unpleasant and proud. She had often caught him staring at her throughout the evening. No doubt he was cataloguing her every fault and misstep.

Mama flicked her fan open and fanned herself with great determination. "Mr. Wickham is here. He spoke with Kitty and Lydia not less than an hour ago."

Why did this news fill Elizabeth with unease? It was unremarkable, save that everyone in Mr. Darcy's party seemed to believe the militia officer was untrustworthy. She tended to disbelieve them, particularly after Mr. Wickham's description of how Mr. Darcy had treated him.

Well, Mr. Wickham scarcely mattered at this moment. She must locate Lydia. Elizabeth and Jane had agreed that their youngest sister should always be supervised at such occasions. But Elizabeth had lost sight of Lydia, and Jane was dancing with Mr. Bingley. Elizabeth wanted to credit Lydia with the wisdom not to slip away with a man, but she could not be certain. The thought sent terror down her spine. *What if a man hurt Lydia? Or disgraced her?* The Bennet family generated quite enough gossip already; they did not need Lydia to ignite a scandal.

Elizabeth grabbed her mother's hand. "We must find her!

Her mother tried to pull free from Elizabeth's grasp. "You do not need me."

Elizabeth would not release her. "Lydia will not heed me. You must help me find her before she does something foolish!"

Mrs. Bennet rolled her eyes, apparently annoyed at the prospect of protecting her daughter's virtue. But finally she heaved a heavy sigh. "Oh, very well!" She allowed herself to be led from the ballroom.

***

Darcy had opened three doors so far. One had proved to be a closet, and two were unused parlors. He was certain the library was along this hallway, but where? Darcy reached the last door in the hallway and opened it. The room was swathed in shadows, but the echoes and musty smell of books revealed that this was the right place. Excellent.

The Netherfield library was a particularly large room, although the collection was unexceptional. It boasted several comfortable chairs, and Darcy eagerly anticipated the escape that books would provide. Perhaps *Romeo and Juliet*…no, a comedy. *Much Ado About Nothing*? *Twelfth Night*?

A faint scuffling emanated from the other side of the room near the windows. Was there another person in the library? Someone who was sitting in the dark?

Darcy experienced a surge of anxiety and anger on Bingley's behalf. Was a guest taking advantage of Bingley's generosity? He could think of no good reason—but a number of bad ones—why someone would lurk in a darkened library.

There had been an oil lamp on the small table in the hallway. After opening the door, Darcy was able to reach out his arm until his fingers closed on the handle. When he pulled the lamp back into the library warm yellow glow illuminated his immediate neighborhood but did not reach the furthest corners of the room.

"Who is there?" Darcy held the lamp aloft so the light could more easily penetrate the darkness. There. He could make out a shadowy figure—or was it two?—in the northwest corner near the door to the back gardens.

The sounds of a muffled curse and the rustling of clothing were followed by a very feminine giggle. Oh, devil take it, had Darcy interrupted an assignation? In the library? Had they no respect? Anger surged through his veins, and he advanced on that corner of the room, hoping to discern more. "Who is there? Show yourself!"

Another curse in a most definitely masculine voice lent credence to Darcy's theory, but he was not near enough to see more than two vague shapes. One moved quickly, and the door creaked open. For a moment a male figure was silhouetted against the moonlit sky, and then he was gone; the door swung shut.

Was the woman still here? Another giggle answered that question. Damnation! Then there was a thump and a moan. *Had the young lady hurt herself? Had the departing man injured her? What if she had been unwilling?*

Coming across another lamp, Darcy hastily lit it and left both blazing on a tall table behind a sofa. Now he could discern the form of a girl slumped near the door, unmoving. *Was she unconscious?*

Darcy quickened his pace. The girl opened her eyes and blinked at him owlishly—more likely foxed than injured. She wrestled herself into a sitting position, and it was then that Darcy realized the top of her bodice was untied, exposing her breasts!

He should help her cover up! No, he should leave at once! He should look! No, he should not! Torn among conflicting impulses, Darcy lurched forward, his footsteps faltering. As he neared the corner, his foot encountered an unexpected obstacle in the form of a chair leg. Darcy tripped spectacularly, falling full length on top of the half-dressed girl.

The girl squealed. "Ow! You oaf! Get off! Move your hands!" Darcy hastened to comply, quickly removing his hands from anything that might resemble a female body part. "Get your hands off me!" the girl shrieked completely unnecessarily.

Darcy scrambled backward, attempting to find purchase and regain his feet.

Then he froze at the most horrible sound in the world: the opening of the library door. A female form entered the library from the hallway, silhouetted by candlelight from behind. "Lydia?" a voice called. Darcy had no trouble identifying its owner. Of all the women at the ball, it had to be Elizabeth Bennet.

Chapter Two

"Here, Lizzy!" the half-dressed girl called to her sister.

Oh, no, no, no! Why did she say anything at all? Why could they not pretend the library was uninhabited?

"I heard someone screaming," Elizabeth said, her voice low with concern.

"Yes, that was me," Lydia admitted, not sounding in the least distressed.

"She is here, Mama!" Elizabeth called down the hallway. "I have found her!"

Darcy's position on the floor had concealed his presence behind various pieces of furniture. His sole object was escape, through the garden door if necessary, before anyone connected him with this awkward and scandalous situation. But every escape route involved standing. So Darcy stood hastily, not even taking a second to straighten his badly disheveled clothes, and gingerly stepped toward the door. Perhaps Elizabeth would not recognize him from the back.

"Mr. Darcy?"

Or perhaps she would.

He turned slowly to face her. There was no purpose to be served in dissembling. Elizabeth's brow furrowed in perplexity as she regarded him.

Then Lydia Bennet stood up, and Elizabeth's mouth gaped open.

Miss Lydia used one hand to preserve her modesty by clutching the front of her unlaced dress to her chest. The dress sagged alarmingly; one sleeve had fallen from her shoulder, and the other was balanced rather precariously. "Lydia, you must cover yourself!" Elizabeth cried, hastening across the room.

Darcy jerked his eyes away so quickly that he had a moment of vertigo. Instead, he was treated to the sight of Mrs. Bennet joining their merry band. She bustled through the doorway officiously but gaped at what she saw.

"Lydia!" Mrs. Bennet shrieked at her youngest daughter.

"Hello, Mama," Lydia slurred drunkenly. "I was looking for a book."

Mrs. Bennet shrieked again, a wordless cry of dismay. Darcy was tempted to cover his ears but could not quite bring himself to be so impolite.

Glancing down at the loosened bodice, Lydia giggled. "No wonder it feels so cold in here!" With a little smirk, she yanked up the sleeves so the bodice did not hang so precariously. Standing behind her sister, Elizabeth hastily tied the laces on the back of Lydia's bodice.

Elizabeth glared at Darcy—at which point he realized that perhaps he should avert his eyes. The carpet. It was a very fine carpet, and no one would object if he stared at it.

Oh, this was not good. Not good. Not good at all. Darcy had been caught in a darkened room with a foxed, partially clad girl from a respectable family. No matter what he said, the circumstances were incriminating. *There must be a way to address this situation before it spins out of control.* But Darcy's mind was not working properly. The combination of naked breasts, Elizabeth's scorn, and Mrs. Bennet's continued shrieking had somehow rendered his mind nonfunctional. He felt like a fox at the end of a fox hunt—surrounded on all sides.

There was a moment of absolute silence while Mrs. Bennet gasped. "W-what were you doing to my daughter? You libertine!" Suddenly, Darcy missed the shrieking. "Oh, I knew it as soon as I saw you! You are the worst kind of rake—a rogue and a scoundrel!"

Darcy was not accustomed to having such language directed at him. "I beg your pardon…?"

"Look at her!" Mrs. Bennet shrieked, gesturing to her youngest daughter. When Darcy glanced in the girl's direction, she cried, "No, do not look at her!"

He turned back to Mrs. Bennet's red, outraged face and took a deep breath before responding. "Nothing happened, Mrs. Bennet. I assure you. I happened upon your daughter as I was in search of a—"

"You came to be alone with my half-dressed sister in a dimly lit library *by accident*?" Elizabeth scoffed. Darcy could not prevent a wince; of all the women at the ball, why was she the one to have discovered him in this ridiculous situation?

Darcy drew himself up and straightened his cravat. "Well, yes." He was aware how absurd the claim sounded, but it was the truth. "When I arrived, Miss Lydia was lying in the corner. I wanted to help her, but I tripped and fell on top…" Darcy's voice petered out. Any details he added at this point would only make the situation worse.

It did not help that Lydia chose that moment to burst into tears.

"I never thought very highly of you, Mr. Darcy," Elizabeth intoned as she put a comforting arm around her sister's shoulders.

Wait, she did not?

"But I at least thought you too honorable to take advantage of girl who is but fifteen!"

Oh, Good Lord! The girl was fifteen?
Georgiana was barely older. Elizabeth's family would think him scarcely better than Wickham. No, it was intolerable!

Darcy rubbed his forehead with the palm of his hand. "I do not molest children!" His voice sounded shrill and strained to his own ears. "Another man was present. He escaped through the door to the gardens! Lydia was already dishabille when I arrived—"

"How convenient for you," Elizabeth sneered. Her words were punctuated by a sob from her sister.

"Ask her!" Darcy demanded. "Ask Miss Lydia. No doubt she arrived here with the man."

Just as the words left his mouth, Darcy realized how badly he had miscalculated. Lydia's hands fell from her tear-streaked face, her eyes wide with horror. She would never admit she had willingly accompanied a man into a darkened room.

Mrs. Bennet and Elizabeth stared at Lydia. "Lydia, what happened?" Elizabeth asked gently.

For a moment Darcy entertained the hope that Lydia would tell the truth, but then she shook her head vigorously. "No! There was never anyone else. I am not that sort of girl!" She dabbed her eyes theatrically with a handkerchief.

Some man had undoubtedly lured her away from the dance with promises and flattery she was too naïve to question. If she were not seeking to tarnish his reputation, Darcy would feel more than a fleeting moment of sympathy.

Mrs. Bennet's shrieks had brought a throng of guests crowding around the library's doorway, including—much to Darcy's horror—Bingley and Mr. Bennet. Behind them stood that fool of a cleric, Elizabeth's cousin. Darcy's stomach clenched and roiled at the sight of so many eyes observing and judging him.

Pushing his way into the room, Bingley shot Darcy a sympathetic glance. "Mrs. Bennet, I am sure it is all a misunderstanding."

"No! No, there is no misunderstanding!" Mrs. Bennet's voice climbed into higher and higher registers. "He has taken advantage of my poor girl! He has ruined her reputation! Everyone will know!"

Darcy refrained from observing that the situation could have been concealed were it not for Mrs. Bennet's shrieks.

Mr. Bennet stepped into the room, his face a grim mask. "I believe there is only one honorable course of action open to you, Mr. Darcy."

A herd of horses galloped through his stomach, and his heart threatened to pound out of his chest. Oh, merciful heavens! Lydia's father expected him to offer marriage. *Let this be some horrible dream!* Darcy paused. Unfortunately, he did not awaken.

Darcy stared at Lydia Bennet: silly, sobbing, foxed, and willing to leave a ball unchaperoned with some unknown man. Without any family position, good understanding, or clever conversation, she met none of his criteria for a wife. In fact, she was the exact opposite in almost every way. If he had wanted a young, empty-headed chit, the *ton* could supply many with impeccable pedigrees.

His eyes brushed past Elizabeth, who glared at him implacably. Asking her to dance was the least of his concerns now. The thought struck him as darkly humorous.

However, he was troubled by the thought that she would think ill of him, that she would see him as capable of seducing and abandoning her sister. She had already declared her low opinion of him; he would hate to confirm it.

Mrs. Bennet wept noisily into her handkerchief while a scowling Mr. Bennet stalked toward Darcy. "Well, Darcy? What will it be?"

If he failed to propose now, Elizabeth and the other onlookers would think him without honor. But the thought of proposing was…profoundly distasteful. Of course, a proposal was not a marriage. If he proposed under duress now, Darcy might later find a way to escape the obligation. The Bennet family might agree to a monetary settlement, but they could hardly discuss such a compromise here, in front of witnesses.

Yes, he would find the means to escape the situation later. For now he need only scrape together the remains of his dignity and live to fight another day. Devil take it!

He turned to the disheveled, red-faced, sobbing fifteen-year-old. "Miss Lydia," he said through gritted teeth.

"Y-yes?" She granted him a quizzical smile and a hiccup.

"Would you do me the honor of being my wife?" Darcy was proud he did not choke on the words. He did not have the slightest hope the chit would reject him; his fortune was too tempting.

"M-marry you?" Lydia laughed.

Laughed!

Darcy failed to see any humor in the situation. "W-why would I want to marry you?" She giggled, swaying a bit on her feet.

Was the girl touched in the head?

A frowning Mr. Bennet advanced on his daughter and took her arm. "Lydia, you *must* accept him," he explained in a low voice. "Your reputation has been compromised."

"But look at him!" She waved wildly at Darcy. "He's so stuffy and formal and *dull*. And he does not even possess a red coat!" A couple of onlookers tittered. Even Mr. Bennet's lips twitched. However, Elizabeth's glare did not relent.

Darcy rubbed the back of his neck. This was a farce in every possible way.

"That may be true, my dear," Mr. Bennet spoke gently to his daughter while staring daggers at Darcy, "but you must accept him anyway."

"I don't want to!" Lydia stamped her foot like a child denied a sweet.

"You must." Mr. Bennet's voice now held a hint of steel. "You would not wish to experience a decrease in your allowance for hats and gloves."

Lydia glared at her father. "Papa, that is unfair!" He crossed his arms and regarded her sternly. Finally, she stepped backward and slumped into a chair with a huff. "Very well! Yes, Mr. Darcy, I accept." Her face arranged itself in a very unattractive pout.

Darcy wondered if there had ever been a less romantic marriage proposal in the history of the world. However, if Lydia possessed that little enthusiasm, perhaps they could reach some sort of agreement which would not leave him leg-shackled. Never before had he been grateful for being considered dull! Of course, he had never before encountered a woman who thought ten thousand a year was dull.

Bingley began to direct guests—all chatting excitedly—toward the library door. Lydia returned to sobbing into her hands. With a scowl at Darcy, Mrs. Bennet swept across the floor to take the chair next to Lydia's. "It will not be so bad, my dear. Mr. Darcy is very rich." Standing next to Lydia, Elizabeth colored at her mother's tactlessness.

Darcy closed his eyes. *This could not possibly be happening.*

"Rich?" Despite being muffled, Lydia's tone was definitely interested.

"Yes!" Mrs. Bennet trilled. "You will have many fine dresses and carriages!"

Lydia peeked through her hands. "More than my sisters?"

"I daresay. They are not liable to find wealthier husbands!"

Lydia clapped in excitement. "La!" she squealed. "How droll!" *She certainly recovered from her mortification quickly.*

Darcy could almost see the hope for an agreement with Lydia slipping further away. Why would the girl accept a fraction of his fortune when she believed she was entitled to all of it?

But there was nothing he could accomplish tonight. Perhaps he could convince Lydia to break off their engagement tomorrow, once she had sobered. Darcy spun on his heel and strode toward the hallway.

He needed a brandy. Or two. Or ten.

Mrs. Bennet's shrill tones followed him as he hurried away. "I daresay you will like being his wife. Mrs. Darcy! Oh, how *well* that sounds!"

"Yes, indeed!" Lydia agreed with a giggle.

Lydia might like being Mrs. Darcy, but Darcy could not conceive how he would survive Lydia.

Chapter Three

Clang!

A servant dropped a set of silver tongs on the floor of the breakfast room, but it was as loud as a church bell to Darcy. He started, dropping his fork on his plate and producing another painfully loud clatter. *Delightful.*

Darcy massaged his temples. Those glasses of brandy—how many had it been?—had seemed an excellent idea the previous evening after he had escaped the debacle in the library. However, his throbbing head and queasy stomach now told him that he should have been more abstemious. He could not help reliving last night's disaster over and over. How had it happened? While attempting to escape one Bennet sister, how had he ended up engaged to another? Surely it was some horrible nightmare.

Foolishly, his mind insisted on repeatedly recollecting the expression on Elizabeth Bennet's face when she thought Darcy had debauched her sister. It was absurd. Given the terrible circumstances, Elizabeth's estimation should be the least of Darcy's concerns. But his memory insisted on producing again and again the image of her horror and disgust. *If only I could explain the circumstances to her! Help her see the truth!* But it was a hopeless wish; he was not liable to see Elizabeth again in a setting which would allow personal confessions. And it was not an easy subject to broach. *By the way, I know you believe I molested your sister, but she actually allowed a* different *man to unlace her bodice.*

Darcy pressed his palms to his eyes. What was he thinking? He did not desire Elizabeth's good opinion, and it was fruitless to hope for it now. He had far greater problems to resolve—such as how he could rid himself of Miss Lydia's claim on his hand. *I have made a complete mull of this.* He stared down at a plateful of breakfast, which made his stomach churn.

Bingley regarded him sympathetically from across the table but had said little to him since Darcy had come down. *What was there to say?* Darcy thought Bingley believed him about the other man in the library, but it did him no good.

Hurst concentrated on shoveling eggs into his mouth. Miss Bingley and Mrs. Hurst had just seated themselves. "Charles told me of the events in the library," Miss Bingley said. "It is a complete travesty! You must not allow it to stand."

Darcy nodded wearily but did not respond. While he was grateful for the outrage on his behalf, it would mean more coming from a woman who was less interested in his fortune.

"You would never run off with a fifteen-year-old country chit. Anyone acquainted with you would know that," she drawled.

Darcy felt damned by faint praise. Perhaps Miss Bingley thought him capable of such despicable behavior with someone slightly older and of a better family.

Any reply he made would not be civil, so he held his tongue.

"It is horrible!" agreed Mrs. Hurst. "I am certain it was all a scheme. Those Bennets probably planned it all. And you fell right into their trap!"

Darcy bristled; he would never have agreed to a betrothal if he had believed the Bennets were entrapping him. "It was not a deliberate trap. There was a man in the library who escaped out the garden door. I did not see his face."

Miss Bingley and her sister exchanged knowing looks. "Whoever he was, he probably colluded with the Bennets in their scheme!"

Feeling thick-witted and disinclined to speak, Darcy was not equal to the task of explaining to Bingley's sister that nobody could have possibly known he would enter the library. Nor did he bother describing Lydia's utter dismay at the prospect of their engagement. *That makes two of us*, he thought darkly.

"I never trusted those Bennets," Mrs. Hurst declared.

"Neither did I, Sister. Neither did I!" Miss Bingley agreed. "You cannot allow this betrothal to stand, Mr. Darcy. It happened under coercion and false pretenses. You must free yourself from the entanglement with all haste and immediately attach yourself to a more suitable young lady."

Her attempt at a coy smile gave a not-so-subtle hint of which young lady she had in mind. Darcy stared at his uneaten food, wondering whether Caroline Bingley would be a better choice than Lydia Bennet. *Perhaps I should emigrate to America.*

Then Miss Bingley turned her cool, appraising gaze onto her brother. "Charles, I think you should take Mr. Darcy's misfortunes as instructive."

Bingley, who had been staring out of the window, blinked in surprise at his sister. "Caroline?"

Miss Bingley spoke slowly as if to a small child. "I know you like Jane Bennet, and she is a sweet girl. But look what her family is capable of! Why, even now they may be scheming how they can ensnare you into marriage!"

"Hmm." Bingley appeared not to mind the idea of being ensnared by Jane Bennet.

Miss Bingley was working herself into high dudgeon. "It is insupportable! You must be free to choose your own wife. And it cannot be Jane Bennet. You should not let another tell you who to marry." Darcy managed not to laugh at the irony.

Miss Bingley gestured forcefully with her fork, sending bits of egg flying all over the table as she addressed her brother. "If you do not care about yourself, at least think of your family! A forced marriage—particularly to someone from that family—would be a disgrace."

Darcy winced. How would he tell this story to Georgiana? Perhaps he could extricate himself from the situation before it was necessary.

Bingley shrank back into his chair as his sister leaned forward to emphasize her point. "Consider how such a disgrace would affect me and Louisa—and Mama. She might have apoplexy if such stories are spread about you!" By now Bingley had turned an alarming shade of white.

Although Darcy did not care for Miss Bingley, she was impressively skilled at manipulating her brother. If only she would turn those talents in a more productive direction. She knew Bingley would not sacrifice his happiness for his own honor, but he would avoid bringing any disgrace on his family. Darcy felt sorry for Bingley. Watching him argue with his sister was a bit like watching someone attempt to fend off a dragon with a butter knife.

He considered intervening, but on the whole, Bingley would be better off without Jane Bennet. Although Darcy could absolve the family of deliberate scheming, he was not charitably inclined toward them at the moment. With the exception of Elizabeth and Jane, they were generally vulgar and far inferior in both birth and manners to anyone in Darcy's circles. Bingley's sisters were most likely correct that he should avoid the clutches of the Bennet family.

"Yes, indeed, Sister!" Mrs. Hurst trilled on cue as if their united front against Bingley had been rehearsed in advance. "We should leave Hertfordshire at once and give those Bennets no more opportunities to scheme against us."

Bingley twisted his napkin nervously in his lap, licking his lips. "But—but—"

Miss Bingley did not allow her brother to formulate his objection. "Indeed, Louisa. That is a brilliant plan! We could pass quite an enjoyable Christmas in town. I would imagine Mr. Darcy is eager to quit Hertfordshire."

She had no idea. "Yes," Darcy said aloud. "I will leave today in any event. I must consult with my solicitor." *And find a way to escape this tangle with my honor intact.*

"But I *like* Jane Bennet." Bingley's plaintive tone suggested he had already conceded the fight.

Miss Bingley patted her brother's hand reassuringly. "We do as well. But her family is so highly undesirable. Just see how they have treated poor Mr. Darcy!"

Darcy shifted in his seat. He disliked being a cautionary tale.

"We must leave immediately!" Mrs. Hurst exclaimed. "Who knows what plots they are scheming even now? They might be planning an afternoon visit today!" Her tone was one customarily reserved for announcements of enemy troop movements.

"Oh yes, Sister!" Miss Bingley's eyes were wide with horror as she turned to Bingley. "You are in grave danger. We must depart now; tomorrow will be too late."

Darcy suppressed a snort of laughter at the ladies' theatrics. However, they were effective. "Very well," Bingley said, rubbing his forehead wearily. "I will have the carriage made ready. We shall leave today."

"Very good." Miss Bingley settled back in her chair with a satisfied smile.

Bingley mopped his brow with a handkerchief. "Perhaps I should call on the Bennets and explain—"

"No!" Miss Bingley practically yelled. "No," she repeated more sedately. "They might be lying in wait for just such an opportunity. I will write a letter to Jane."

Bingley's expression remained dubious, but he nodded. "Very well."

***

Elizabeth knocked on the door of the room Lydia shared with Kitty. "Come in!" Lydia's voice lilted. *Well, at least she is not traumatized after her adventure last night*, Elizabeth thought. ·

Kitty was not there, but Lydia sat in bed, eagerly devouring the contents of the breakfast tray before her. "See what Mama had Hill bring up?" Lydia beamed. "Usually I only receive a breakfast tray when I am sick!"

Elizabeth nodded, happy to see her sister in good spirits but experiencing some uneasiness nonetheless. Her hands balled into fists every time she thought of Mr. Darcy in the library with her sister. If only she were a man, then she could challenge him to a duel to avenge her sister's honor. Yet the previous night in bed she had considered the odd circumstances in the library. Mr. Darcy was rude and unpleasant, but he had not demonstrated the least interest in dallying with any woman, not even Miss Bingley, who was obviously fascinated by him—or at least his fortune.

And Lydia had appeared so horrified at the prospect of marrying him that Elizabeth wondered why she had slipped off with him at all. They were such an …improbable couple. Before last night, Elizabeth would not have been certain Mr. Darcy even knew Lydia's name.

Perhaps she could gain some clarity by speaking with Lydia. "How are you feeling?" Elizabeth asked.

"Better now." Lydia practically bounced as she nodded vigorously. "I had a bad headache when I first awoke, but Hill's coffee helped. And I had Kitty draw the drapes again. The sunshine is unusually bright today." She took a large bite from a piece of toast.

Those symptoms sounded familiar. "How much wine punch did you drink last night?"

"La! How would I know?" Lydia chewed more toast.

Oh, merciful heavens! Had Mr. Darcy procured punch to make her foxed? "Did Mr. Darcy find you punch to drink?"

"Mr. Darcy?" Lydia's tone suggested the absurdity of this idea. "No! It was—" Lydia clapped her hands over her mouth.

Elizabeth regarded her sister closely. "Someone else gave you the wine punch?"

Lydia waved the toast about airily. "I do not recollect precisely. The night is hazy in my memory."

"But Mr. Darcy did *not* get you the punch?"

"No!" Lydia said scornfully. "I drank it between sets while I was dancing. Lord, dancing makes me so thirsty! And of course I never danced with Mr. Darcy!" She made a face.

Elizabeth was struck by the truth of this statement. She had not noticed Mr. Darcy dancing with anyone at the Netherfield ball. He had observed Elizabeth herself for several minutes, and Charlotte had speculated that he might request a set of her. But then he had disappeared.

Lydia's mouth was full of toast, but that did not stop the torrent of words. "I danced with so many men! Five of them officers! Did you see me?"

Elizabeth made no reply; instead, she considered Mr. Darcy's assertion that another man had consorted with Lydia. "How did you arrive in the library with Mr. Darcy?" she asked.

"I do not recollect precisely," Lydia said with a shrug. "Really, the evening is all a blur."

What if Lydia *had* accompanied someone else to the library? What if Mr. Darcy had happened upon her after some other man tried to take advantage of her virtue? As much as Elizabeth disliked the idea of her sister committing such an impropriety, she was forced to admit that Lydia could have been vulnerable to a predatory man.

Elizabeth frowned as she considered the implications. The circumstances had seemed so blatantly obvious last night that she had discounted Mr. Darcy's protestations. But spiriting away a young girl from a dance did not seem…likely for Mr. Darcy. Although Elizabeth did not care for him, he seemed too proud and too aware of his family's position to stoop to debauchery—particularly in his friend's library. And he had appeared so horrified by the accusation….

But if not Mr. Darcy, then who? Lydia would not have stolen into the library with a stranger, would she? Although she was likely acquainted with a number of militia officers she considered to be "friends."

If only Elizabeth knew more! She tapped a finger on her chin as Lydia swallowed more coffee. "Did you dance with Mr. Wickham last night?"

Lydia's hand jerked, spilling coffee all over her breakfast tray and night rail. "Look what you made me do, Lizzy!"

"I am sorry." Elizabeth picked up a napkin from the tray to blot Lydia's garment.

Lydia pushed her hands away. "Never mind that. I must change clothes anyway. Kitty and I are walking into Meryton to see some of the officers and have some laughs." She stood and opened the door to her closet to peruse her choice of dresses.

Elizabeth dropped the napkin on the tray. "You cannot flirt with officers now, Lydia. You are betrothed to Mr. Darcy."

"I remember, silly!" Lydia waved away this objection as she shrugged off her night rail and donned her dress. "I shan't *kiss* anyone! But I must have some fun before I marry that stodgy old man."

Elizabeth was not an admirer of Mr. Darcy's, but she would hardly describe him as stodgy or old. "Engaged women must behave with greater discretion," she said.

"I can be discreet!" Lydia declared. "I shall have discretion shooting out of my ears!" Elizabeth winced at this image as she laced up her sister's dress.

Once her dress was fastened, Lydia flopped back onto her bed. "Although honestly, Lizzy, I wish I were *not* engaged to Mr. Darcy. I agreed to marry him because everyone said I must, but I always wanted an officer. They are so dashing and so much fun! Mr. Darcy almost never smiles and never laughs."

Elizabeth pulled Lydia into a standing position before she could wrinkle her dress. "I understand, my dear. But the circumstances last night were…quite bad. You are betrothed now, and you must make the best of it."

"That is what Mama said, and she reminded me of Mr. Darcy's fortune." Lydia sighed. "If only he were more dashing…Although I suppose I shall comfort myself with jewels and hats…"

"Yes, indeed," Elizabeth said. She hardly approved of such an obviously mercenary approach to marriage, but Lydia must not break off the engagement. Her reputation was in tatters.

"I cannot wait to tell everyone in Meryton about Mr. Darcy's ten thousand a year!" Lydia giggled.

Elizabeth's righteous anger at Mr. Darcy was gradually transforming into an amorphous regret. Last night she had been so certain of his guilt, but now…if what she suspected was true, he had been wronged, and Elizabeth had helped to wrong him.

Moreover, she did not need to learn more of his character to be certain that he was spectacularly ill-suited to be Lydia's husband; most likely they would both be miserable in the marriage. Elizabeth rubbed suddenly sweaty palms on her gown. *What can I do?* She had nothing but suspicions and no way of confirming them without Lydia's cooperation.

"I shan't let anyone forget I have a fiancé. A *very wealthy* fiancé!" Lydia dashed from the room and down the stairs. Elizabeth followed at a slower pace.

At the bottom of the stairs, however, they both encountered Hill, followed by the tall figure of Mr. Darcy. He bowed to the two ladies. "Forgive the intrusion at such an early hour," he said. "But I was hoping to have a word with Miss Lydia."

Elizabeth's first reaction was alarm. Surely he was not suggesting she leave them alone! But then she recalled that they were betrothed, and it was appropriate for betrothed couples to enjoy some privacy. Although she could not imagine what two such different people would say to each other.

Lydia pouted. "I am bound for Meryton with Kitty!"

Elizabeth barely refrained from chastising her sister. How could Lydia treat her fiancé so rudely?

Mr. Darcy looked affronted. "I shall be departing from Hertfordshire within the hour."

Lydia heaved a great sigh. "Very well, I suppose I have time for a brief conversation."

"Thank you for making time for me." Mr. Darcy's tone was so dry that Elizabeth could not discern if he was being sardonic.

"I suppose I must, for I am your fiancée!" She gave Elizabeth a sidelong glance and giggled. "Isn't that such a grand word: fiancée?" Elizabeth rolled her eyes, but Lydia mistook the gesture. "Don't worry, Lizzy," she patted her sister's hand, "I am sure someday a man will want to marry you as well."

Mr. Darcy regarded the sisters with a carefully blank expression. Did he also believe Elizabeth would be lucky to procure a husband?

"You are too good," Elizabeth murmured to Lydia. Mr. Darcy made a strangled sound that turned into a cough.

"I know." Lydia tossed her head so her curls bounced. "Mr. Darcy, shall we retire to the drawing room?"

He nodded mutely.

Lydia turned to the housekeeper. "Hill, please have some tea brought in." Hill scowled at Lydia's imperious tone, but Lydia was reaching for the drawing room door and did not notice.

Mr. Darcy followed Lydia and closed the door behind him. Elizabeth lingered by the door for a moment, reluctant to leave for some reason. Slowly, she became aware of the source of her unease. When had she ceased worrying about Mr. Darcy's influence over Lydia and started worrying about Lydia's influence over him?

***

Lydia flopped inelegantly into a chair the moment they entered the drawing room. "Lord, I am so tired! All that dancing wore me out!"

Darcy suspected her fatigue had more to do with what she had imbibed rather than how much she had danced, but he stood by the door and said nothing. How could he broach the subjects which needed discussion?

Lydia regarded him sharply. "Will you buy me lace?"

"I beg your pardon?"

"I want my wedding dress to have real lace that was made in Belgium. None of my friends have real lace from Belgium!"

This is what she wished to discuss? "Perhaps there are shops in London—"

She did not allow him to finish the sentence. "What kind of carriages do you have?"

Darcy's hand worried the edge of his hat. He took a deep breath. "Well, there is a phaeton, a barouche, a—"

"Is your estate very grand?" she interrupted.

Darcy blinked at the rapid shifts in conversation. "My family house is Pemberley..." he temporized. Did she wish him to brag about his possessions? He found the thought distasteful.

"How many rooms does it possess?"

He rubbed his forehead. This was not how he had imagined his first conversation with his fiancée. "Two hundred and twelve."

Lydia clapped her hands as if she had received a sweet. "Two hundred and twelve! How wonderful! There should be plenty of space for my friends to visit. There is Maria and Helen and—"

Darcy disliked interrupting people, but he could not tolerate any more. "Are you certain they would all like to travel to Derbyshire to visit you?"

Lydia's eyes grew wide. "Pembleton is in Derbyshire? But that is so far away!" she squealed. "It must be closer. That is impossible!"

Darcy sighed. "Unfortunately, I cannot relocate my family's estate to a more convenient location."

Lydia waggled her head. "How vexing!" But then she sat up straighter. "Do you have a house in town?"

"Of course."

"Then I shall live there most of the year, and I will not need to go all the way to Peckerly!" she declared triumphantly.

"If you wish." Darcy silently resigned himself to years of avoiding London.

"It will be wonderful!" Lydia clasped both hands to her bosom. "I shall host the most elegant balls in all of London. And I shan't invite anyone who has been cruel to me."

He needed to redirect the conversation. "About the—"

"And I shall have ostrich feathers for my hair!"

Darcy had never given a moment's consideration to what women wore in their hair. "If you wish—"

"And I—"

Darcy was not sure when this conversation had gone wrong, but he must regain control. She would never stop spinning fantasies in her head. "Lydia, you and I both know there was another man with you."

Lydia froze, suddenly wary. "I am sure I do not know what you mean," she sniffed.

Darcy stepped closer, deliberately looming over her. "I must know the man's identity."

"There was no man." Lydia's voice quavered as she stared straight ahead, refusing to meet Darcy's eyes.

"You did not untie your bodice yourself. Nor did I. I never touched you, save inadvertently when I fell on you." Lydia clamped her lips together tightly. Darcy raised his voice. "I agreed to a betrothal to salvage your reputation, but we cannot marry. You must marry the man who is actually responsible for your plight."

Lydia jumped up from her chair. "Mama says it will be a great scandal if you do not marry me! You cannot renege on your promise!"

Darcy scrubbed his hands over his face. Lydia was correct about the scandal, unless Darcy found the other man and persuaded him to marry her. If she jilted Darcy, it would be a minor contretemps, but if he did not keep his word, the Darcy name would suffer. He prayed that the other man was not already married— and that he would be susceptible to monetary inducement if necessary.

Lydia's lower lip protruded stubbornly. It was time for a different tactic. "Miss Lydia, please see reason. We do not suit each other."

"Of course we suit each other!" she cried. "You shall buy me jewels! And I can be very charming!" She gave him a winsome smile. Darcy shook his head, endeavoring to think of an appropriate argument if such was Lydia's notion of compatibility. "And I shall be a good hostess for your elegant balls!"

The Darcy family had not hosted a ball since his mother's death, and he had no intention of remedying that situation. He sighed. "I could not make you happy."

Lydia slumped into her chair, pouting in a most unladylike manner. "Am I not pretty enough?"

Darcy sighed. This was like arguing with Georgiana at age ten—and at her most petulant. "That is not the issue at all."

Her eyes glistened. "I know I do not have Jane's beauty or Elizabeth's eyes, but—"

"I pray you, do not misunderstand me. You are very pretty." Lydia preened. *Oh, Good Lord!* "You are…very young—a full thirteen years younger than me."

She shrugged. "Sir William Lucas and his second wife are sixteen years apart!"

Darcy rubbed his forehead. "Being mistress of Pemberley carries with it a great deal of responsibility…the servants, the tenants, societal obligations…"

She fluttered her hands in a dismissive gesture, a motion that reminded Darcy unpleasantly of her mother. "Who manages it now? Your housekeeper?"

"My housekeeper, and my sister, Georgiana, helps."

"A sister!" Lydia clapped her hands together in glee. "How old is she?"

"Sh-she is just sixteen."

"We are almost the same age!" she exclaimed with a bright smile. "Oh, what fun! We will have a grand time visiting dress shops and sharing gossip! Does she like regimentals, too?" Red coats were definitely not one of Georgiana's favorite subjects of conversation. *I will need to keep them separated at least until Georgiana is married.*

"Oh, and I may chaperone her when she makes her come out!" She clapped her hands in glee.

Lydia had all the restraint of a rabbit in springtime. She would not make a suitable chaperone for a barmaid. Darcy pinched the bridge of his nose, endeavoring to imagine informing Georgiana that he intended to wed a girl younger than she—and utterly failing. *I must escape this somehow!*

"You must tell me the name of the man who was with you in the library!" he demanded sternly.

"I am sure I do not know what you mean." Lydia pursed her lips stubbornly.

Darcy paced to the fireplace and back. How could he compel her to produce the man's name?

"How much longer must you visit, Mr. Darcy?" Lydia's voice had acquired an unpleasant whiny tone. "I do wish to visit Meryton. The milliner is expecting new ribbons, and if we do not go at once, all the pretty ones will be purchased."

How could I listen to such discourse for the rest of my life?

Darcy stared out of the window. Clearly she would not yield. He could achieve nothing in this visit. Upon his arrival in London, he would consult with his solicitor. Perhaps they could devise other inducements.

"I suppose we are finished," he said.

"La! Finally!" Lydia slid from her seat and scurried from the room before Darcy could utter another word.

Chapter Four

Elizabeth descended the stairs, wondering, not for the first time, how Mr. Darcy and Lydia fared. It was almost impossible to imagine a conversation between them. Mr. Darcy could be severe and have a sharp tongue, but Lydia paid little heed to what others thought of her. That attitude would no doubt distress Mr. Darcy. On the other hand, he might tire of discussing red coats and ruffles.

Hearing no voices emanating from the drawing room, Elizabeth decided to investigate whether Mr. Darcy had departed. To her amazement, when she opened the door she found Mr. Darcy alone. He sat in the far corner with his head in his hands but rushed to his feet when she entered.

"I beg your pardon, Miss Elizabeth. Lydia left for Meryton a few minutes ago." *Of course she had.* Only Lydia would depart the house and leave her guest alone. Perhaps she would have remained if Mr. Darcy wore regimentals.

When Elizabeth turned her scrutiny on Mr. Darcy, she discovered her anger from the previous evening had melted away. It was impossible to maintain in the face of his obvious distress. His hair was disheveled, and dark circles showed under his eyes. His face was impassive, yet there were signs of strain around his mouth.

He shifted uneasily on his feet. "You need not feel under an obligation to receive me...."

Why would I not—? Oh. Abruptly, Elizabeth recollected their encounter in Netherfield's library. She had been very vociferous, and he might easily believe she was still angry with him. At the time, the evidence of his guilt and reprehensible moral character seemed irrefutable. Now she was not so certain. At that moment Hill arrived with the tea service.

Mr. Darcy glanced from Hill to Elizabeth. "I-I should return to Netherfield," he stammered.

Elizabeth found herself in the odd position of wishing she might do something to alleviate Mr. Darcy's distress. Indeed, he might very well be an inadvertent victim of Lydia's thoughtlessness rather than a scoundrel who sought to take advantage of it. If so, he deserved Elizabeth's consideration, although she could do little to help him. "Please, stay for tea," she murmured.

Mr. Darcy hesitated but then seated himself once again. She poured out a cup, added the sugar she had noticed he preferred, and handed it to him. Then she poured one for herself and took an adjacent chair. Mr. Darcy hunched miserably in his chair as he sipped.

Elizabeth considered how she could demonstrate that she had reconsidered her opinion of him. However, it was a difficult subject to broach. How does one say, "I may have been mistaken in thinking you debauched my younger sister?"

For a long moment silence reigned. Finally, Elizabeth said, "I would like to hear your account of the events of last night."

Mr. Darcy's eyebrows rose. "You were present, Miss Elizabeth. Surely you do not need me to..." He shifted uneasily in his chair.

"You said there was another man with Lydia."

"And you said I must have been false." His tone was level, but his eyes narrowed slightly.

Elizabeth disliked admitting *anything* to such an unpleasant man, particularly that she might have been in error, but he deserved the truth. "Something Lydia said this morning suggested that someone else had escorted her to the library."

He leaned forward, nearly spilling his tea. "Did she give a name?"

Elizabeth shook her head. "She said nothing directly. I am only surmising based on what she did not say."

"But you believe me?" His gaze on her was very intent. *Why should my opinion be of any importance to him?*

Elizabeth felt like a disloyal sister, but she suspected Mr. Darcy had not been treated fairly. "I believe your story is possible…"

"Thank God!" He slumped back into the chair.

She shrugged, more than a little puzzled by his reaction. "It is not as if my convictions will materially affect your situation." Unless the other man was identified, Elizabeth could hardly condone any efforts to break the engagement, for that would leave Lydia disgraced and unwed.

"I am simply pleased you believe me." He gave her a weary smile.

Elizabeth stared down at the hands clasped in her lap. She owed Mr. Darcy a full account of her thoughts on the subject, but they did her no credit. "I apologize for being hasty in drawing conclusions. I was inclined to believe…that is, in conversation with Mr. Wickham—"

"Wickham?" Mr. Darcy's face darkened. "What did that scoundrel say about me?"

Elizabeth wished she were anywhere else. Why must she be the one to share such stories with Mr. Darcy?

Her fingers twisted together in her lap as the words emerged in a rush. "He-he said you had refused him the living your father had promised and thus left him penniless." She omitted Mr. Wickham's colorful characterization of Mr. Darcy's temperament.

Mr. Darcy exploded from his chair and started pacing the length of the room. "*This* is what everyone in Meryton believes of me? Small wonder they fancied me capable of seducing a girl of fifteen." Tightness around his mouth suggested that her news pained him. "My *sister* is barely past fifteen." He shook his head in disgust. Elizabeth's belief in his innocence increased.

Mr. Darcy came to rest near the window, staring out at the grounds of Longbourn without apparently seeing them. "Wickham came to me and expressed his disinterest in taking orders, so I compensated him for the living, and he departed from Pemberley."

"Oh!" Elizabeth's hand rose to her mouth. *Why was I so quick to believe Mr. Wickham's version of the story?*

"He may also have failed to mention that he attempted to seduce...a female relative of mine and convince her to elope with him. Of course, he only wanted her dowry. When I arrived unexpectedly, it ruined his scheme."

"How horrible!" Elizabeth was ashamed she had ever believed Mr. Wickham.

"Do you believe me?" Mr. Darcy regarded her sharply.

Elizabeth spoke without thinking. "Of course!"

He cocked a quizzical eyebrow at her. "You believe my version of events over Wickham's?"

"Yes." She paused a moment as she struggled to articulate why. "I do not believe you would trouble yourself to tell me a false story."

Mr. Darcy gave a bark of laughter. "So I am too proud to stoop to lying to you?"

She shrugged helplessly. That was not the message she had intended to convey, but it was not wholly inaccurate.

"I *am* pleased you believe me to be honorable."
Again he watched her with alarming intensity. "At
least some good has come from this farce, although too
late."

What on earth did this cryptic statement mean?

A half smile quirked one side of Mr. Darcy's
mouth. "The circumstances last night did not favor my
innocence. In your position I might have made the
same judgment."

"What will be your next course of action?"
Elizabeth asked him.

Mr. Darcy crossed the room and sank into his
chair again before responding. "I must locate the man
who *was* with your sister, but she will not even admit
his existence." Rather than anger, Elizabeth now saw
weariness and anxiety in his face.

"I can question her again, but she is not likely to
confide in me," she offered.

His mouth was set in a straight line. "I would
not ask you to spy against your sister."

It was an admirable conviction, particularly
given the circumstances. She responded without
hesitation. "And I would not have you enter an
unwanted marriage because of my sister's...folly. This
other man should take responsibility for his behavior."

"It is enough that you believe in my innocence,
Miss Elizabeth. Your faith in me is...most welcome."
He stared at the fireplace and seemed to have difficulty
articulating his thoughts. "However, I would not set
sister against sister."

Before Elizabeth could respond, Darcy stood
and straightened his coat. "I must speak with your
father, and I will return to London today. But I will
perforce return to Hertfordshire before long." He gave
her a very precise bow. "I bid you good day."

He strode to the door and disappeared within seconds.

Elizabeth remained in the drawing room, considering Mr. Darcy for some minutes. He was a most puzzling man. Lydia's behavior had caused him endless trouble, yet he was insistent that Elizabeth not violate her sister's trust.

Just as Elizabeth contemplated taking up her long-neglected embroidery, a grim-faced Jane slipped into the room, clutching a letter in one hand. "Lizzy, may we talk for a moment?" Elizabeth felt a touch of anxiety. Such distress was most unlike Jane.

Jane sank onto a settee, biting her lip as she smoothed the letter on her lap. "I had a note from Caroline Bingley informing me that the whole party has removed to London."

This was a blow indeed; Jane had been so pleased by Mr. Bingley's attentions. But— "I am sure Mr. Bingley will be back to see you within a fortnight," Elizabeth said.

Jane shook her head slowly, blinking back tears. "Caroline writes that he has no intention of returning to Netherfield and will probably give it up as soon as he receives an eligible offer!" She dabbed her eyes with her handkerchief. "She also implies that Mr. Bingley is interested in Mr. Darcy's sister."

Elizabeth could scarcely credit the news. Mr. Bingley had seemed so enchanted with Jane; they were so perfectly matched. What possibly could have happened?

"Oh." Understanding struck.

"What is it, Lizzy?" Jane asked as she folded the letter into smaller and smaller squares.

Elizabeth rubbed her hand over her lips. "Perhaps this results from the events of last night—with Mr. Darcy."

Jane's brow furrowed.

"Mr. Darcy was angry last night at being forced to propose to Lydia." *With good reason most likely.* "Nor can Mr. Bingley's sisters look favorably on what occurred. Perhaps they are concerned you mean to entrap their brother."

Jane turned white. "I would never—!"

"I know, dearest!" Elizabeth patted her sister's hand reassuringly. "I daresay Mr. Bingley knows it as well." *At least I hope he does.* "But his sisters do not…trust easily."

A small sigh escaped from Jane. "I cannot possibly convince them otherwise if they are not in Hertfordshire."

"No," Elizabeth agreed, silently castigating herself. *By judging Mr. Darcy too hastily, I may have helped to ruin all of Jane's hopes!* Elizabeth's stomach churned uneasily.

She swiftly considered and discarded various possibilities for rectifying the situation. *Mr. Darcy seemed relieved that I believed his account of the events. Perhaps if I speak with him, he could…but he is now* en route *to London, no doubt full of dark thoughts about the Bennet family.* Not that such thoughts were completely unwarranted.

What have I done?

Chapter Five

Lydia had managed to slip away from Kitty and Maria Lucas while they were admiring items in the milliner's shop. She only had a few minutes to find Wickham before the other girls sought her out. He had not been at his lodgings with Denny, so Lydia guessed he would be at his favorite pub, the Drowsy Pig.

She hesitated outside the door. A pub was hardly the best place for a girl; she had been warned repeatedly not to visit one alone. *But*, she reasoned, *there is no choice. And I have never viewed the inside of a pub.* Squaring her shoulders, Lydia strolled inside. She squinted around the dim interior until she found Wickham, occupying a corner table and nursing a pint.

As she claimed the seat opposite him, Wickham scowled. "We must not be seen together. Get you gone!"

Her hand inched across the table until it grasped his. "We did not have an opportunity to finish what we started last night." She produced the coy smile that seemed so effective with him.

He jerked his hand out of reach again. *What was the matter?* "Did you tell anyone I was with you last night?" he whispered.

"Of course not!" Lydia was indignant. "I can keep a secret…most of the time…Well, more than half the time."

Wickham rolled his eyes. "You must not tell anyone. It is vitally important!"

Oh, she had something he wanted. Lydia knew how to play this game. "What will you give me?" She gave a toss of her head.

His eyes narrowed. "What do you want?"

"I do not want to marry Mr. Darcy."

"Are you a fool? Do you know how much he is worth?"

Lydia shrugged. "I do not care two figs about that. You are a lot more fun. I want *you*." She batted her lashes at him.

For a moment a look of panic crossed Wickham's face, but it was quickly replaced by his usual easy humor—and Lydia was unsure if she had seen it at all. "Of course you do. Darcy is as interesting as dirt."

She leaned forward so he could see down the front of her dress. Men were fools about that sort of thing. Sure enough, Wickham's eyes were drawn to the sight; he licked his lips. "Will you be my hero and rescue me from Mr. Darcy?"

"Certainly." His voice had that dazed quality she so enjoyed. "But-but, not immediately. It will take some time for me to…organize everything. In the meantime, you may enjoy being Darcy's fiancée," Wickham said to her bosom.

"I do not want to wait." She pouted.

Wickham's eyes sparkled. "His family is loaded with jewelry."

Hmm. Now that was intriguing. "Very well, I will wait if you insist."

"It is necessary." He regarded her with heavily lidded eyes. "But that does not mean we cannot enjoy ourselves now and then."

One corner of her mouth curled up. "What did you have in mind?"

"There is this secluded spot right behind the pub…"

She ran her tongue over her lips—something else men liked. "Please, show me."

***

Life was good, Wickham decided. Life was very, very good. The previous night he had escaped Netherfield's library without being observed, and he had ensured the Bennet girl's silence about his identity.

Of course, the best part of last night—Wickham laughed whenever he thought of it—was that *Darcy* had been blamed for seducing the girl! Wickham could not have conceived of a better revenge on the man. So proud and haughty, convinced of his own superiority! Wickham almost wished he *had* orchestrated the circumstances himself; then he could have arranged to see Darcy's face when he was trapped into proposing to the empty-headed chit. They would make a proper pair! Darcy with the stick up his arse, and Lydia Bennet with all the self-restraint of a dog in heat.

Wickham had experienced a moment of panic when Lydia had found him at the pub, but the place had been dim and mostly empty, so he doubted anyone had seen them together. Of course, he had no intention of following through on his almost-promise to Lydia that he would rescue her from Darcy. She had next to no dowry! But if she believed he would run away with her, at least she would keep his secret. What a shame her friends had arrived at the pub before they reached the most fun part of their tryst. Thankfully, they had not seen Wickham, but he really could have used a good roll in the hay.

Wickham's own schemes were progressing nicely as well. Mary King seemed quite taken with his tales of brave militia service. Another week of wooing her and she should be ready to run off to Gretna Green. Then he could quit the militia with its tedious regulations and unreasonable expectations; they expected far too much labor from him.

There was one thing, and it was more of a puzzlement than a genuine obstacle. He felt in his pocket for the note he had received this morning from Sir William Lucas. Wickham had been introduced to the man, but they had never had a private conversation. Why would the man summon Wickham to Lucas Lodge?

However, Wickham had no reason to avoid the man, and the visit might be to his advantage. Thus, after a long, cold ride, he knocked on the door of Lucas Lodge. A footman opened the door, took his coat, and ushered him into a book-lined room which must have been Sir William's study.

Behind the large oak desk, Sir William greeted Wickham and invited him to sit. Then he fell silent, steadily regarding Wickham from behind steepled fingers.

Finally, the silence irritated Wickham. "Sir William? Did you have a matter you wished to discuss?"

"Yes, Mr. Wickham." Sir William rubbed his hand over his mostly bald head. "I had a very interesting experience last night." He paused for Wickham's reaction.

"Oh?" Wickham could not imagine how this related to him.

"Yes." Sir William laid his hands flat on the desk before him. "I grew too warm in the Netherfield ballroom—too much dancing, I suppose." Wickham nodded agreeably, attempting to forget the sight of Sir William dancing; it was a bit like watching a cow do a jig. "So I retreated outside—to Netherfield's back garden, as a matter of fact."

Wickham froze.

"And I came across a most peculiar sight. There is a door at the back of Netherfield, almost hidden in shadows, but I happen to know that it leads to the library. I saw a man slip out of the door and steal his way around to the front of the house where he could rejoin the festivities."

"Did you?" Wickham examined his nails with studied disinterest. Perhaps Sir William was not certain of the man's identity.

"The moon was bright, and I caught a good glimpse of the man's face." Sir William paused, but Wickham said nothing. "It was you."

Wickham blustered. "How could you possibly know that—?"

Sir William chuckled. "Oh, it was you, no doubt about it. I did not realize the import of what I had witnessed until I returned to the ball and learned that *Mr. Darcy* had been forced to propose to a certain young lady he encountered in the library."

Wickham said nothing, but he could feel the back of his neck growing hot. He licked his suddenly dry lips. Sir William wanted something from him. Hopefully not money, since he had precious little of it.

"I think Bennet would be quite interested to know the actual identity of the man who accompanied his daughter last night. The Bennets were so very good at bringing Darcy up to scratch. What would they do with the man who actually *had* debauched their daughter—and then fled the scene?"

Sweat had broken out on Wickham's brow, but he dared not mop it with his handkerchief and demonstrate his anxiety.

Sir William settled back into his chair, an amiable smile on his face. "I can imagine it now: Mrs. Bennet shrieking and fainting. Lydia Bennet giggling and squealing. And Mr. Bennet glaring at you through his spectacles before returning to his study." Sir William paused briefly to allow the images to settle into Wickham's mind. "Of course, the Bennet girl would confirm your identity; you would be engaged before you knew it!"

Wickham could not prevent a wince. Lydia was pretty enough and fun for a romp in the hay—not that he had romped very much the night before. But she was also demanding and so damned chatty. An hour of her incessant chatter the previous night had Wickham contemplating suicide—or murder. He could not survive a lifetime with her.

Sir William's hand toyed with a letter opener on the desk. "Of course, *Mr. Darcy* would be the most interested in this information. It would help him escape the engagement. He would be highly motivated to see you engaged to Miss Lydia."

"What do you want from me?"

The other man smiled. "I am pleased we understand each other. You see, I have a problem with which you can help me." Wickham nodded warily. "I have a daughter, Charlotte, who is eight and twenty." Wickham did not hide his wince. A woman was close to being on the shelf by that age. "An unfortunate cold prevented her from attending the ball last night." Sir William cleared his throat. She is the daughter of my first wife. And my second wife would…like to see her out of the house."

Wickham frowned, shifting uneasily in his seat. "I will not marry your daughter simply to—"

The other man interrupted. "You will be well compensated. She has a generous dowry. In addition, I will pay off your creditors in Meryton."

Now the conversation was growing more interesting! Wickham raised an eyebrow. "How generous?"

Sir William wrote a sum on a slip of paper and slid it across the desk to Wickham, who read it eagerly. It was not as much as Mary King's dowry, but it was not a paltry sum. And success with Mary King was hardly certain while Lucas's daughter was guaranteed. On the other hand, Miss Lucas probably had a face like a horse and a disposition to match; she was still unwed for a reason. Miss King at least was pretty despite the freckles.

"I should take some time to consider…"

Lucas's features hardened. "I want your agreement now, Wickham, or I will go straight to Bennet and tell him all I know."

Wickham ran his hands through his hair. Hellfire! His mind worked furiously to find a way out of this trap, but it was futile. Lydia Bennet brought almost no dowry, so Miss Lucas was infinitely preferable, no matter which barnyard animal she resembled. Wickham sighed. "Very well, I will marry your daughter."

Sir William gave him a wide grin. "Capital! Capital! Return tomorrow, and I will arrange for you to meet Charlotte; you may make the proposal then."

Why must the blasted man move so quickly? Would a couple of days at this point make Charlotte Lucas any less withered? But Wickham could not afford to anger the man. "My pleasure." He smiled through gritted teeth.

He would see how unpalatable Charlotte Lucas was; if the picture was particularly grim…well, he would find some way to escape the marriage.

Chapter Six

Collins was perplexed.

He disliked being perplexed. Life should be simple. After all, right and wrong were easy to distinguish. Good and bad behaviors were clearly delineated by society. Moral decisions were simple as long as Collins followed the guidance of his higher power: Lady Catherine de Bourgh. He was thankful for her invaluable advice every day.

When she had sagely determined it was time for him to obtain a wife, she suggested he find someone who was not brought up too high but was also an active, useful sort of woman. It had been Collins's happy thought to choose a wife from among his cousin's daughters since they would lose their home when he inherited it.

It was an elegant solution. It helped to mitigate his guilt, and it complied in every respect with Lady Catherine's deman—suggestion. Above all, it was extremely convenient; Collins did not wish to fuss overly long about this business of finding a wife. Like most things, it should be simple and straightforward.

When Collins first arrived at Longbourn, he had fixed his attentions on Jane Bennet, who was a lovely, serene creature. But Mrs. Bennet had mentioned that her eldest was already attached to the nearby owner of Netherfield. So Collins had turned his attention to the second daughter, Miss Elizabeth, who was happily unattached. Being both active and useful, she also met the criteria Lady Catherine had enumerated. She was also healthy and strong of limb—and had all of her own teeth. She was neither too tall nor too short. And she did not wear feathers in her hair; Collins particularly disliked hair feathers. In all respects, she was admirably suited to his purposes.

Collins had been quite happy with his decision until he actually proposed to Miss Elizabeth—once he got her alone in Longbourn's drawing room. There his plans encountered an unanticipated obstacle. He had laid out all of his considerations quite rationally, assured her that he would not berate her for her lack of dowry, and embellished his proposal with all the extravagant declarations of love that women expected.

And yet she appeared to have refused him.

It was not possible she had *actually* refused him; that would fly in the face of reason. And Miss Elizabeth seemed to be an eminently sensible woman.

And so very pretty. Not as elegant as Lady Catherine or her daughter, but—

Aha! Collins realized what was happening as he returned his attention to the events in the drawing room. He again listed the great advantages of the match. "I must therefore conclude that you are not serious in your rejection of me. I shall choose to attribute it to your wish of increasing my love by suspense, according to the usual practice of elegant females," he informed her.

Collins expected her to laugh and bat her eyelashes, admitting that he had caught her at her game. But instead her lips—pressed firmly together—turned white, and her face grew red. Were those good signs? "I assure you, sir, that I have no pretensions whatever to that kind of elegance which consists in tormenting a respectable man." Her voice held an odd tone he could not decipher. "I would rather be paid the compliment of being believed sincere."

Collins frowned. What was her meaning? What sort of game was she playing? Perhaps it was best to be blunt. "You should take into consideration that in spite of your manifold attractions, it is by no means certain that another offer of marriage may ever be made to you," he warned her.

Her mouth hung open for a moment. Then she closed her mouth and swallowed, a uniformly charming gesture. "No, sir. You could not make me happy, and I am convinced that I am the last woman in the world who could make you so."

He smiled at her. "Your modesty does you credit, Cousin. But—"

"Really, Mr. Collins," she interrupted him, "I know not how to express my refusal in such a way as to convince you of its being one. Can I speak plainer? Do not consider me now as an elegant female intending to plague you but as a rational creature, speaking the truth from her heart."

This greatly resembled a refusal, but Collins knew it was not. There was no reason—no reason at all—that she would refuse him. Therefore, it could not be. Perhaps—ah, perhaps—the problem was a lack of formality! He knelt down somewhat awkwardly on one knee. "You are uniformly charming!" he cried, bravely ignoring the pain in his knee. "And I am persuaded that when sanctioned by the express authority of both of your excellent parents, my proposal will not fail of being acceptable."

Collins looked up to see how this speech had been received. Surely Miss Elizabeth was now prepared to admit she intended to accept him. However, the room was empty.

Really! This was taking the practices of elegant females a bit far! Collins regained his feet with the help of a conveniently located chair and strode through the open door into the hallway, which was completely devoid of inhabitants. Was she hoping he would pursue her? He had never heard of such a game, but he had never proposed before.

Perhaps he needed a pet name for her of the sort which was acceptable between husbands and wives. My precious peacock? My dearest cherub? My honey blossom? He could test them—each in turn—to discover which she liked the best. Or when he was her husband, perhaps he should simply select one for her?

Rapid footsteps sounded from the direction of Mr. Bennet's study. Ah, she had consulted with her father, and he had demanded she cease these silly games! However, it was Mrs. Bennet rather than Elizabeth who entered the room. Collins blinked in confusion.

Mrs. Bennet's hands fluttered about her like a pair of butterflies. "Oh, Mr. Collins!" she cried when she saw him.

Collins drew up to his full height, straightening his coat. "My precious honey blossom appears to have refused my suit, but I am not daunted! I have scaled higher castle walls than these. I shall cross the moat and brave the crocodiles—" Mrs. Bennet stared at him, her mouth agape.

She swallowed as her eyes darted about the room. "Lizzy can be quite stubborn in matters such as these," Mrs. Bennet admitted.

"Stubborn?" Collins frowned. "That is not a quality Lady Catherine wishes in my wife."

Mrs. Bennet glanced over her shoulder at the hallway and then stepped a little closer to Collins, lowering her voice. "In truth, Mr. Collins, Lizzy may not be the best choice for you."

He was confused; Elizabeth was his love bunny! "But—"

"Jane's hopes for Mr. Bingley have been dashed to pieces, and she is dearly in need of a... rescuer—a knight, as it were."

Collins considered this for a moment. Yes, he would dearly love to be a rescuer. He could easily envision himself sitting tall on horseback with sunlight gleaming off his armor. What a noble role to play! And Miss Jane would be so pleased by his attentions, so grateful. Much more grateful than Elizabeth, who did not yet know heartache. The more he thought on it, the more he liked the idea.

Mrs. Bennet smiled brightly. "Jane would, I daresay, make an excellent clergyman's wife. She is sweet, modest, and a good housekeeper." Mrs. Bennet kept her voice low. Did she not wish her second daughter to hear her praising the elder?

Collins blinked rapidly. He was not accustomed to redirecting his thoughts so quickly, and he must remember Lady Catherine's criteria. "But is she active and useful?" he asked.

Mrs. Bennet stared at him blankly for a moment. "Yes, yes, of course! Very active and very useful."

Collins meditated on Jane Bennet's face. She was quite the prettiest of the sisters and had a soothing serenity that would be appropriate for a clergyman's wife. Lady Catherine would find her acceptable. And after all, Miss Jane was in need of a rescuer…

He smiled. He would show the Bennet family how flexible and magnanimous he could be; he was not too fixed on one woman as his choice of wife. "Very well, I am sure Miss Bennet would be eminently acceptable."

Mrs. Bennet's shoulders sagged in relief. "Very good! Please remain here in the drawing room, and I will send Jane in directly."

***

Jane was reading with Kitty and Lydia in the blue parlor when her mother arrived. Her favorite poetry was no consolation today; any poem about love made her melancholy. She had switched to a popular novel, but it waxed eloquent about the love between two characters, bringing tears to her eyes. Finally, in despair, Jane had picked up Fordyce's *Sermons*, which did not remind her of Mr. Bingley but did little to hold her attention.

Her mother burst through the door, startling all three inhabitants of the room. "Jane, come quickly! Mr. Collins wishes to speak with you!"

Kitty and Lydia exchanged a look and giggled.

Mr. Collins? What could he possibly have to say to me? However, Jane obediently closed her book and stood. "I do not understand." She had suspected their cousin intended to ask for Lizzy's hand, but Jane knew Lizzy's temperament and knew his suit would be in vain.

"You need not understand!" her mother responded in a vexed tone. "Just come!"

Shrugging, Jane followed her mother into the hallway and through the door to the drawing room, where indeed Mr. Collins was sitting.

Mama took Jane's hand and stared meaningfully into her eyes. "Mr. Collins has had a trying day. We must do *everything* in our power to make him happy." Then she winked at Jane. What could her mother possibly mean?

Mama gave Mr. Collins a little smile and a wave of her handkerchief. Then...*oh, merciful heavens!* She quitted the room, closing the door behind her and leaving Jane *alone* with Mr. Collins.

Mystified and more than a little anxious, Jane seated herself on the sofa closest to the fireplace and gave Mr. Collins a tentative smile. "You wished to speak with me?"

"Yes." He took a deep breath. "Er…" He cleared his throat noisily. "Um…almost since the first day in this house I singled you out as the companion of my future life."

It took Jane a moment to decipher his convoluted syntax. *Oh, Good Lord! He is proposing to me!*

Jane's first impulse was to race for the door so she need not respond to Mr. Collins's proposal. Her feet twitched with the need to flee. But of course, she could never bring herself to be so impolite, so she willed her feet to immobility.

She realized Mr. Collins was still speaking. "But before I am run away with my feelings on the subject, perhaps it would be advisable for me to state my reasons for marrying…"

Jane stifled the impulse to laugh at the thought that Mr. Collins would ever allow his feelings to run away with him. As the man recited his reasons for marrying, Jane considered him. *Lizzy is correct; this man is a bore and pompous as well.*

"And thirdly, which perhaps I ought to have mentioned earlier, marriage is the particular recommendation of my patroness, Lady Catherine de Bourgh…"

Jane tried to concentrate on Mr. Collins's words. She really did, but it was so difficult. Why was he not saying these words to Lizzy? She was the object of his attentions but could easily say no to him.

In a sudden rush of horror, Jane realized why some of Mr. Collins's words sounded rehearsed. He had already proposed to Lizzy and been turned down! And now Mama wanted Jane to accept in her place.

Jane's stomach did a slow flip, which had nothing to do with what she had eaten for lunch. Whenever Jane thought of marriage, of walking down the middle of the Meryton church, she pictured Mr. Bingley's face at the end of the aisle. But now that was not to be.

Jane had finished shedding tears over it. She had. She was perhaps still a trifle melancholy, for Mr. Bingley was the most amiable man of her acquaintance. But she would never see him again. Netherfield would be let by another family, and someday Mr. Collins would inherit Longbourn—when he would be free to turn Jane's mother and her unmarried sisters into the hedgerows.

A little sigh escaped Jane, but Mr. Collins did not notice. What did it matter who she wed if she could not wed Mr. Bingley? She could not imagine falling in love with another man. The experience had been too painful; in the future, Jane would guard her heart.

"Let her be a gentlewoman for my sake, and for your own, let her be an active, useful sort of woman, not brought up too high and able to make a small income go a good way…"

Oh, heavens! Mr. Collins was still speaking about Lady Catherine. But Jane had no doubt she would rub along tolerably with Mr. Collins's patroness; no one ever disliked her. In this way, she supposed, she was better suited to marry Mr. Collins than Lizzy would be.

And marrying Mr. Collins would bring so much joy to so many. Her mother would be happy for the security. Her sisters would be excited that they need not leave Longbourn when Papa died. Mr. Collins would be happy to secure a bride who would be acceptable to his patroness.

Jane tried not to consider Lizzy's reaction.

Jane could not have Mr. Bingley. She could not have happiness. But if she married to secure her family's future, perhaps she could have contentment. Providing for her family would bring its own kind of happiness.

"And now nothing remains but for me to assure you in the most animated language of the violence of my affection." He landed on his knees before Jane's sofa, almost as if he were at the end of a carnival act.

Had he uttered these same words to Lizzy? She supposed he had. Well, it mattered little. Despite his passionate declarations, Jane had few illusions about Mr. Collins's sentiments. Still, he was willing to fake affection, and perhaps that was a start. Jane could pretend the affection was real and could respond with false affection of her own. He might never know the difference. Surely that was better than nothing.

Mr. Collins regarded her expectantly. Now was the time. She must make a decision. She could postpone it no longer. Jane closed her eyes and said a little prayer for forgiveness. Then she opened them and looked down at him. "Yes, Mr. Collins, I will marry you."

***

Bingley stood at the top of the steps, waiting as the carriage pulled to a stop before his townhouse. Then he hurried down the stairs, nearly reaching the carriage door before the footman, although he was in time to hold his mother's hand as she alighted from the vehicle.

"Thank you, Charles. It is wonderful to see you!" She gave him a sweet smile and drew him into a warm hug. Bingley squeezed her tight, conveying his love and happiness at seeing his mother again.

However, she felt smaller and frailer in his arms. Had she actually lost weight, or was it his imagination?

"Six months is too long, Mama," he said as he finally released her. "Next time you travel, I pray you, do not make it such a lengthy trip."

"I do not have any future travel plans," she responded in a quiet voice. Where had her usual exuberance gone? People often compared her temperament to Bingley's own.

As always, he offered her his arm on the steps into Bingley House, but for the first time she actually leaned on him as they ascended. She stumbled twice and would have fallen the second time if Bingley had not caught her hand. It was disturbing. Of course, his mother was aging just like everyone else, but Bingley had never expected her to grow *old*.

"Louisa and Caroline are visiting Uncle Robert in Scarborough," he said once they had attained the front portico. "But I have written to them that you are back in England."

"It will be nice to see them," his mother responded.

As they approached, the butler whisked the door to Bingley House open, and Bingley escorted his mother into the front hallway. "Would you like to go to your room and freshen up?" he asked.

"No. I have not seen you for so long, and letters only convey so much. I will rest later." His mother took decisive steps toward the front drawing room.

Bingley shrugged. "As you wish." He sent the butler for tea and followed her. As he helped situate her on the sofa, the very fact that she did not object to his overly solicitous behavior bothered him.

"Your letters made Italy sound fascinating." He smiled at her after he had taken a seat.

His mother clapped her hands almost like a small child. "Oh, it was! The weather was delightful. And the sculptures—oh, lovely statuary everywhere you look! Your Aunt Margaret was enthralled by the food, as you can imagine."

Bingley chuckled. "If Italy was that delightful, I am surprised you returned so soon."

He meant the words as a jest, but his mother appeared unexpectedly grim. "I would have been pleased to remain longer."

Bingley's heart beat a little faster. "What do you mean? Nothing compelled you to return. I know you miss us, but—"

"Of course not. But, Charles, I...I am ill."

Bingley's heart plunged into his feet. "Ill?" he croaked.

"I experienced some fainting spells. The doctor in Italy speculated that it was my heart. He bade me return home and order my affairs."

Bingley swallowed, wishing to deny the doctor's every word. "How long...d-does he think—?" He could not bring himself to finish.

She shrugged. "He could not say. It could be years. It could be days."

Bingley blew out a breath. "Oh, Mama." He moved to sit next to her on the sofa and enveloped her in another hug. Somehow she had become even frailer in the past few minutes. "We must have you examined by a doctor here in London."

"Yes," she squeezed his hand, "but I am at peace with whatever happens, Charles. Perishing at eight and fifty would hardly be considered a life cut tragically short."

Bingley's eyes ached, and he rubbed them with his free hand. "I-I am n-not prepared to lose you."

"You will be fine." She patted his arm reassuringly. "You have stepped into your father's shoes rather well. You are a son I can be proud of."

"Thank you." Bingley blinked rapidly. "Are you in pain? What may I do to help?"

"I have occasional chest pain, not severe. But there is one thing…"

His hand enclosed hers. "Anything," he breathed.

She smoothed his hair away from his face. "I pray you, tell me you made an offer to that nice Bennet lady you described in your letters."

Bingley froze in place. His muscles locked up and prevented him from moving so much as an inch. "Offer?"

"You wrote how you were considering proposing, and on the ship from Italy my thoughts were preoccupied with the hope that you had done so. A wife will help you build a family and order your life. You are too old to flit about England, changing your mind like your sister changes clothes."

"A wife." Bingley swallowed.

She rubbed his cheek affectionately. "From your letters it seems Miss Bennet appreciates your fine qualities. I thought you might be married by the time I arrived."

His mother's eyes brimmed over with excitement and hope. The thought of extinguishing that hope crushed him. "No, not married," he admitted.

"But you did propose?" his mother asked, watching him closely.

How could he reveal the truth? That he had abandoned Jane based on unfounded suspicions? That he had yielded to his sisters' pressure and likely caused the woman he loved endless heartache? Every night he lay in bed, meditating on Jane Bennet's face and wondering if fleeing Netherfield had been the best choice. But he was too much of a coward to rectify his mistake.

Her pale blue eyes regarded him so earnestly that he could not bear to disappoint her.

No. After breaking his own heart, and likely Jane's, he could not break his mother's as well. What if her disappointment prompted a heart seizure? He could not risk worsening her health.

Bingley remained absolutely still as a moment of clarity washed over him. His mother wished to see him married. Now he realized that above all else he wished to *be* married. These weeks away from Jane had been colorless and bleak. Away from his sisters' constant criticism, Bingley had become dubious that the Bennets had sought to entrap him—and more convinced of Jane's true feelings.

Over the past weeks, Bingley's feelings for Jane Bennet had not dissipated as they had in his previous affaires de coeur. The persistence of such emotion proved his niggling suspicion: he was in love with her and should have proposed to her.

He was seized by an overwhelming urge to saddle his horse and gallop to Hertfordshire without delay. True, Jane might refuse him, but he did not think that likely. Surely she returned his affections.

He was decided. He would visit Hertfordshire and beg Jane's hand, in which case he need not reveal to his mother how he had abandoned his love at his sisters' behest. He was heartily ashamed of himself.

Therefore, if he told his mother he had proposed to Jane, it would merely be…premature—not an actual lie.

Bingley shoved his fingers through his hair, noting the sweat breaking out on his brow. He had never uttered such a falseho—premature declaration in his life. But his mind was decided. "You will love her, Mama. She is an angel."

"So she accepted you?"

It is for her own benefit, Bingley reminded himself. "Yes. She has the sweetest temperament—never a harsh word to say about anyone."

"She sounds well suited to you, Charles." His mother smiled beatifically at him.

He shrugged, hoping he appeared modest rather than ashamed. "She is far better than I deserve." *Particularly given how I have treated her.*

But Jane was a forgiving creature. Surely she would understand his reservations, and they could swiftly relegate all the unpleasantness to the past. Bingley would return to Longbourn and propose immediately. Then his mother would happily witness his wedding, none the wiser about when the proposal had occurred.

He was certain…almost certain…well, mostly certain that Jane loved him and wanted to marry him. It had only been a few weeks since he had quitted Hertfordshire. Surely she would not have forgotten him so soon. He could beg her forgiveness and ask for her hand. She was an angel; she would forgive him, and they would wed.

His mother sighed blissfully. "It sounds perfect." Bingley fervently hoped it would be.

Chapter Seven

"Mr. Wickham wishes to speak with you, my dear."

At her father's words Charlotte Lucas diverted her attention from her needlework.

Wickham let loose his most stunning smile, the one that had persuaded Lydia Bennet to grant him access to her bodice. Miss Lucas, however, frowned as if wondering why he would be smiling at her.

"Mr. Wickham?" she echoed dubiously.

"Yes, my dear." Her father nodded vigorously. "I shall leave you two to talk."

Her brow furrowed as her father closed the drawing room door. "How very odd," she murmured. Then she resumed her stitching. "What did you wish to speak about, Mr. Wickham? I should not think we have much in common."

Wickham cleared his throat. She was an exceedingly…direct young lady. Surely she understood why a father would leave his daughter alone with an eligible man. Had she been on the shelf so long that she did not even hope for an offer?

Wickham could not deny she was plain. Her hair was a mousy shade of brown and pulled severely back from her face without any attempt at styling. Her face was round and pale. Her dress was so drab that she was easily overshadowed by the colorful pattern of the settee she occupied. Most noticeably, she granted him none of those coy glances he was accustomed to receiving from young women.

Wickham felt like an accomplished hunter who was faced with a bizarre new quarry for the first time.

He summoned to mind the figure on Sir William's slip of paper and forged ahead. "I was hoping you would do me the very great honor of being my wife." He braced himself for an excess of enthusiasm; she might hug him or erupt into high-pitched squeals.

Nothing happened. Except she paused in her stitching…and then resumed. Had she even heard him?

After a long pause he prompted, "What is your response?"

"Oh!" Her eyes met his again. "I was not certain you had finished speaking. I thank you for the great honor, Mr. Wickham, but I must decline."

Wickham mopped his brow with a handkerchief. *Damn these uniforms—always too hot!* Decline? Such a possibility had not occurred to him. "W-why?" he asked shakily.

"Oh." She knotted off a thread and selected a different color. "We are not well acquainted, are we? And I do not believe I would like being the wife of an officer. I would like a comfortable home, a permanent one."

He cleared his throat. This conversation was not proceeding at all as he had expected. She would not even look at him! That never happened. Women were *always* pleased to gaze on his features. *Is the girl simple? Or have I somehow lost my appeal?* Wickham had a sudden desire to find a mirror.

Reordering his thoughts, he swallowed convulsively. "You need not follow the drum. We could purchase a house where you could reside when I am gone. I have some funds."

"You mean my father is providing a generous dowry." Her matter-of-fact tone suggested the dowry held little interest for her.

Wickham was sufficiently off kilter to answer honestly. "Well, yes."

Tilting her head to the side, she frowned at him as if he presented a puzzle to be solved. After a moment, she shook her head. "I am not sure you would make a good husband."

What? Wickham's pride was pricked. Women *always* wanted him! He was charming. *Charming* is what he did! Well, and attractive. How could she be so blind?

I shall show her.

Suppressing a premature grin, Wickham slid from his seat and settled next to Charlotte on the settee. She did not lay down her damn needlework, and he did not like playing second fiddle to embroidery.

He inspected her gown. A serviceable muslin, it was more modest than most dresses he encountered— which unfortunately meant less skin was available. But he could rise to this challenge. He leaned close enough to smell her faint honeysuckle scent and kissed his way down her neck.

She paused her needlework.

And then resumed.

Aside from a small furrow in her brow, his actions did not appear to have attracted her notice at all. Damnation! What was wrong with the woman? That maneuver should have earned him a shiver, a deep sigh, and perhaps some kisses in return.

He ran a finger under the edge of her neckline, right on the top of her shoulder. Perhaps she needed verbal seduction. "You are very beautiful."

This provoked a reaction but not quite the one he expected. She turned toward him, frowning. "No, I am not. Why would you say so?"

Wickham blinked and allowed his hand to drop. Every woman loved being told she was beautiful, did she not? He swallowed, attempting to reestablish his equilibrium. "You are beautiful to me," he murmured.

She pursed her lips. "I sincerely doubt that, Mr. Wickham. You are acquainted with many prettier women." She moved the position of her embroidery to get better light.

Very well. It was time for heavy artillery. He leaned forward until his lips nearly touched her ear. "I love you."

She snorted. "Do not be absurd. You barely know me."

Wickham recoiled.

Why couldn't she simply accept him and be done with it? Damn it all! Did she not understand he needed the money? A spinster of eight and twenty should fall into his hands like a ripe plum. How vexing!

Increasingly desperate, he breathed in her ear while simultaneously and expertly kneading her breast. She stopped stitching but uttered no protest. *Progress, at last!* Then she giggled. "Mr. Wickham, that tickles!"

Tickles? That maneuver had convinced Marianne Smith to visit his room last week!

But Wickham persisted. Placing one hand behind Charlotte's neck and the other on her face, he kissed her very thoroughly—using tongue and lips and every trick he knew. When he finally released her, he was panting and proud of himself. Now she could not ignore him!

Her lips were slightly open, her cheeks were flushed, and her needlework was abandoned on her lap. She raised her eyebrows and licked her lips. "You are very good at kissing, Mr. Wickham. You must have practiced quite a bit." *Was that a veiled insult, suggesting I am a man of loose morals? Of course I am, but how impolite!*

Miss Lucas bent her head to her needlework once more. Wickham barely restrained himself from swearing in the presence of a lady. Would nothing move this woman? Despite his most charming maneuvers, she had brushed him away like a fly.

He stewed silently for a minute. How could he convince this woman to accept his suit? Without her, he faced certain ruin.

Unexpectedly, Charlotte looked up at him again. "Do you like children?" Her eyebrows were raised quizzically.

Children? What was she on about? Really, this woman was the most vexing he had ever encountered. He shrugged. "I suppose."

"Would you be willing to give me children?"

"Of course." He didn't much care about the actual children, but the begetting part was a specialty of his.

"I would dearly like to have children." These were the most emotional words Miss Lucas had uttered in his presence. "Would you leave me alone once I had a sufficient number of children?"

Wickham had the odd feeling he was negotiating his proposal like a business transaction. *Leave her alone? In bed?* "Very well." He would have no difficulty finding companionship elsewhere.

She regarded him sharply. "And if we wed, would you allow me to run the household as I see fit?"

"Certainly." Wickham had no interest in children or households; she was welcome to the responsibility.

She rubbed her chin as she contemplated him. "I suppose I could make it work."

"Make what work?" he asked.

She shrugged. "A marriage, even though I do not find you particularly attractive." Wickham's jaw dropped open. "And your character *is* somewhat lacking." This had to be the most humiliating marriage proposal in the history of the world! Miss Lucas continued, "But no one else has proposed, and I would like to have children and my own household. So I suppose you will suffice—if you agree to my conditions."

Wickham mopped his brow again. "Yes," he managed to croak.

"Good." She stuck out her hand, and Wickham shook it automatically. "Then, Mr. Wickham, I accept your proposal."

***

Elizabeth kicked a stone that lay in her path as she walked along the road, returning home after visiting Oakham Mount. Usually the lovely view lifted her spirits, but it had not done so today. Nearly a month had passed since the ill-fated Netherfield ball, and still the various consequences of that evening disturbed her.

Lydia had made no further confessions about another man and insisted that Mr. Darcy was the only man present. However, she refused to act like an engaged woman. She still enjoyed flirtations with many of the officers, including Mr. Denny, who seemed decent if dull, and Mr. Wickham, who regarded Lydia with a sly smile that Elizabeth heartily disliked. Why had she ever thought the man handsome and honorable? Clearly he was untrustworthy in the extreme!

Elizabeth had repeatedly begged her parents to curb Lydia's reckless behavior, but her father deemed it too much trouble, and her mother believed Lydia should enjoy her freedom before she wed. No one seemed concerned about Mr. Darcy's opinion about such openly flirtatious behavior or whether Lydia's wildness would reflect poorly on her fiancé. It was most unfair to Mr. Darcy! He had not desired the betrothal, and Elizabeth increasingly believed he had done nothing to deserve it. Although Elizabeth had initially disliked Mr. Darcy, she experienced great sympathy for him.

Elizabeth and Jane had both spoken to Lydia about her wild behavior, with little success. She insisted on "having some laughs" before she was shackled to one man. In fact, Elizabeth was far more concerned about the future of her marriage than was Lydia herself. When she spoke of her future husband, Lydia only complained about his lack of fun, or she imagined the jewels, clothes, and carriages he would provide. She viewed the wedding as some future event that would occur in a few years.

Their father had heard nothing from Mr. Darcy. Did that mean he did not intend to honor his promise to Lydia, or was he simply biding his time? Elizabeth was torn about which outcome she preferred. While ordinarily she believed a man should honor his promise to marry a woman, she admitted to a sense of relief at the thought that Mr. Darcy would not wed Lydia since it seemed likely they would both be miserable. She could think of few people so ill-suited to marry than Lydia and Mr. Darcy.

Elizabeth drew her shawl more closely about her shoulders as her thoughts turned to Jane. She had been horrified when Jane accepted Mr. Collins's offer. If she had thought that he might propose to Jane—and she might accept—Elizabeth would have accepted him herself. Far better for Elizabeth to make that sacrifice than her gentle, loving sister.

While Jane had the gentlest, most forbearing nature of any woman in England, even she could not possibly withstand the assault that years of stupidity would provoke. Elizabeth had begged Jane to reconsider, but Jane was determined to preserve Longbourn for their family and was certain that she would never love again. The betrothal had been created, and—much to her chagrin— Elizabeth could not unmake it if both principals did not cooperate.

Elizabeth was cross with their mother for having placed Jane in such a position. Mama certainly knew that Elizabeth and Papa would have opposed such a marriage for Jane, so she had arranged for a hasty proposal without their knowledge. By the time they had learned of Mr. Collins's intentions, Jane had already accepted.

Thus, Elizabeth and her mother were barely on speaking terms. Her father had been similarly outraged at the time; however, he had been more philosophical in his acceptance of the situation.

Jane had tried to talk Elizabeth out of her rage. "You must make allowances for differences in temperament," she insisted. "Not everyone is romantic, Lizzy."

"No," Elizabeth had countered, "but *you* are."

Jane had not denied the truth of Elizabeth's assertion, but she had obviously surrendered any hope of loving again. Even now the thought of Jane giving in to despair and shackling herself to that oaf brought tears to Elizabeth's eyes.

She entertained little hope that the situation could be improved. If both Jane and Mr. Collins were determined to wed, what could possibly convince them otherwise?

It was the fault of those interfering Bingley sisters. If they had not forced Mr. Bingley to leave Hertfordshire, then Jane would not have plunged into the despair that rendered her vulnerable to Mr. Collins's blandishments.

Enough of these gloomy thoughts! I embarked on this walk to distract myself from these troubles, and here I am carrying them with me! Elizabeth had arrived at the edge of the Longbourn estate, marked by a large pond where the stable boys sometimes watered the cows. However, today the pond lacked visitors, save for a few ducks. Stepping off the road, Elizabeth followed the short dirt path to the pond's edge.

Perhaps throwing something would help ease her frustrations.

Bending down, Elizabeth selected a small, flat, round stone. With a flick of her wrist, she sent it skimming across the surface of the pond, scaring the ducks into flight. One, two, three skips before the stone sank into the water. *I can do better than that!* She selected another stone and sent this one across the pond. Four skips this time. Another stone yielded a disappointing three skips again, but the next one skipped five times! Elizabeth laughed aloud at her triumph.

"Miss Elizabeth?"

Elizabeth started so violently that she was forced to grab a sapling near the edge of the pond to avoid falling into the water. Regaining her footing, she turned toward the road—where she spied Mr. Bingley dismounting from his horse. She had always liked Mr. Bingley, although she was disappointed at the way he had treated Jane.

"Mr. Bingley." As he approached, she gave a small curtsey. "What brings you to Hertfordshire?" She could hear the coolness in her own voice.

He returned with his usual warm, open smile. "I have returned to Netherfield for a few days and thought I would call at Longbourn."

Elizabeth frowned. "But I understood you planned to relinquish Netherfield as soon as an eligible offer was made."

Mr. Bingley raised his eyebrows. "I did— I do?"

"Your sister so informed Jane in her letter."

He blinked rapidly. "Oh…er, my plans regarding Netherfield are not yet fixed." He wiped his hands nervously on his breeches.

"I see." Elizabeth returned her eyes to the pond to avoid that earnest blue gaze. "Did your sisters accompany you…or Mr. Darcy?"

Mr. Bingley also enjoyed the meager view afforded by the pond. "No…um…this is a solo visit. Last minute, as it were." He licked his lips. "Sometimes I am impulsive like that."

She nodded. He returned his gaze to her face, eagerness warring with anxiety. "How fares your family?"

Elizabeth's stomach twisted. Must she be the one to tell him about Jane's situation? She heaved a resigned sigh. It would be best if he arrived at Longbourn armed with knowledge about Jane's engagement. Presumably he would rather receive the news from Elizabeth than from Jane herself.

She swallowed, looking everywhere but at Mr. Bingley. "Everyone is enjoying excellent health." He nodded vigorously. "And of course, you are aware of Lydia's betrothal to Mr. Darcy." He frowned a little at this but said nothing. "And…um…well, there was news of another betrothal as well." There was no way to soften the blow; she could make it as quick as possible. Elizabeth closed her eyes and said the last part in a rush. "Jane accepted an offer of marriage from our cousin, Mr. Collins."

Opening her eyes, Elizabeth watched the news sink into Mr. Bingley's awareness. His open smile faltered and disappeared as his mouth fell open and his eyes widened. "M-Mr. Collins?" His lower lip trembled. Abruptly, Mr. Bingley stumbled backward as if his knees could no longer hold him, and he fell against a large boulder near the edge of the pond. He sat heavily on it—his head in his hands. If Elizabeth had ever harbored doubts that Mr. Bingley loved Jane, she did so no longer. "She is e-engaged to Mr. C-Collins?"

Elizabeth felt like she had just kicked a puppy. "I am afraid so." His distress was so clear that she was sorely tempted—despite the impropriety—to put her arms around him for comfort. How could she account for Jane's decision and alleviate his distress? Was it even possible? "Mr. Collins is to inherit Longbourn upon my father's passing." Mr. Bingley nodded jerkily. "He wished to choose a wife from among my father's daughters as recompense…." There was no need to reveal how Elizabeth herself had refused him. "I believe Jane felt obligated to help secure the family's future."

"She does not love him?" Mr. Bingley's voice was hoarse and strained.

Would that make the news easier or more difficult for him to accept? Elizabeth did not know; it was best to simply tell the truth. "I believe she has friendly feelings toward him, but she does not love him."

Had Mr. Bingley returned to Hertfordshire to make Jane an offer? *Why did I not accept Mr. Collins? Then Jane would be free! I should have foreseen Mr. Bingley's return.*

Mr. Bingley finally raised his head, displaying red-rimmed eyes. "I-I returned to Netherfield to—well, it hardly matters now."

Elizabeth nodded. Should she encourage Mr. Bingley to speak with Jane? She was not the kind to break a promise, particularly not one of such import. But she might still harbor feelings for him.

"I am a fool." Bitterness saturated Mr. Bingley's voice.

"No—"

"I should not have been persuaded to leave Netherfield."

"I am very sorry."

He stood, staring bleakly over the lake. "It is my own doing. It is right that I should suffer for it."

"No!"

He gave a wan smile but did not turn in her direction. "You are too forgiving."

"You will meet another woman someday."

He was shaking his head even before she finished speaking. "I have met many women; none have affected me like Jane." A cold breeze blew, and Mr. Bingley wrapped both arms around his chest. "And there is the matter of my m-mother."

"Your mother?" Elizabeth's brows drew together.

He looked down as his boot idly kicked a few loose stones. "She is ill. Her heart." Elizabeth nodded, still mystified. "I told her…I allowed her to believe…I am already engaged." Elizabeth gaped at him. "It was foolish. I thought I could ride to Longbourn, beg Jane's forgiveness, and make my lie a reality. But now—" He swallowed convulsively. "What would a revelation of the truth do to my mother? Not only am I not engaged, but I lied to her! Would it hasten her demise?"

Elizabeth could think of nothing to say in response. Mr. Bingley turned a bleak face to her, staring for such a long moment that she grew uncomfortable and looked away.

"Unless...yes!" A new note of hope in his voice drew her attention back to him. "Unless I could be betrothed to a *different* Miss Bennet..."

Elizabeth frowned at him. *What is he suggesting? Lydia is already engaged, and he barely knows Kitty or Mary... Oh.*

"Mr. Bingley!" She gasped.

He closed the distance between them. "It would be the perfect solution, unless...is your heart engaged elsewhere?"

For some reason Mr. Darcy's face flashed into Elizabeth's mind; she knew not why. Although their last encounter had been cordial, he was customarily cold and unpleasant. "No, my heart is not engaged."

Mr. Bingley took one of her hands in his. "Then would you consent to a betrothal? Even if it is a temporary one? Under such circumstances, at least I might present a Miss Bennet to my mother. She will find your wit and beauty quite pleasing, I am sure."

A refusal was on the tip of her tongue, but despite the circumstances, Elizabeth was flattered by his words. "Temporary?" she asked.

"We do not know each other well. If you later decide we do not suit, I will not hold you to the promise. It can be a long engagement."

"But your mother—"

He frowned. "I believe Mama will simply be pleased I plan to wed. That will make her happy for now."

Elizabeth tucked a loose lock of hair behind her ear. "I dislike deceiving people."

"It is not a deception if you would actually consider marrying me." He grinned and gave her a sidelong glance. "I daresay our chances of happiness are greater than Darcy and Miss Lydia's."

Or Jane and Mr. Collins's. But Elizabeth did not say it aloud.

He graced her with one of his engaging puppy smiles. "I like you, Elizabeth. I believe you and I would rub along quite well."

Yes, except that you are in love with my sister, she thought darkly. But perhaps such feelings would fade with time. He had spoken of a long engagement...

Biting her lip, Elizabeth deliberated. She could not help considering Mr. Bingley's five thousand a year. Elizabeth had hoped to marry for love, but she must view her family's situation realistically. While Jane's marriage would secure Longbourn for the family, the Bennet sisters still had little in the way of dowries—and Lydia's marriage to Mr. Darcy was far from certain. If Elizabeth married a wealthy man, it would provide security for the whole family.

Mr. Bingley was a very pleasant man with extremely amiable manners. Being married to him would be far preferable to marrying Mr. Collins. This thought occasioned another twinge of guilt over having refused the parson. If Elizabeth had agreed to his offer, Jane would be free to accept Mr. Bingley now.

I do not wish Mr. Bingley's feelings for Jane to fade, Elizabeth realized. *I want them both to have the happiness they deserve. Therefore, I should not accept his offer.*

However, if Elizabeth declined, Mr. Bingley would no doubt return to London immediately, and they might never encounter him again. If she accepted, perhaps she could effect a reconciliation between the lovers and encourage Jane to break her engagement.

"If I do this, it will provide you with an opportunity to speak with Jane. I would be pleased if you could persuade her to marry you instead of Mr. Collins." Elizabeth held his gaze. "You would make her happy."

Mr. Bingley's mouth fell open slightly. "So you will accept me on the condition that I persuade your sister to marry me?"

"I would like her to have the opportunity to reconsider her engagement, yes. I believe she would be far happier with you."

Mr. Bingley paused before he answered. "Surely this must be the strangest betrothal agreement ever." He laughed, and she joined him. "However, I will gladly make the attempt. But Jane has strong principles; she would not take such a commitment lightly." Elizabeth nodded her understanding. Mr. Bingley took her hands in his. "And I do think we would do well together. What say you to my proposal, then?"

Elizabeth took a deep breath. "Yes, Mr. Bingley, I will marry you."

Chapter Eight

"Perhaps I ought not to have agreed," Elizabeth said to Jane for the third time. As they readied themselves for bed, Elizabeth had related her conversation with Mr. Bingley. Jane's face was very still, and her eyes were suspiciously shiny, but she maintained her composure.

"No, Lizzy, you did the right thing." Jane swallowed. "I want you and Char—Mr. Bingley to be happy. You will suit very well."

"Dearest," Elizabeth sat on the bed and slid her arm around Jane's shoulder, "I would not have agreed if I did not hope that this course might lead him back to you. He still cares for you—very much."

Jane kneaded the crumpled handkerchief in her hands. "I cannot break my promise to Mr. Collins. He has done nothing to deserve such treatment, and marrying him will bring the family much happiness."

Elizabeth nodded, having expected this response from her responsible older sister. She fought the impulse to shake Jane and convince her that she did not owe Mama and Mr. Collins all of her happiness. Jane often made decisions slowly, particularly when she worried about causing pain to others. And she had been devastated by Mr. Bingley's abandonment.

Elizabeth could only hope that when Mr. Bingley visited Longbourn again, Jane's feelings would be re-kindled—and she would send Mr. Collins scurrying back to Kent. Elizabeth squeezed her sister's shoulder reassuringly. "Mr. Bingley will visit tomorrow. That may help you sort out your feelings."

Jane wiped her eyes with shaky hands. "There is nothing to sort out, Lizzy. We are divided forever."

Elizabeth's heart clenched, but still she clung to hope. Many things might come to pass when Jane and Mr. Bingley were together again.

Elizabeth stood, intending to change into her night clothes, but Jane lifted her head expectantly. "Yes, dearest?" Elizabeth asked.

"Do you think—would you—" Jane lowered her head again and fell silent.

"Would I do what?" Elizabeth prompted.

"Would you marry Mr. Bingley?"

Elizabeth considered. This was a question she had asked herself many times since the proposal that afternoon. She shrugged. "I do not know. Perhaps. I think I could be…content with him…. But I am less certain he could be happy with me." Jane winced. Elizabeth took Jane's hands in hers. "I would far rather see him marry you. Then I could live with you and become your children's vexing spinster aunt."

Jane gave her a somewhat watery smile. "That will not come to pass, Lizzy, but it is a nice fantasy."

Elizabeth shrugged. "You never know what might happen." Jane did not respond but climbed into bed and pulled up the covers. Elizabeth blew out the candle and likewise settled herself.

After a long pause, Jane spoke again in a strained voice. "You should marry Charles, Lizzy."

Elizabeth's heart sank at Jane's defeated tone. "Oh?"

"You would make him an excellent wife, and he deserves to be happy."

You would make him a better wife. But Elizabeth did not say this aloud. Instead, she kept her tone neutral. "We shall see. Goodnight, Jane."

"Goodnight, Lizzy."

***

The following morning, Mr. Bingley called on Longbourn as early as was socially acceptable. Elizabeth had hoped she might receive him alone, but her mother and Kitty were also in the drawing room when he arrived. Much to Elizabeth's dismay, Mama received Mr. Bingley with cold civility, no doubt still vexed over the perceived snub of her eldest daughter.

"So, Mr. Bingley, you are come back to the neighborhood," her mother said by way of greeting.

"Indeed, ma'am." Mr. Bingley bowed quite correctly as all the women curtsied.

When he had taken the seat she indicated, Mama said, "We understood you were not to return to Netherfield and would take the first offer you received."

Mr. Bingley fidgeted with the hat in his lap. "I know Caroline wrote as much to Miss Bennet, but she was…mistaken about my intentions. I have no desire to quit Hertfordshire altogether. Business merely took me to London."

Mrs. Bennet nodded, slightly mollified he had not intended to slight the entire neighborhood.

"Well, we have had a bit of excitement since you went away." Her mother's tone was triumphant. "Jane accepted an offer from Mr. Collins. He is the parson at Hunsford, with the patronage of Lady Catherine de Bourgh herself."

A shadow passed over Mr. Bingley's face. "So I heard, ma'am." At Mrs. Bennet's shocked expression, he explained, "I encountered Miss Elizabeth on the road yesterday."

"Oh." Elizabeth's mother seemed disappointed to have been deprived of the opportunity to provoke greater despair from their visitor.

Mr. Bingley rubbed his palms on the legs of his trousers. "I was hoping for an opportunity to give Miss Bennet my good wishes." He shot Elizabeth a meaningful look. Elizabeth shook her head ever so slightly, and Mr. Bingley's face fell.

"Jane is about somewhere." Mrs. Bennet waved airily. "I am certain she will join us soon."

Mr. Bingley stared at the carpet for a moment, but when he glanced back up, his cheerful mask was firmly in place. "In that case, is Mr. Bennet about? I have a matter of business to discuss with him."

"Mr. Bennet?" Elizabeth's mother blinked in surprise. "Yes, I believe he is in his study."

Mr. Bingley stood. "I will take my leave, then." With a quick bow, he slipped through the door, closing it softly behind him.

"Papa will not like being disturbed so early in the day," Kitty said.

Elizabeth nodded. Her father did not care for visitors on the best of days but particularly abhorred them before noon. Still, he must know Elizabeth had agreed to Mr. Bingley's offer.

"What business could he have with Papa?" Kitty wondered.

Elizabeth knew but said nothing. She was too busy quelling her misgivings.

"Lizzy," their mother intoned, looking up from her embroidery. "You had best go to Meryton with Kitty this afternoon and call upon the militia soldiers. You might strike someone's fancy. And the men are all so dashing!"

"I do not believe that is necessary, Mama." The irony threatened to choke Elizabeth.

"You are not growing any younger," her mother retorted. Elizabeth rolled her eyes but refrained from speaking.

Silence reigned as the three women did their needlework. Then a maid entered, quietly requesting the mistress's presence in the study. With a lift of her brows, Mrs. Bennet hurried from the room.

After her departure, Elizabeth started counting under her breath. "Thirty, twenty-nine, twenty-eight…"

When she reached twenty, Kitty asked peevishly, "Why are you counting?"

Elizabeth merely smiled and shook her head, continuing to count.

"Three, two, one." Right on cue, the shrieking began. "Oh, Lizzy! Oh! Oh! I had not the least idea!"

Quick footsteps pattered down the hallway, and then the drawing room door was thrown wide open. Her mother, red-faced and out-of-breath, occupied the entire doorway. "Oh, you are a sly one! I had not the least suspicion! Five thousand a year!"

Kitty looked from Elizabeth to her mother. "Mama, what are you going on about?"

"Mr. Bingley just asked your father for permission to marry Lizzy!"

Elizabeth gave her mother what she hoped was a serene smile. "Papa gave his permission?"

Her mother gestured expansively. "Of course he did! He would not refuse Mr. Bingley anything!" Apparently the owner of Netherfield was now forgiven for any past transgressions.

Mama swept into the room, giving her second eldest daughter an overly enthusiastic hug and a kiss. "Oh, Lizzy! What fine clothes you will have! What jewels! What carriages! Not as fine as Lydia's, but still very fine!"

Mr. Bingley appeared in the doorway, and Mama emitted a squeal of joy. "Oh, Mr. Bingley! Let me give you a kiss!" He blushed endearingly as she kissed his cheek. "What do you like best for luncheon?" she asked as she drew him into the room and seated him beside Elizabeth. "I will make sure we have your favorites!"

"I am happy with anything," Mr. Bingley replied.

"Beef! We must have a nice beefsteak for luncheon!" Mrs. Bennet cried and rushed from the room.

Jane appeared in the doorway, and abruptly Mr. Bingley's smile disappeared. "I heard Mama's voice. What has happened?" She blanched upon seeing Mr. Bingley. "H-hello, Mr. Bingley." She gave a curtsey, and he returned a bow.

"Mr. Bingley is to marry Lizzy!" Kitty declared.

Jane's mouth tightened. Her eyes looked everywhere in the room but at Mr. Bingley. Mr. Bingley, however, could not tear his gaze from her face.

"Perhaps we should walk in the garden," Elizabeth suggested.

"Now?" Kitty cried, wrinkling her nose. "It is much too cold."

"We need only stay out for a short time."

Kitty sighed and rolled her eyes. Elizabeth gave her sister a stern look which she somehow understood. "Very well," Kitty conceded.

They moved into the hallway, where they all donned coats and wraps. Finally, everyone emerged from the house into the bright winter sunshine and cold air which seemed to sear the lungs with every breath.

Elizabeth had taken her time tying Kitty's bonnet ribbons, allowing Jane and Mr. Bingley to exit the house first.

"Caroline wrote and told you that I intended to give up Netherfield?" Elizabeth heard Mr. Bingley ask Jane.

Jane's voice was practically a whisper. "Yes."

"That was not my intention," Mr. Bingley said. "I intend to…"

As they turned left down the garden path, Mr. Bingley offered his arm, and Jane took it in a gesture so natural that Elizabeth wondered if either had noticed it.

Kitty watched with a frown. "Lizzy! She is walking off with your fiancé!"

Elizabeth nodded. "Shall we go this direction?" She pointed to her right.

***

Jane kept her eyes averted from Mr. Bingley and instead swept her gaze over the bushes and vines of the Longbourn garden. Truthfully it was becoming a little overgrown. Papa could only afford to hire one gardener, and the work exceeded his efforts. She noticed a dead branch on a boxwood hedge and took her hand from Mr. Bingley's arm to investigate, hoping to determine what had killed it.

"Jane!" Mr. Bingley's voice was a strangled whisper.

Jane started at the sound but willed herself not to turn around. If she so much as glanced at him, she might shatter into pieces.

"Did Elizabeth describe the circumstances of our engagement to you?" His voice was quite close.

Her eyes fixed on the boxwood, Jane nodded, not trusting herself to speak.

"It is to help me. My mother is not well and dearly wishes to see me wed."

"Yes," Jane's voice broke, and she cleared her throat. "Yes, Lizzy explained. You are very good to your mother."

"Elizabeth only agreed for my sake. She does not have feelings for me. Nor I toward her—well, not *those* sorts of feelings." His voice was so earnest, begging her to believe him.

Despite her resolve otherwise, Jane felt a ray of hope pierce her heart. Ruthlessly, she tamped it down. *This changes nothing*, she reminded herself.

"I believe she was hoping to persuade you to accept me in her stead." Mr. Bingley was so close his breath tickled her neck.

She straightened and turned quickly, forcing him to stumble back a step. "Please do not say such things!"

"But I lo—"

Jane held up her hands. "No! Do not say *that*! I cannot—I am engaged to another. I made a promise to Mr. Collins, and he is an honorable man. I cannot break faith with him."

Mr. Bingley caught up one of her hands. "Please, Jane! I know you do not love him. You cannot marry him!"

For a moment Jane allowed herself to indulge in the sensations of her hand in his. But then she withdrew; it was far too tempting. Sternly, she reminded herself that circumstances had been resolved for the best; both she and Lizzy would have comfortable homes. Jane had a far more suitable temperament for marrying Mr. Collins than did Lizzy, who would do very well with Mr. Bingley.

"You-you should marry—" Jane swallowed. Why was it suddenly so hard to speak? "—Marry Lizzy. She would make you a splendid wife, Mr. Bingley." He winced as she addressed him so formally. "She does not deserve to be unwed and homeless."

"Elizabeth would be quite happy to see you accept my hand." He uttered the words with an unexpected vehemence.

Jane could only imagine what the neighbors would say if she jilted Mr. Collins in order to marry her sister's erstwhile fiancé. It would be talked about for months, if not years. However, the potential for gossip was irrelevant. She had made a promise to Mr. Collins and always believed that one should not break one's word.

A little voice in the back of her mind also could not help questioning Mr. Bingley's sincerity. He had left her without a word. Was his sudden interest prompted by the necessity of his mother's illness, or was it sincere affection?

Jane gave herself a little shake. It hardly mattered. She would keep her promise; it was the safest and easiest course—and at least she could take solace in her principles.

"I am sorry to cause you pain, Mr. Bingley." Unable to meet his eyes, Jane focused her gaze on the rose bush behind him. "But I think it best if we not speak of this again."

"Please!" Mr. Bingley's voice took on a pleading note. "I pray you, at least consider it."

She turned her face toward the house so his anguished features would no longer be visible to her. "It is rather chilly. I think I will return to the house." Deliberately averting her eyes from Mr. Bingley, Jane set a brisk pace back up the path.

***

The next day Elizabeth required an extremely long walk. Being a man had its advantages, she noted; they could turn to pugilism to alleviate their frustrations. Hitting something today would be immensely satisfying. Instead, she could only channel that angry energy into walking.

The previous night, Jane had admitted that Mr. Bingley had broached the subject of marriage. When pressed, Jane even confessed to still possessing "some feelings" for him, but she steadfastly refused to act on those feelings. She repeated "I made Mr. Collins a promise" a half-dozen times.

Thus, when Mrs. Bennet escorted her other daughters on a shopping excursion to Meryton, Elizabeth declined in favor of a bracing walk. It was an improvement on yelling at her sister.

She returned to Longbourn only slightly less vexed but much the worse for wear. It had rained the day before, and the roads had been muddy. Elizabeth's boots were crusted with mud, and her skirt was sprinkled with brown droplets. On an impulse, she had removed her bonnet, allowing the wind to play merry havoc with her hair.

When she peered into the front hall mirror, she noticed a streak of mud she had somehow managed to smear on her left cheek. *A bath and change of clothes must be my first task.*

However, before she reached the stairs, Hill accosted her. "Miss Elizabeth! Thank goodness you have returned. Mr. Darcy arrived to call upon Miss Lydia, but she is in Meryton with your mother. He said he would wait in the drawing room, but they could be a while still."

Elizabeth suppressed a groan. When he learned everyone was from home, Mr. Darcy should have departed, but since he remained, Elizabeth must be the hostess. A guest must be received by a member of the family.

Elizabeth rubbed her cheek, hoping she removed the mud. "Very well, I will see to him." Perhaps she could welcome him, ascertain his business with Lydia, and then retreat upstairs for a change of clothes. Although an impish part of her character looked forward to shocking Mr. Darcy with such evidence of country life.

Mr. Darcy stood immediately upon her entrance and bowed quite correctly. His eyes scanned her from head to toe, noting every detail of her appearance, and she felt her face warm with a blush. But his gaze was not disapproving; some other, indecipherable emotion burned in his eyes. Elizabeth lifted her chin a little, restraining the impulse to retreat from the room, and examined Mr. Darcy in turn. He actually appeared…unwell. His eyes were ringed by dark circles, and his skin had a grayish pallor. Had he lost weight?

"Lydia and the rest of the family have gone into Meryton for a bit of shopping and some luncheon." Elizabeth consulted the mantel clock. "They should return within an hour."

Mr. Darcy nodded.

Remaining in the man's presence was awkward to say the least, but leaving him alone would hardly show her to be a good hostess—and he had experienced insults enough from the Bennets. However, he regarded her with that unnerving intensity once again, no doubt cataloguing every one of her flaws and missteps. She was increasingly conscious of her hair and the mud on her hem.

Mr. Darcy cleared his throat, and Elizabeth realized she had been hesitating, staring at him for a long time. Heavens, what would he think of her?

Say something! Anything.

"Are you visiting to discuss wedding plans with Lydia?" she asked.

Mr. Darcy winced. "I wished to speak with her, yes."

"I see." She gestured for him to sit and took the chair opposite.

They sat in silence for a moment. Mr. Darcy coughed. Elizabeth fidgeted. Should she inquire about the state of the roads or the weather in London? It seemed hopelessly trivial under the circumstances.

Mr. Darcy's fingers clenched and unclenched where they rested on the arms of the chair. Why was he anxious? "Has your sister revealed any more information about the man who took her to the library?" he asked.

Elizabeth smoothed her hair nervously with one hand. "No, unfortunately not."

He said nothing, but his shoulders slumped ever so slightly. Then he gave her a sharp look. "Please do not misunderstand me. I appreciate your assistance in this matter—and your faith in me. It is simply that…this has been an extremely…trying time."

Elizabeth was not accustomed to thinking of Mr. Darcy possessing the same emotions and sensitivities as other people. When the mask of the serious, proud Mr. Darcy slipped, however, it was clear that he did. And the accusations about his behavior with Lydia obviously bothered him. "I can well imagine," she said warmly.

Still, Elizabeth was mystified. *Why is Mr. Darcy showing this side of his personality to me? Why am I granted these glimpses into his true character?* She gave herself a little shake. *It matters not. I must concern myself with Lydia's wellbeing. Mr. Darcy can take care of himself.*

"Do you plan to end the betrothal?" Elizabeth was ambivalent about such a prospect. Although they were not well-suited for marriage, she feared for Lydia's reputation should they not wed.

Mr. Darcy frowned and directed his gaze out of the window. "I would prefer to find the man from the library and induce him to marry her. Then it would simply appear to be the transfer of her affections."

Thus saving Lydia's reputation. That was very considerate of Mr. Darcy. He could simply break the engagement and leave Lydia—and her family—to suffer the slings and arrows of outrageous gossip.

"And if you cannot find him?" Elizabeth asked. "Are you...determined to break the engagement? Under any circumstances?"

His eyes swung back to her. "I am loath to leave Miss Lydia and y—her family in a difficult position."

Elizabeth felt her cheeks growing warm. "That is very good of you." Why did his gaze make her so self-conscious?

"I am not averse to matrimony," he said hastily. "With another woman, I might not hurry to dissolve the engagement. However, I am convinced your sister and I could not make each other happy."

"I ...see..." He seemed intent on making a point, but the significance escaped her.

His eyes were fixed on her as if she held all the secrets of life. "Someone with a different temperament perhaps." His words were full of a meaning Elizabeth felt she was missing. He cleared his throat self-consciously. "Or...for example...a woman closer to my age."

"I see," she said faintly, although she did not. Not at all.

Chapter Nine

Damnation! I did not mean to say that aloud!
Darcy could not think of enough foul curses to level at
himself. This entire conversation had been a disaster.
Her forthrightness and faith in him were so distracting
that they had completely destroyed his discretion.
*Devil take it! If Elizabeth had not guessed of my
interest in her before, she certainly will now. And I am
still engaged to her sister. What will she think of me?*

She was staring at the door. Pretending she had
not noticed his horrible indiscretion? Or perhaps
hoping someone would arrive to rescue her from this
disastrous conversation.

She was very lovely in profile, with her slender
neck and pale skin, offset by masses of beautiful dark
hair.

*I should have proposed to her when I had the
opportunity.* Why had he foolishly fought his
obsession? She was unlikely to look kindly on a
proposal from him *now*—even if he could disentangle
himself from the engagement to Lydia. If she married
her sister's former fiancé, the neighborhood would
gossip about it for years. Once again Darcy cursed the
fate that had brought him into the path of a loosely
moraled country girl. Only when he had lost his chance
with Elizabeth had he realized what a prize he had
squandered.

Nevertheless, just being in the same room with
her kindled those desperate, hopeless dreams. He could
not completely rein in his hopes. If he could discover
the identity of Lydia's suitor and convince—or pay—
him to marry her, perhaps Elizabeth would consider
him. At least she appeared inclined to believe in his
truthfulness. Perhaps all was not lost.

Darcy emerged from his musings as he noticed Elizabeth turn toward the sound of footsteps in the hallway. The maid entered and announced, "Mr. Bingley, miss."

Bingley! This was a stroke of good fortune. Darcy had learned Bingley was at Netherfield and had written to inquire if he might stay, but he had not received a reply before leaving London.

"Darcy!" Bingley gave his friend an enthusiastic handshake. "Well met!"

Darcy echoed the statement.

"I did not know you were in Hertfordshire!" Bingley exclaimed.

"I sent you a letter two days ago."

"Oh." Bingley ran a hand through his hair, ducking his head. "I, er, have been distracted and have not attended to my post as I should." Was he actually blushing? For heaven's sake, why?

Bingley then turned to Elizabeth, who had stood upon his entrance. She blushed, and Bingley hesitated as if unsure how to greet her. What was wrong? Why were they behaving so strangely? Bingley often frustrated Darcy, but he was usually at ease in company.

Finally, Bingley took one of her hands and murmured, "Elizabeth," before kissing it. Darcy frowned. When had Bingley started employing such gallant gestures? And why was he calling her by her Christian name? Should he not reserve such familiarity for *Jane* Bennet?

Elizabeth's face was bright red, and her eyes darted uneasily to Darcy before she gestured Bingley to the chair next to hers.

"You are visiting Miss Lydia, eh?" Bingley asked Darcy.

Before Darcy had the chance to reply, the drawing room door swept open. Mrs. Bennet sailed in, followed by her other daughters—like ducklings following a mama duck.

"Mr. Darcy, my apologies for not being present to welcome you when you arrived." She fluttered her hands in response to his bow. "And Mr. Bingley! How delightful to see you again so soon!"

The various Bennets settled themselves about the room. Darcy expected Jane Bennet to seat herself near Bingley, but she chose a chair in the far corner and deliberately avoided his eye when he glanced her way. Had the two quarreled? What could two such amiable souls have possibly disagreed about?

"Well, Mr. Darcy!" Mrs. Bennet exclaimed. "So much has happened since you left Hertfordshire! Jane is engaged to Mr. Collins."

Darcy felt his body jolt. Now he understood Miss Bennet's choice of seat. He examined Bingley for signs of despondency, but his friend was smiling, although it seemed a trifle forced. Darcy would have sworn Bingley harbored a real affection for her and would have expected him to be devastated by the news. In point of fact, why was he bothering to visit Longbourn at all? Why did Bingley not return to London at once upon hearing of Miss Bennet's engagement?

Oh. Mrs. Bennet had paused, allowing Darcy to voice typical words of congratulations, which he did.

But Mrs. Bennet was still bursting with chatter. "And...just yesterday, our dearest Lizzy became betrothed to your friend, Mr. Bingley!"

Darcy had a swooping sensation in his stomach—as if he had fallen off a high swing. "What?" he exclaimed. That could not be. It was not... The swooping feeling intensified. Darcy had leaned so far forward in his chair that he was in danger of tipping out of it. He grabbed the chair arms just in time and pulled himself back. All eyes in the room were upon him, watching with varying degrees of alarm and amusement. A familiar prickling on the back of his neck told Darcy he was blushing.

Darcy coughed. He must have heard wrong. Mrs. Bennet must have said "Kitty." Kitty sounded much like Lizzy if one mumbled. Or perhaps she had said "Mary." Bingley would not let glasses and a sour disposition stand in his way, would he? No, Mrs. Bennet could not have possibly said Bingley was engaged to Elizabeth!

"I beg your pardon?" he asked Mrs. Bennet, pleased his voice only cracked once.

"Lizzy. Will. Marry. Mr. Bingley," Mrs. Bennet said slowly as if he were hard of hearing.

No, this cannot be…

But now Bingley took Elizabeth's hand and smiled at her.

Then he regarded Darcy with a furrowed brow. Had Darcy moaned?

"Er, congratulations," Darcy managed to mumble. "This is a surprise." Of course, Bingley knew nothing of Darcy's interest in Elizabeth; Darcy had not even admitted to himself. Bingley would have known no reason why he could not attach himself to Elizabeth.

Suddenly, the drawing room seemed much smaller. Was it possible the walls were actually moving closer? Elizabeth was his! He had planned to propose—he was almost certain of it—once he was no longer engaged. Then the absurdity of that thought struck him forcefully. Darcy was engaged; how could he have any hopes of Elizabeth or any other woman?

Elizabeth and Bingley! It was like his worst nightmare come to life. If it had been another man, a stranger, Darcy would have been prepared to fight for her—well, once he was no longer engaged to Lydia. However, he could not do battle with his friend!

Oh, Good Lord, how had his life come to this pass? Darcy's lungs had stopped working, yet he must say something to Bingley. His friend must not guess that a black pit had opened in Darcy's chest.

Abruptly, Darcy was angry. How much additional misfortune would fate pile on him? First he was accused of debauchery and forced to propose to an empty-headed girl, and now the woman he wanted was engaged to his dearest friend! "I thought Miss Jane Bennet was the object of your admiration." The words emerged as a growl.

Every head in the room was now turned in his direction. Belatedly, Darcy realized he should not have uttered such words in a public setting.

Mrs. Bennet looked appalled while Miss Jane kept her eyes focused on the floor. Elizabeth turned red with anger. Bingley blinked. "Yes…Miss Bennet…is a very pretty…I like her…but she is…er…engaged to Mr. Collins," he stammered.

Suddenly, Miss Jane stood and rushed from the room, her hand covering her mouth. Oh, Good Lord! Darcy massaged his forehead with one hand as he closed his eyes briefly. He had caused her distress. Of course, she would rather marry Bingley than Collins, and Darcy had reminded her of that—while also reminding the others of her shameful abandonment by Bingley.

Darcy cursed himself for a fool. The shock of the announcement had prompted him to think only of his own loss without considering how it would affect others.

From the thunderous look on Elizabeth's face, he was not the only one cursing himself. She glared at

Darcy before throwing down her needlework and racing from the room after her sister.

Oh, I am doing an excellent job of improving her opinion of me, Darcy thought. *Perhaps if I work a little harder, I might drive her to strike me.*

***

Elizabeth hurried after Jane, who was striding toward the front door and its promise of an escape to the outside. Elizabeth understood her sister's need to escape but was worried that she would venture out without a cloak or a bonnet.

"Jane! Jane, dearest!" she called. "Please wait!"

Jane's pace did not slow, and she quickly slipped through the front door. Elizabeth grabbed her sister's cloak and bonnet from the pegs near the door, but as she sought the exit, her way was blocked by a group of people entering the house.

Elizabeth tried to push her way past but instead became hopelessly entangled with the visitors. "Miss Eliza!" exclaimed one of the figures with whom she collided, and Elizabeth vaguely recognized the tall form of Miss Bingley. Elizabeth suppressed an urge to say a most unladylike curse. She could not ignore Mr. Bingley's sister to run out into the garden. In fact, she now realized, Miss Bingley would be her future sister-in-law! *Perhaps I did not consider this engagement as thoroughly as I should have.*

"I beg your pardon," she murmured as she shuffled back into the hallway and replaced Jane's garments on the pegs. Unwilling to face Miss Bingley and her companions, Elizabeth turned toward the drawing room, painfully aware of her dirty, disheveled clothes and tangled hair.

Mr. Bingley and Mr. Darcy had already reached the hallway. At the sight of the new arrivals, Mr. Bingley's mouth gaped open. But Mr. Darcy's eyes were focused on Elizabeth.

"Perhaps *I* should speak with Miss Bennet?" he asked.

"I believe you have said quite enough, thank you!" she growled at him before retreating into the drawing room. As she slammed the door, Elizabeth briefly wondered whom Miss Bingley had brought to visit Longbourn.

***

For a moment everyone stood frozen, staring at the drawing room door. Then Darcy cursed under his breath, sweeping his way down the hallway and out of the front door.

Things could be worse, Bingley assured himself. *No one was dying, and no one had been challenged to a duel. So there was a bright side.*

Bingley was forced to reevaluate that opinion when he turned to Longbourn's newest arrivals. His sister, Louisa, looking appalled, stood on one side of the Bennets' hallway while Caroline, a vindicated expression on her face, stood on the other. And between them was… his mother, quite confused.

"Is she your fiancée?" Mrs. Bingley asked.

"Yes, Mama." He rubbed his eyes, aware that Elizabeth had not created the best first impression.

"You said she is beautiful and has the temperament of an angel." His mother's tone expressed nothing but bewilderment.

"She is! She does!" All three women regarded Bingley skeptically. He cleared his throat. "She is not having a good day."

"I can see that," his mother murmured. "You described her hair as blonde."

"It is darker in the winter," Bingley said. Substituting Elizabeth for Jane was beginning to look like a mistake.

"Charles," Caroline's voice was practically a whine, "why are you engaged to Elizabeth Bennet? I thought you were interested in Ja—"

Bingley leaned forward as if to give her a brotherly kiss and trod very hard on his sister's foot. "Ow! Charles! Mind where you are stepping."

He spoke quickly to prevent her from returning to her previous subject. "Why are you here in Hertfordshire?" His eyes darted from Caroline to Louisa and back.

Caroline drew herself up to her full height. "When we returned home from Scarborough, thankfully earlier than we had planned, Mama shared this alarming report about your betrothal to Miss Bennet. We hastened to Longbourn at once to prove it false!"

Bingley gritted his teeth. "It is true, as you see."

"But—" Caroline started, no doubt marshalling further objections about Jane.

Bingley interrupted ruthlessly, looking at his mother. "Mama, now is not a good time for the Bennets; they are having a bit of a trying day. What possessed you to visit unannounced—without me—when you have not been introduced?"

His mother frowned. "Caroline said the Bennets love to have unexpected visitors," she murmured.

"Did she?" Bingley glared at Caroline. "Not today."

Caroline lifted her chin. "Miss Bennet is not a suitable match for you! Mama should meet her at once and judge for herself."

"This is hardly the place to discuss it, Caroline." Bingley ran both hands through his already disheveled hair. He had expected that when he introduced his fiancée—be it Elizabeth or Jane—to his mother, he would enjoy plenty of time to prepare her. For now he could only keep them apart and remove his sisters from Longbourn if they insisted on insulting the Bennet family in their front hallway.

Bingley took his mother's elbow and guided her toward the front door. "Let us return to Netherfield and visit the Bennets another day." He had not bade farewell to the Bennets, but under the circumstances, he thought it an acceptable—not to mention prudent— transgression.

His mother uttered a few words of protest but then followed his lead. Bingley said a silent prayer of thanks. They departed Longbourn with no further incidents.

***

Darcy stood in Longbourn's garden feeling like a fool. When he had quitted the house, he had planned to find Miss Bennet and apologize for his intemperate words. But once he was outside, she had not been visible, and Darcy had not the faintest idea where she might go. Was she a great walker like Elizabeth, or had she slipped up the back stairs to cry in her room? He had circled the property in search of her and finally wound up in the garden, which was as equally devoid of people as the rest of Longbourn.

He should return to the drawing room and seek a private audience with Lydia. It was, after all, the cause that had prompted his journey to Hertfordshire. However, the drawing room also contained Elizabeth. An angry Elizabeth. Angry at him, with good cause.

The conversation had been proceeding so well! They had carried on an amiable conversation, and Elizabeth appeared to enjoy his company. But then Darcy, like an idiot, had to remind Jane of her abandonment. If he rejoined the group in the drawing room, Elizabeth would glare and make cutting remarks. Some days he might withstand such barbs. But today he had no stomach for Elizabeth's wrath.

If only he could depart for Netherfield and return to do battle another day, but he could not depart without a proper farewell to the family. That would require facing an irate Elizabeth, which gave him cold sweats when he imagined it.

He perched on the cold, stone bench and wondered how his life had spun out of control so quickly.

The crunch of gravel roused him from his reverie. He shot to his feet. Perhaps the footsteps belonged to Elizabeth, coming to berate his ill manners. Or perhaps it was Miss Bennet—providing an opportunity for him to apologize.

But the visitor proved to be neither. It was Lydia, scowling and bundled up in a wool shawl. "Mama bade me speak with you since you traveled all this way." She shrugged carelessly. "Do you even wish to speak with me?"

"Yes, it is why I visited Longbourn." He ground his teeth at the necessity. His solicitor had been unable to find a legal means of escaping the agreement without a messy scandal.

Lydia shivered theatrically. "But it is so dreadfully cold! Let us go inside to talk."

Inside meant Elizabeth and her frowning disapproval. Not to mention other family members who should not hear his words to Lydia. "I would prefer to remain out here."

She rolled her eyes and tossed her head. "Very well, I hope you talk quickly."

Just what I always hoped my future wife would say to me. Darcy sighed. "I do—"

Lydia immediately interrupted. "Oh! Did you bring me jewelry?"

Darcy blinked. "No." Could he have possibly given her the mistaken impression that he would bring her gifts?

She pouted prettily. "But that is what wealthy men do! They give their fiancées jewelry, Mama said. Usually a very valuable piece that has been in their family for generations."

Over my dead body. "I did not bring you jewelry."

"Will you bring me jewelry the next time?" She bounced on her feet. "I would like a necklace with real rubies—or maybe sapphires."

Darcy rubbed his face with both hands, deciding to ignore the subject of jewelry and get to the point. "I do not believe you and I are well-suited for marital happiness," he said in a rush before she could interrupt him.

She shrugged, idly playing with one of her bonnet ribbons. "That cannot be helped."

Darcy itched to shake some sense into the girl but clenched his fists to his sides. "I believe you would be happier marrying the man who…escorted you to the library. Clearly you were attracted to each other." *Please do not let him be married!*

Lydia regarded him warily. "I do not know who you mean."

Darcy sighed. Although he had expected no different answer. "I believe your chances of happiness with him are far greater than with me."

She waved away his concerns. "You have ten thousand a year. That will make me *extremely* happy."

His first plan had failed, so it was time for his second. "I have two houses in London."

Now he had her attention. "You do?"

"Yes. Darcy House, and then a townhouse which is smaller but still quite lovely—in a fashionable neighborhood. If you agree to dissolve our engagement, I will give the townhouse to you and your…friend after you marry."

Lydia squinted at him in the bright winter sunshine. "If I reveal his name?" Darcy nodded. "But then I won't get the jewels and gowns and carriages."

Does this girl think of nothing else? "I will give you a sum of money with which you may purchase such things."

"But not as many as if I were Mrs. Darcy."

Darcy could not prevent a shudder at the sound of that name on her lips.

"You should take some time to consider it," he said, holding onto his temper by a thread. "Discuss it with your…friend."

"No!" She stamped her foot. "You just wish to renege on your promise—and cheat me out of what is rightfully mine.

The thread snapped. "Not rightfully!" he cried. "You have done nothing to deserve it. By rights I should be proposing to the woman I love!"

Lydia's mouth dropped open, and she stared at him for a moment. Had he finally penetrated her veil of self-regard? Then a sob emerged from her throat. He took a step toward her, but she whirled away and hurried along the path toward the house—sobbing loudly.

Darcy sank back down on the bench, cradling his head in his hands. He disliked losing control and its attendant sense of shame. But he knew he should feel more regret at having brought Lydia to tears. She was so difficult and selfish that he could find little sympathy for her in his heart. *Apparently she brings out the worst in me; what an excellent quality in one's future wife.*

He took a deep breath, willing his racing heart to calm. If he were truthful with himself, the real reason he had lost control with Lydia and been so unforgivably rude to Jane Bennet was the news about Elizabeth and Bingley's engagement. He should be pleased for them. They were both excellent people and would no doubt be very happy together. He would be a world-class cad to be anything less than happy for them.

Until Mrs. Bennet's announcement, Darcy had not noticed his reliance on the hope that Elizabeth might accept him once he was free of Lydia. Now he knew how vain such hope was. Apparently she had been harboring her own hopes, but of his best friend. What a fool he had been!

Darcy barely registered the sound of approaching footsteps until Elizabeth was already in sight, rounding a bend in the path. Darcy pinched the bridge of his nose, reminding himself not to lose his temper.

"I saw Lydia running into the house. What happened?" Elizabeth asked.

Darcy took a deep breath. The truth was unpleasant. "I provoked her to tears—which makes two of your sisters in one afternoon. Perhaps you should invite Miss Kitty and Miss Mary out here, and we shall see how quickly I might reduce them to tears as well." He regretted the words almost as soon as they were out of his mouth; sarcasm was hardly appropriate in this situation.

To his astonishment, Elizabeth chuckled. "Lydia weeps whenever things do not go her way. It is hardly unusual."

"I am sorry for my words about Miss Bennet. It was…thoughtless. I was…" *Appalled at the news of your engagement.* "Surprised by Bingley's change of heart."

She nodded but said nothing. He had been half hoping she would explain when she and Bingley had come to care for each other. But perhaps it was best if he did not know.

Darcy swallowed and attempted to push aside a sense of betrayal. Neither Bingley nor Elizabeth had any inkling of his feelings. In any event, it was done and could not be undone.

"Jane has returned to the house, a bit embarrassed at her outburst," Elizabeth said.

Darcy stood. "I should tender my apologies, then."

She gazed at him for a moment. "Yes. It would help her, though she will claim there is no need. She is the most forgiving creature in the world."

No doubt Miss Bennet would prefer to marry Bingley than that fool Collins. Darcy experienced a brief moment of kindred feeling for her. Yet she appeared to bear her sister no ill will. "An ideal sister," he remarked.

She smiled fondly. "I cannot imagine a better one."

Darcy indulged himself and offered Elizabeth his arm. They fell silent as they walked into the house.

***

The Bingley carriage rattled over stones in the road, and Bingley's mother made a face, saying something to Louisa beside her—no doubt a complaint. Bingley must speak with the coachman; the carriage was not nearly as well sprung as it should be. Fortunately, the noise effectively masked anything Bingley said to Caroline when he leaned over and murmured, "You must not tell Mama I was at first interested in Jane Bennet."

Caroline gave him a sidelong glance, raising her eyebrow skeptically. "Why should I not? Jane Bennet was bad enough, but Elizabeth—!"

Bingley gritted his teeth. "She is my choice. You must abide by it, Caroline."

She rolled her eyes. "But it does not follow that I must remain silent on the subject of Jane Bennet."

"Mother is unwell," he hissed. "It would distress her to think I was marrying the wrong woman!"

Caroline examined her gloved hand. "It would distress her further if you *did* marry the wrong woman. Did those Bennets entrap you the way they trapped Mr. Darcy?"

"Of course not! It was entirely my idea to propose to Elizabeth." Bingley scowled.

Caroline pursed her lips. "Are you certain? Elizabeth could have used her arts and allurements to draw you in—"

Bingley had to laugh. "That is not her way."

"No." His sister shook her head. "I think Mama and I must intervene since you are obviously not in your right mind."

Merciful heavens! "You cannot do this!" Bingley pleaded. "Caroline, please!"

Caroline sat up straight and considered his plea. "Two ball gowns."

Bingley blinked, not immediately grasping her meaning. Oh yes. A few weeks ago, he had refused to purchase her any more ball gowns. He had just wanted to marry his beloved and make his mother happy. How had it all spun out of control so quickly? Now he was reduced to bribing his own sister to keep her quiet.

Two ball gowns! It was a big expense.

"One ball gown," he countered.

She considered this. "One ball gown, a new hat, gloves, stockings, and reticule."

Merciful heavens! Bingley prayed for strength. "A gown, gloves, and reticule but no hat or stockings."

Caroline pursed her lips. "Very well."

Bingley settled back into the seat with the sense he had emerged from battle relatively unscathed.

Caroline regarded her gloves again. "Of course, Louisa knows about Jane Bennet as well. And I am certain she would also like a new ball gown…"

Bingley groaned.

Chapter Ten

The next day Bingley again visited Longbourn, this time with no relatives in tow. Jane declined to come down to the drawing room, but the other Bennet ladies joined him. After an hour of pleasant conversation about the weather, the state of the roads, the dishes for dinner, and the weather again, Bingley invited Elizabeth for a private walk in the garden. Given the much-discussed unseasonably cold temperatures, the other sisters declined to join them.

Once they were alone on the garden path, gravel crunching under their feet, Elizabeth said, "I must apologize for my behavior yesterday. I did not realize the arriving visitors were your mother and sisters. I was angry with Mr. Darcy, but I should not have—"

Bingley patted her hand where it rested on his arm. "Do not be uneasy about it. My family ought not to have descended on Longbourn without prior notice. It was all Caroline's doing."

Elizabeth nodded, having suspected as much. They walked on a few paces in companionable silence. "Did your sisters reveal the truth about your interest in Jane?"

Bingley winced. "I secured promises from them not to mention it to Mother."

"Good," Elizabeth said. Silence reigned for a moment.

Mr. Bingley's eyes stared without noticing any of the trees and plants around them. Finally, he asked, "Was Jane very distressed yesterday?"

"She cried for a while after returning home, but I believe it is for the best."

"For the best?" Mr. Bingley's tone was indignant.

Elizabeth did not recall ever seeing such a scowl on his face. "I simply meant that misery might convince Jane to break off her engagement with Mr. Collins."

Mr. Bingley shook his head. "I do not wish to see Jane miserable."

"Nor do I," Elizabeth acknowledged. "But I would like seeing her married to Mr. Collins even less."

He was grinding his teeth and staring at the floor. "Jane asked me not to importune her again."

"Oh." That was a blow. How could he convince her to marry him if he was forbidden to raise the subject? "What will you do?" Would he give up hope and return to London? The thought sent cold chills down Elizabeth's back.

Mr. Bingley raised his chin. "I shall remain at Netherfield, biding my time and awaiting another opportunity."

"Good."

"Our engagement provides a perfect excuse for staying in Hertfordshire," he said. Elizabeth nodded.

After a long moment of silence, Mr. Bingley rubbed his forehead with his free hand. "My sisters suggested holding a ball at Netherfield to celebrate our engagement."

"They did?" Elizabeth could not keep the astonishment from her voice.

"They think to provoke me. Perhaps they hope I will give you up." He grimaced. "Or perhaps they merely wish to flaunt their new ball gowns."

Elizabeth tilted her head to one side as she considered. "A ball? I believe it is an excellent idea!"

"It is?" Mr. Bingley scratched his head. "Will you not be uncomfortable?"

She shrugged. "The salient fact is that Mr. Collins is in Kent while Jane is *here*." Elizabeth smiled conspiratorially. "She would not miss a ball held in my honor. You could dance and converse with her freely."

"It is extremely odd to have my fiancée play matchmaker," Mr. Bingley observed with a quirk of his lips.

Elizabeth laughed. "I am only your fiancée until we can convince Jane to take up the role."

Mr. Bingley stopped suddenly, turning to Elizabeth and clasping both her hands in his. "And what if we cannot? Would you still be my fiancée if she marries your cousin?"

Elizabeth was a little startled by his suddenly somber mood. "Would you like me to be?"

Mr. Bingley's eyes had a faraway look. "I think I might. If that would suit you."

Once again Mr. Darcy's face flashed inexplicably into Elizabeth's mind. It was ridiculous! If he managed to extricate himself from Lydia, Mr. Darcy would waste no time in riding for London. However, Mr. Bingley was everything kind and amiable. "Yes, I think it might suit me as well."

"Good." Mr. Bingley's smile did not reach his eyes.

"And I believe an engagement ball at Netherfield is an excellent notion."

Mr. Bingley nodded. "Very well."

***

As usual before a ball, the Bennet household was in a frenzy. Jane helped Elizabeth pin the final ribbons and tiny flowers into her hair. "Thank you, Jane. It looks exquisite." Elizabeth admired Jane's handiwork in the mirror of their dressing table. "I wish you would let me place flowers in your hair. You will be quite the prettiest woman in the room."

Jane averted her eyes but not before Elizabeth observed that all-too-familiar haunted look. "No. My ribbon will be sufficient."

"Mr. Bingley will ask you to dance with him," Elizabeth said.

Jane closed her eyes briefly. "Lizzy, he is your fiancé!"

"He would be yours if you let him."

"Then you will have no one to marry, for I do not believe you would take Mr. Collins."

Elizabeth shuddered. "No, indeed. You are far more tolerant than I. While he bragged about Rosings Park, I might be tempted to push him out one of the expensively glazed windows."

Jane covered her mouth as she laughed. "Do not say such things!" But her eyes were dancing.

Elizabeth sobered. "I do not want you to worry on my account, Jane. If I never marry, I will be quite content. I would rather see you happy."

"You are too good to me."

"I am just as good as you deserve." When Jane did not reply, Elizabeth sighed. "Will you at least agree to dance with Mr. Bingley if he asks you? It would make him very happy."

Jane's shoulders relaxed slightly. "Yes, of course I will."

Elizabeth stood. "Perhaps we should go down. The coach will be—"

She was interrupted by the sound of their mother's voice. "Oh my! Jane! Jane, dear! What a surprise! Come down at once!"

Jane lifted her eyebrows in inquiry at Elizabeth, who simply shrugged. Who knew what had caused their mother's latest attack of nerves?

Elizabeth followed her sister down the stairs but gasped in dismay when she saw who waited in the front hallway.

"My dearest honeysuckle rose!" Mr. Collins exclaimed as he took Jane's hand and kissed it so vigorously that it must have grown quite moist. "Your most delightful mother wrote to me about the ball at Netherfield, and I thought to surprise you with a visit. Now you will have a partner for the dancing!"

As if Jane ever lacked for partners! Elizabeth clamped her lips shut lest some unladylike words emerge.

"This is indeed a surprise. You are too kind, sir," Jane murmured.

"And I must confess to a selfish motive as well. I missed you with my whole heart and body. My arms have longed to reach out for you—to…hold your hand…And my lips tingle just thinking about your…kiss." Jane's eyes widened. "Not that you have kissed me, of course. That would be highly inappropriate until we are wed, but my lips have been imagining it…for some time."

Elizabeth turned a laugh into a cough. Jane appeared more alarmed than amused, but she merely nodded.

"It was very good of you to come, Mr. Collins," Mrs. Bennet cooed at him.

Why had her mother written to Mr. Collins? Why had he come? *Well, I must simply ensure that Jane dances with Mr. Bingley despite her fiancé's inconvenient presence, even if I am forced to dance with Mr. Collins myself.* It would be worth a few bruised toes!

Elizabeth's father entered the hall, looking at his pocket watch. "It is past time we departed."

"How right you are, Mr. Bennet!" Her mother cried. "Mary! Lydia! Kitty!" she called up the stairs. "Those girls are always late," she complained to no one in particular.

The younger girls arrived, and everyone donned their outer garments. "Now, Lydia, Mr. Darcy shall be there," their mother admonished. "Be sure to smile sweetly at him."

Lydia made a face at their mother. "I don't see why I must. We are already engaged, and he's an old bore."

Elizabeth found Mr. Darcy to be many things, but boring was never one of them. *Were I engaged to Mr. Darcy, I would happily pass the entire ball by his side.* Elizabeth blinked. Where had that thought come from? How odd. She refocused her attention on Lydia. "Your behavior should reflect well on him," she said.

"What about his behavior reflecting well on me? Hmm? Nobody worries about that! What shall my friends think when I am accompanied by such an old fellow?" She pouted. "It is such a trial while I wait for—" Suddenly, she clapped both hands over her mouth.

"For what?" Elizabeth asked.

Lydia swallowed. "For us to be married. That shall be great fun!"

"Hmm." Elizabeth was sure Lydia had been about to say something else. "Perhaps you can find something you and Mr. Darcy both enjoy at the ball."

Lydia rolled her eyes. "To be sure, there are no things we enjoy in common. I am not certain he even knows how to laugh." Then her eyes widened. "Oh, I know! I shall cure him of that! It shall be my scheme for the evening. I will teach Mr. Darcy to have fun and be more carefree. I am certain he is capable of it. It shouldn't take long."

Elizabeth winced. "Mr. Darcy may not feel he is in need of change."

Lydia lifted her chin. "He simply needs someone to demonstrate how to have fun. Miss Bingley and Mrs. Hurst are too proud and proper; they know nothing about fun." Lydia did a little dance step. "But I am an expert!"

Elizabeth suspected the result of Lydia attempting to teach Mr. Darcy anything would be rather unpleasant. She did not know why she felt so responsible for the man, but she had a strong impulse to rescue him from Lydia.

I suppose I must dance with him myself. Although the idea was not as unwelcome as she would have expected. Elizabeth had seen him dance with Miss Bingley and knew he was a good dancer, so rescuing him from Lydia's ministrations would not be unpleasant. Of course, it was socially acceptable to dance only two sets with the same partner, which was a shame. *Wait, when did I begin to look forward to dancing with Mr. Darcy?*

With this disturbing thought in her mind, she followed Lydia out to the carriage.

***

The ball had been underway for an hour, but it easily seemed like a day to Darcy. He had managed to avoid the entire Bennet family, although his eyes frequently wandered in Elizabeth's direction.

At the moment he was conversing with Miss Bingley—for the simple reason that doing so prevented him from staring at the object of his affections and seething with jealousy at Bingley. Caroline Bingley had been complaining to him about her brother's attachment to "that Bennet family" when abruptly she recalled that Darcy was also connected to that family. She had turned red and fanned herself rapidly, casting about for a new topic of conversation. "What a shame Lord Pippinworth was unable to attend," she drawled.

Darcy nodded absently, wondering who the devil Lord Pippinworth was.

A shrill feminine voice called from behind him. "Fitzie! Fitzie!" *Who is the poor unfortunate saddled with such a pet name?* he wondered. When his arm was grabbed unexpectedly, he nearly toppled over. He looked down to identify his assailant and discovered the dark head of Miss Lydia Bennet.

Darcy was proud of himself for not groaning aloud.

"There you are!" she exclaimed breathlessly. Had she run the entire length of the ballroom? "Didn't you hear me calling you, Fitzie?"

Fitzie? What fresh horror was this?

Darcy took a deep breath. "I did not realize you were referencing me."

"Fitzwilliam is too old and stuffy." She made a face of mock solemnity. "With a more fun name, you will have a better time at the ball!"

Miss Bingley gave Lydia her best supercilious look. "You call Mr. Darcy Fitzie?" she inquired in the same tone as she might ask, "You enjoy eating slugs?"

Unabashed—or perhaps simply unaware—Lydia grinned impudently at the other woman. "Isn't it a darling name? I thought of it myself!"

"Imagine my surprise," Miss Bingley murmured faintly.

Lydia hung on Darcy's arm. "My dear fiancé simply must relax and learn to have fun. And I am here to help him!"

Oh, Good Lord, no, Darcy thought. *I am her "project."* Before Lydia's appearance, Darcy had worried what others would think if she ignored him and flirted with other men. Now he wished she would.

"Have you had the wine punch?" she continued, oblivious to his expression of horror. "Netherfield always has excellent punch—the first step toward having a good time! We should get you a couple of glasses. Then you will not be so proud and pompous." She giggled.

"How fortunate you have a fiancée who is willing to help you with your 'affliction,'" Miss Bingley drawled to Darcy.

"It is my pleasure!" Lydia waved airily. "He is my darling Fitzie, after all. Just think what fun we will have once we are married!" She squeezed his arm and glanced up at him with a smile.

"Indeed," Darcy responded. Miss Bingley almost spilled her drink concealing a snort of laughter. "Dare I ask what else this plan entails?" Darcy almost managed to conceal his flinch.

"Well you may ask." Lydia tapped her fan on her chin thoughtfully as Elizabeth silently joined their party. "I considered my plans during the carriage ride here, and the most marvelous idea came to me. Do you know who has the most fun at balls and soirées?"

"No." Darcy dreaded the answer.

"The militia officers!" she cried triumphantly. "Especially Mr. Denny and Mr. Wickham. I should introduce them to you. Wickham is so charming and always has a good time wherever he goes. You could use him as a model for your behavior!"

Miss Bingley was having a coughing fit. Elizabeth glared at Lydia. Darcy ground his teeth as he tried to rein in his temper. "I will not emulate Wickham in any respect," he said firmly to Lydia.

"But you don't even know—" Lydia started.

Elizabeth interrupted. "Lydia, Mr. Denny was searching for you. I believe he hoped for a dance."

Lydia's eyes lit up, all thoughts of reforming Darcy temporarily forgotten. "Where was he?"

Elizabeth gestured in the general vicinity of the ballroom's entrance. "Ooh!" Lydia squealed and rushed away immediately. Miss Bingley then received an invitation to dance from Mr. Hurst, so Darcy was left alone with Elizabeth.

Elizabeth gave Darcy a rueful look. "I apologize. Lydia knows nothing of your family's history with Mr. Wickham."

"So I surmised," Darcy said.

Elizabeth's face fell; did she think he was rebuking her? "I will take my leave—" She gave a brief curtsey and turned away. No. He could not allow her to believe he thought so little of her.

His hand reached out to touch her arm. "Would you do me the honor of the next set?" he asked.

Elizabeth turned back to him, her eyes wide. She might well be surprised. He had only danced with Miss Bingley and Mrs. Hurst since arriving in Hertfordshire. "Uh…yes. I-I am not engaged with anyone else," she stuttered.

"Excellent!" Darcy smiled and offered her his arm. "The set is forming now. Shall we go?"

***

Dancing with Mr. Darcy was not like dancing with anyone else. He was particularly light on his feet and attentive to his partner's movements. Compared to him, partnering another man was like dancing with a horse. Elizabeth's anxieties about Lydia, Jane, and Mr. Bingley had quickly faded as she became the sole focus of Mr. Darcy's attention. While they danced, his eyes never left her. To him, apparently, there were no other couples or a room full of revelers. The rest of the world had fallen away, and only she remained. Elizabeth was quite dizzy from his interest.

Although Elizabeth had once vowed to never dance with Mr. Darcy, she had never been so pleased to break a vow. She had once believed him to be proud and taciturn, but now she could see the unspoken emotions lurking in every gaze. Why had she ever thought him to be unemotional?

What were those emotions? She thought she glimpsed affection…yearning. But...that could not be right. No, he was offering her friendship, nothing more. And of course, she wanted nothing more from him.

Mr. Darcy did not maintain a steady discourse about the occasion, the company, or the number of couples. In fact, he said little. But somehow she did not mind. She felt he was talking to her without using words. But most likely she was deceiving herself.

The set ended with a curtsey and a bow, and then Mr. Darcy had taken her hand to lead her from the dance floor. Elizabeth found herself oddly reluctant to release his hand. She should have been pleased to escape the company of a man she had long considered to be proud and unpleasant, but now she felt quite the opposite. It caused a pang of loss to think that he would soon seek out another partner, and they would go their separate ways.

"Perhaps some punch?" he inquired.

"Yes," she breathed. Anything to prolong the moment.

A shy, surprised smile flickered over his face. He guided her through the throngs of people into the anteroom where the punch was being served. After procuring glasses, he handed one to Elizabeth, but she was immediately bumped from behind, nearly spilling her punch.

She laughed self-consciously. "There may be a few too many people."

"Indeed. Miss Bingley would have been well served to limit her guest list." Mr. Darcy's eyes scanned the room. "Here, there is an alcove few know about."

He guided her by her elbow to a section of wall covered by draperies, but when he pulled one back, she realized there was indeed a hidden alcove. "Oh!" she exclaimed. It was actually an entryway to a back hallway, probably an unused servants' entrance to the ballroom. There were no furnishings, save a single wooden chair with a broken arm. The draperies hid them from the ballroom, and no one in the hallway could see them without standing in the precisely right location and peering carefully into the shadows.

"Now you may drink your punch in peace," Mr. Darcy said triumphantly.

"Indeed. I thank you." Elizabeth clenched her cup in both hands as she sipped, suddenly aware that she was alone with an unmarried man. Although they could easily hear the din from the ballroom, they were completely secluded. As she made an innocuous remark about the temperature in the ballroom, what disturbed Elizabeth the most was that she did not find the circumstances more distressing. She enjoyed Mr. Darcy's company and found it pleasant to be alone with him.

She set her empty cup next to Mr. Darcy's on the broken chair and gazed up at him. His eyes were locked on her face; had he been staring at her this whole time? Slowly, his hand reached up, and he brushed his trembling fingertips along her cheek. The touch was light, and yet she felt burned by fire.

"You are so…" His voice dropped off as he shook his head slowly. What was he about to say? Beautiful? Lovely? Elizabeth had heard such compliments before, but for some reason they would mean more coming from this man.

He stroked her cheek again. "You are so…quick."

Quick? Elizabeth blinked. He could not possibly mean fast; he had hardly observed her in many footraces.

"You are so quick to understand—to grasp the subtleties of a situation." His voice held a soft wonder while his hand gently stroked the curls of hair that framed her face. "It is so…attractive." He sighed out the word. "I do not understand why all the men of Meryton are not falling at your feet."

Many women might consider that an odd compliment, but it warmed Elizabeth from the inside; such words from him meant more than twenty compliments on her face and figure. His other hand brushed up the length of her arm to cup her shoulder. She shivered at the touch.

A tiny voice in the back of her head warned that no man should touch her in this way, but it felt so *right*. It was the right moment. He was the right man. She could not bring herself to prevent him.

He bent his head, his lips a little parted as his eyes held hers. *Asking permission?* Elizabeth experienced a thrill of excitement. Mr. Darcy would kiss her, and she could think of nothing she wanted more.

Chapter Eleven

Mr. Darcy would kiss her!

Elizabeth pulled away with a jerk. What was she thinking? Mr. Darcy was engaged to Lydia! Her own sister. And this was her engagement ball! To celebrate her betrothal to Mr. Bingley. She did not believe she would actually marry him, but that did not give her license to wantonly kiss other men!

What is wrong with me that I could contemplate, even for a second, kissing this man when we are both promised to others?

Elizabeth ducked her head and stepped backward. Mr. Darcy's hands instantly dropped to his side. The spell was broken. For a moment neither spoke. Elizabeth stared at her shoes. *I must leave immediately, or I might be tempted again to let him kiss me.*

"I...ah...should find...Mr. Bing-Charles," Elizabeth stammered as she collected the punch cups. "He will wonder where I am."

"Yes, yes, of course," Mr. Darcy said. He had turned from her and was running both his hands through his hair.

Elizabeth slipped through the draperies, daring to peek back at Mr. Darcy at the last minute. He had dropped into the chair, his head in his hands. She desperately wanted to put her arms around him and comfort him. But she continued to move forward, letting the drapes fall. It was not her place.

***

What is wrong with me? Darcy stared at the wall. Perhaps if he banged his head against it, he might jar his reason into functioning once more. *How could I have been such a fool?*

He slouched back in the chair, staring at the ceiling. For a few perfect, crystalline moments everything had seemed just right. Elizabeth had been under his hands; he had touched her shoulders, her cheek, her magnificent hair... The glorious feeling of her silky strands in his fingers. He closed his eyes on the memory. He must forget it. He should never have touched her hair at all. Darcy's face grew hot with mortification, although there was no one to see him.

Perhaps it was not so surprising that in the face of Elizabeth's beauty and surrounded by her elusive rosewater scent, his betrothal to her sister had faded from his memory. But how could he have forgotten her engagement to Bingley?

There was no genuine affection between him and Lydia, and Darcy had no intention of marrying the girl. Nonetheless, he should not consider kissing another woman until he was free of such entanglements. But Bingley had not been forced to make an offer for Elizabeth; he would not have proposed if he had no genuine affection for her. And now Darcy was lusting after his friend's fiancée. He should be shot!

But...Elizabeth. Her eyes had sparkled so brilliantly in the lights of the ballroom. And when she was genuinely amused, she laughed so...freely, as if her whole body enjoyed the joke. Nor had Darcy ever danced with a partner who suited him so well. Their set had been...transcendent.

Darcy staggered to his feet. *I must not think like this! It is dangerous, a path leading only to mortification and pain. I am betrothed. Elizabeth is betrothed. Most likely she would never wish to speak with him again after his egregious behavior. That might make it easier for me to forget her, although I doubt it.*

Darcy had been prepared to kiss her, and she knew it. Undoubtedly, he could somehow have made a worse impression on the object of his affections, but Darcy would be hard-pressed to think of how.

Would Elizabeth tell Bingley of the incident? Bingley would be completely justified in challenging Darcy to a duel—not that he was the type of man who would. No, Bingley would not turn to violence, but Darcy would necessarily lose his friendship. Darcy's fists twitched by his sides. If only he could pace! But the small alcove barely provided enough room to stand.

Fresh air. That was what he required. He needed to escape outside before the warmth—and the guilt—stifled him.

***

Had Mr. Darcy been about to kiss her, or had she misinterpreted his intentions? Did he consider her odd for having left so abruptly?

Why was she worried about Mr. Darcy's intentions? The far bigger problem was Elizabeth's reaction to him. She had wanted him to kiss her. It was undeniable. She had gazed at his lips and imagined how they would feel pressed against hers. She had envisioned how his arms would wrap around her waist, holding her body against his…

She should not imagine Mr. Darcy so. It was inappropriate in so many ways that Elizabeth could barely count them. *Still, if he broke his engagement to Lydia, and if I were no longer betrothed to Mr. Bingley…no, such thoughts were absurd!* If Mr. Darcy ever freed himself from Lydia, he would run far and fast from the entire Bennet family.

Nothing had occurred in the alcove, save that Elizabeth had fooled herself into believing Mr. Darcy might kiss her, but that was disturbing enough.

Needing distraction, Elizabeth helped herself to another cup of punch and sought out Charlotte Lucas in the crowd. Charlotte was always a soothing presence and the voice of moderation, although Elizabeth had no intention of admitting to the precise source of her consternation.

She found Charlotte, and they watched the dancing for several minutes as they talked about happenings in Meryton. Elizabeth's equanimity started to return. "Who is that terribly handsome man dancing with Jane?" Charlotte asked.

Elizabeth peered through the crowds. Had Mr. Bingley finally convinced Jane to dance with him? But no, there he was dancing with Kitty. Who could Jane be partnering that Charlotte would not recognize?

Finally, Elizabeth espied Jane amidst the throng of dancers and saw her partner was…Mr. Collins.

"With Jane?" She checked with Charlotte to ensure she had heard correctly. Her friend nodded eagerly. "Er, that is Mr. Collins, our cousin," Elizabeth murmured in a low tone. Was it possible Charlotte's description of the man was sardonic? No, Charlotte never teased. "I had forgotten you were ill and missed the last Netherfield ball, or you would have made his acquaintance then."

"Handsome" was not the first adjective Elizabeth would use to describe the parson. In fact, it would not even be the last—it would not be on the list at all. Did Charlotte actually find greasy hair, an obsequious smile, and beady eyes attractive?

"He seems very wholesome," Charlotte observed, her eyes still fixed on the clergyman.

"I suppose…"

"And his clothing…I have always liked men of the cloth." Charlotte sighed.

Elizabeth struggled for positive words to describe the man. "Mr. Collins always has much to say on any subject, and he is very proper with his manners. Apparently he is very willing to perform all of the services his parishioners need. He informed us of that himself."

"I see," Charlotte murmured approvingly.

"Um…he is…very knowledgeable about Rosings Park in Kent." Charlotte nodded. "I could make an introduction after this set."

Charlotte turned to Elizabeth with shining eyes. "Oh, would you? He seems most intriguing."

"He is betrothed to Jane," Elizabeth reminded Charlotte gently.

"I know." Charlotte nodded impatiently. "And I am betrothed to Mr. Wickham, but—"

"You are betrothed to Mr. Wickham?" Elizabeth cried. "I did not know!"

Charlotte shrugged. "The contract was only signed two days ago."

Elizabeth grabbed her friend's arm. "Charlotte, I do not believe that man can be trusted."

Charlotte laughed. "Oh, I do not trust him. Do not be absurd, Lizzy." Elizabeth blinked in confusion. "He will give me babies and a nice cozy house. It is all I ask from life."

"But I fear Mr. Wickham is not at all a respectable—"

"I know, Lizzy. He has debts and a loose relationship with the truth. But I can manage him."

Charlotte must be in love with Mr. Wickham! There was no other explanation for her decision. Now Elizabeth struggled for positive words about Mr. Wickham. "He is very attractive."

Charlotte regarded her in surprise. "I suppose. He is no Mr. Collins, but he will do."

With some difficulty, Elizabeth managed not to laugh.

The set had ended, and Mr. Collins led Jane to Elizabeth. She took the opportunity to gesture to Charlotte. "Mr. Collins, may I introduce my friend, Charlotte Lucas?"

"I am exceedingly charmed." Mr. Collins bowed low and kissed Charlotte's hand. She giggled.

Giggled? When had Charlotte Lucas ever giggled?

"My cousins indeed have exquisite taste in friends—as well as in family." He gifted Charlotte with his most insincere smile. "And may I say how lovely your gown is, Miss Lucas?" he continued without pause. "That particular color puts me in mind of the drapes in the southern sitting room at Rosings Park, which is the home of my most esteemed patroness, Lady Catherine de Bourgh."

"How wonderful to have such a patron!" Charlotte exclaimed, her eyes wide. "What is she like? Pray, tell me more."

Elizabeth exchanged glances with Jane. Now Charlotte was in trouble.

"I would happily tell you more about the noble family of de Bourgh. Would you perhaps honor me with the next set?" Mr. Collins inquired.

"Oh yes! That would be wonderful," Charlotte replied breathlessly.

Jane and Elizabeth watched in disbelief as Mr. Collins escorted a smiling Charlotte onto the dance floor. "I suppose it is good that someone wishes to hear more about Rosings Park," Jane said faintly.

Elizabeth turned to her sister. "I know Mr. Bingley wished to dance with you. Perhaps now would be a good time to seek him out."

Jane was still regarding the retreating figures with bemusement. "Indeed."

***

Miss Lucas was uniformly charming, Collins decided. She did not complain when he misstepped or trod on her toes. "My dear Miss Lucas," he declared after his third mistake, "I do apologize. I was blinded by your beauty." This was a compliment that had worked quite nicely when he had made a misstep with others, although it occurred with such frequency that some partners appeared not to believe him. When his cousin, Kitty, had complained about her sore toes, he had informed her that it was all part of the process of dancing, but she had appeared not to credit his words.

Miss Lucas giggled at the compliment, which made her lovely face even more charming. He again admired the simplicity of her dress. She was a modest woman and dressed modestly. How refreshing.

"And I must be allowed to tell you how this shade of green, er, blue...greenish-blue complements your complexion." This was another bon mot that was always acceptable to the ladies.

Miss Lucas colored and smiled demurely. But the next time they met in the middle, she met his eyes boldly. "I have always found clerical garb to be most becoming on a gentleman."

Collins was struck dumb, which was a completely foreign experience. No one had ever said such a thing to him. Was it proper? He felt flattered. But was it proper that he felt flattered? But she smiled in such a becoming way that it was hard to remember not to feel flattered. Oh, it was all so bewildering!

"Other girls prefer regimentals," she continued, "but I think a parson's wardrobe is much more...alluring."

She was awaiting his response. He cleared his throat. "Indeed? How...interesting." The shine in her eyes made his heart beat faster, which was quite a feat given how fast it was pumping from the exertion of the dance.

I have a fiancée, he reminded himself. But he was certain—well, almost certain—that Jane's eyes had never held a light like Miss Lucas's. He did not make it a practice to view Miss Bennet's eyes at every moment she was in his presence. What if he was doing her a disservice? Then he stole another look at Miss Lucas and was certain he had never seen that glow before.

Miss Bennet was, of course, lovely and all that was good. But she was...serene. She never seemed to experience Miss Lucas's thrill in his presence. And Collins had learned from the younger Miss Bennets that Sir William had given his daughter a generous dowry. Collins was not mercenary, not in the least. However, the dowry did...add to Miss Lucas's other charms. But of course, he had a fiancée.

Collins felt the need to hold his end—and perhaps some of her end—of the conversation. It would not hurt to impress her with his connections. "Have I, er, told you about the chimney piece at Rosings Park, the home of Lady Catherine de Bourgh? Or the glazing on the windows? It is quite impressive."

Her eyes lit with excitement. How wonderful to find an appreciative audience, he thought. "No. Please do!" she exclaimed. "How interesting."

As Collins launched into his description of the chimney and Rosings Park, he reminded himself that he had been quite correct in choosing a wife from among Thomas Bennet's daughters. Miss Bennet would make him an eminently suitable bride, although she did not look at him in such a way. Why did she not? After all, he was connected to the noble family of de Bourgh.

He could not fail to notice the naked admiration in Miss Lucas's glances, and he mourned what could have been.

***

I must not dance with Char—Mr. Bingley again, Jane vowed. Not because the experience was unpleasant. Quite the opposite. As they finished the set and he led her from the dance floor, she experienced a dangerous sense of exhilaration. No other partner had ever complemented her as well as Mr. Bingley. It was like dancing in a dream.

She had forbidden him to mention the subject of marriage again, but his eyes spoke eloquently enough. With every look, he suggested his yearning for her.

However, he was not her fiancé, and dancing with him made her wish he was. At moments during the dancing, Jane had even allowed herself to pretend that he was her betrothed. And that was dangerous. It made her recollect how easily he could be hers. She need simply tell Mr. Collins that they would not suit, and Mr. Bingley had sworn he would visit her on bended knee the next day. It was such a tempting vision.

As she had done before, Jane pushed aside that vision and reminded herself that she could not sacrifice her principles or her mother's happiness—or leave her sister without a fiancé. She had reasons—good, practical reasons—for marrying Mr. Collins. *I must focus my thoughts on him.* The memory of their last conversation came to mind. Well, perhaps not on him precisely but on my reasons for marrying him.

"Would you like some punch?" Mr. Bingley asked, and Jane found herself agreeing merely so she could steal a few more moments in his presence. Although she had resolved not to dance with him again, she could indulge herself now.

But before they reached the punch table, Mr. Collins appeared, looming over her, a cup of wine punch in each hand. He had partnered Charlotte Lucas in the previous two sets and was quite sweaty and red in the face. He swayed unsteadily. How much punch has he imbibed?

"Miss Jane, you will dance the next set with me." His words were more an order than a question.

She could not lose her opportunity to spend a little more time with Mr. Bingley. "Oh, I am thirsty and somewhat fatigued. Perhaps I might sit out this set."

Mr. Collins glared at Mr. Bingley, who was still holding her hand. Jane attempted to withdraw it discreetly, but he clutched it more tightly.

Mr. Collins stood straighter. "You are my fiancée. We should be seen dancing." His tone was stern, but then he added "love blossom" as an afterthought.

"We did dance earlier," she reminded him. What had come over Mr. Collins?

"You never look at me with shining eyes," Mr. Collins said, slurring the last words. "You do not ask questions about Lady Catherine or Rosings Park. And you do not giggle when I give you compliments. Why is that?"

"Mr. Collins?" Jane asked helplessly. Where were these questions coming from? Shining eyes?

He took a lurching step toward her, and Mr. Bingley held out his hand as if to halt the other man's progress. Mr. Collins ignored him. "I have been quite good to you, Jane." He finished off the last of his punch and set the cup on a nearby table. "I will allow you to return to your ancestral home. I have not chastised you over your lack of dowry—"

"Now, see here!" Mr. Bingley said sternly, pushing his way between Jane and Mr. Collins. "That is no way to speak with a—"

"Nor have I scolded you for your unfortunate tendency toward excessive smiling," Mr. Collins continued as if Mr. Bingley were not present, craning his head to peer at her around the other man's body.

"Excessive smiling?" Jane repeated blankly.

"You have no cause to insult Jane in such a way! She is an angel. A perfect angel!" Mr. Bingley's hands clenched into fists as he glared at Mr. Collins.

Her fiancé focused on Mr. Bingley for the first time. "If she is so perfect, then why does she not regard me with shining eyes?" Mr. Collins shook his head wildly. "No, I would say she is quite imperfect."

And that was when Mr. Bingley punched Mr. Collins.

Chapter Twelve

Lydia took Darcy's arm as they left the dance floor. She held her head high, scanning the crowd, no doubt to ensure that others noticed who escorted her.

"Will you give me a ring?" she asked, not removing her eyes from the surrounding revelers. Darcy did not respond. "A ring for our engagement? That would be very handsome of you."

"I had not given it much thought," he replied truthfully, massaging the back of his neck where a headache threatened to appear.

Lydia bestowed a brilliant smile on a young man they passed. "I think presenting a ring to one's fiancée is a lovely tradition. They say rings symbolize the eternity of our love."

Darcy tried to prevent the laughter that bubbled up in his throat; instead, it emerged as a rather strangled gasp. Fortunately, Lydia inhabited her own world and did not notice. "I would dearly love a ring," Lydia continued. "Then I could show it to my friends, and they would know you really did plan to marry me."

So much for the eternity of love.

"There is Maria Lucas!" Lydia exclaimed and dragged him over to a girl a year or two older than she. "Maria, this is Mr. Darcy, my fiancé. He owns Pimbersly in Derbyshire and is worth ten thousand a year." Darcy cringed inwardly.

Maria's eyes were wide as she curtsied. "Mr. Darcy," she murmured.

Lydia had been intent on plying him with punch "to help him relax," but her absence would help him relax most readily. Despite having spent little time with the girl, he was already able to identify that gnawing pain in the back of his neck as his "Lydia headache."

"You may speak with your friend, and I will obtain punch." He managed to smile at Lydia as he said this.

"La! How wonderful!" Lydia exclaimed and promptly turned her back on him to whisper in her friend's ear.

Darcy did not care; he was rid of the girl for the moment. If he never returned with the punch, she probably would not notice.

Throughout their dance, Lydia had encouraged Darcy to "smile more" and "have more fun" as if fun were something one could conjure up at will. He supposed this subject of discourse was an improvement on her constant questions about gifts of jewelry, but Darcy found himself equally irritated.

Darcy needed counsel and thought Bingley might help. He had spied his friend over by the punch table talking to Mr. Collins and Miss Bennet. However, as Darcy neared the group, Bingley drew his arm back and punched the oafish parson on the chin.

"What the devil?" Darcy muttered, hastening forward. While Darcy had often fantasized about striking the supercilious parson—or perhaps pushing him into a convenient lake—he could not imagine what had provoked Bingley. His friend rarely lost his temper and never resorted to violence. What had Collins said?

When Darcy arrived, Collins was tottering on his feet, pure astonishment on his face. The contents of the cup he held sloshed dangerously. Bingley was preparing for another punch, but Darcy hastily grabbed his friend's arm. Wickham appeared on Bingley's other side to capture his other arm.

Bingley pulled fiercely, trying to tug his arms out of their hold as he growled wordlessly and glared at his adversary. Finally, Collins fainted, pouring punch down the front of his waistcoat in the process.

"Damn fool!" Bingley muttered in disgust, shaking off Darcy's hold and stepping away from Wickham.

Two of Netherfield's footmen appeared, and Darcy gave instructions for Collins to be removed to another room and to summon a doctor if necessary. Darcy suspected Collins was merely suffering from an excess of drink, but they would need to ensure that Bingley had not caused any lasting harm.

By the time Darcy returned his attention to Bingley, the man was facing Jane Bennet, who had gone quite white in the face. "Charles! What were you thinking? You struck him!" she cried.

"He insulted you!" Bingley said.

Miss Bennet stared at him wide-eyed for a moment. She opened her mouth to speak but then shut it and whirled away, striding from the room without another word.

Wickham doubled over with laughter. "She is properly angry with you! Well done, Bingley!"

Bingley scowled at the other man, which provoked more laughter from Wickham. The sound grated on Darcy's nerves even more than usual.

"Keep your mouth shut, Wickham!" Darcy warned.

Wickham smirked again, and Darcy wondered if the militia officer was foxed. "I cannot blame you, Bingley. Miss Bennet is a toothsome morsel," Wickham slurred. Bingley growled, but Darcy restrained him with a hand on his arm. "The whole lot of them are quite the eyeful. Lydia's a pretty enough wench." Darcy glared but did not rise to Wickham's bait. He had no interest in defending Lydia's honor; if Wickham wished to provoke Darcy's jealousy, he would fail.

Wickham laughed giddily and stumbled sideways but caught himself on the edge of a table before falling. *Definitely foxed.* "But for my money…" Wickham slurred, "the best of them is Elizabeth."

Wickham now had Darcy's full attention. "Wickham…" Darcy growled a warning.

Wickham appeared not to notice. He grinned drunkenly as he spoke. "With those eyes and that hair…and have you seen her bosom?" Wickham gestured obscenely.

That was when Darcy punched Wickham.

***

Mrs. Long had hastened to inform Elizabeth about the contretemps between Mr. Bingley and Mr. Collins. Elizabeth was immediately torn between pity for Mr. Bingley and exasperation, but her duty was to rush to her fiancé's side. The small crowd that had formed near the punch table indicated his location. She arrived just in time to witness Mr. Darcy punching Mr. Wickham.

What was wrong with the gentlemen tonight?

Rushing toward the crowd from the other direction, Lydia screamed "Wickham!" as if the man were being murdered in the Netherfield ballroom. Mr. Darcy landed another punch in Mr. Wickham's stomach before the man crumpled to the floor.

By the time Elizabeth reached the combatants, Mr. Bingley was restraining Mr. Darcy while Mr. Wickham rolled on the floor, holding his stomach and groaning. Lydia knelt next to him, wringing her hands and loudly imploring him, "Please be all right! Whatever you do, don't die!"

Mr. Darcy let out a noise that could have been a laugh, causing Lydia to glare accusingly at him. "You have killed him!"

Mr. Darcy strained to reach Mr. Wickham yet again, but Mr. Bingley would not release him. "Darcy," he hissed in his friend's ear, "you are making a scene!" The other man shook his head and continued to struggle. Perhaps Elizabeth could be of assistance to Mr. Bingley.

She approached Mr. Darcy, attempting to catch and hold his gaze. "Mr. Wickham is on the floor. He is no longer a threat," she said gently. What had the militia officer done to provoke such an assault? Mr. Wickham and Mr. Darcy were not friendly, but they had tolerated each other's presence in the past.

Mr. Darcy's eyes fixed on Elizabeth's face and grew wide with horror. He took in his surroundings, and abruptly all the fight drained out of him. He sagged in Mr. Bingley's hold until his friend released him.

Lydia worried over Wickham until he pushed her hands away and sat up. "For God's sake's, girl. Don't make a fuss!" he hissed.

"But Wicky--!" Lydia wailed.

Wicky? Elizabeth thought.

Lydia glared accusingly at Mr. Darcy. "I know you are jealous, but he does not deserve to be killed for my sake!"

Mr. Darcy barked a laugh. "It was not you—" He stopped and glanced guiltily at Elizabeth. Was he embarrassed she had witnessed his loss of control? He rubbed his forehead and sighed. "I will not kill him," he told Lydia.

"And you never brought me my punch!" she wailed at him. Mr. Darcy rolled his eyes.

Two Netherfield footmen appeared, staring dubiously at Mr. Wickham on the floor. "Another?" one footman exclaimed in disbelief.

Mr. Bingley gestured for them to collect Mr. Wickham. "Take him to another room to recover."

The two men pulled Mr. Wickham to his feet, but he shook off their hold. "I can walk, damn you!" Before they could lead him anywhere, he had disappeared into the crowd with Lydia trailing behind him. Mr. Bingley waved his servants away, and they, too, departed.

Mr. Bingley turned a concerned look on his friend. "Darcy, what is wrong with you?"

Mr. Darcy glared sullenly at the floor. "Wickham is a blackguard and a scoundrel. He disgusts me."

"But it is not like you to lose control so easily," Mr. Bingley persisted.

Mr. Darcy gave a bitter laugh. "You are one to talk."

Mr. Bingley flushed and glanced away. Apparently Mrs. Long had been correct that he had been brawling as well. Elizabeth shook her head in disgust. *What were the men about?*

In the next moment, she reminded herself that it hardly signified. This was her engagement ball, and she must do what she could to dissipate the crowds of gawkers and return it to normality. She turned to Mr. Bingley. "This has caused quite a commotion." From the corner of her eye, she saw Mr. Darcy's shoulders sag a bit as if he were mortified by her observation. "We should all join the final set of the night and encourage the guests to return to their revels."

"An excellent idea, Lizzy!" Mr. Bingley grinned at her and then sent his friend a sharp glare.

"Perhaps you should seek out Lydia?" Mr. Darcy nodded sheepishly.

As they walked to the dance floor, they passed Wickham, who had Charlotte on his arm and was practically dragging her to join the dancing. Then right before the set began, Mr. Collins stumbled up, bruised in numerous places, with a very unhappy looking Jane. Lydia and Mr. Darcy slipped in at the last minute.

By the time the music commenced, there were four betrothed couples standing up together. No one was smiling.

***

Ordinarily Darcy enjoyed dancing, but at the moment he felt as if he had been locked into prison, and Lydia was his jailer. Dancing at Netherfield, with the eyes of all the revelers upon him, was torture. Lydia danced with far more enthusiasm and energy than skill, and Darcy had difficulty encouraging her to focus on the dance steps.

Moreover, five minutes had not been sufficient to recover from his anger and mortification. *How could I have lost control like that?* Over and over he reviewed that moment when Wickham had insulted Elizabeth, but each time the blinding rage descended once again.

Dancing with Lydia was about as enjoyable as a funeral. But following such a display of temper, Darcy must appear to be his own master and devoted to his fiancée. Hopefully, he was fooling their observers; however, he had never felt less like touching a woman in his life. Every time their hands met, a little shudder of anger and disgust coursed through him.

A set with Darcy had not been Lydia's fondest wish either. She had only agreed after extracting a promise from Darcy that he would not hit "dear Wicky" again that evening.

After her recent behavior toward Wickham, Darcy suspected the militia officer had been the other man in the library. He would have laughed at the irony if he had not been so angry. *Of course it was Wickham; he is destined to ever be a thorn in my side.* Furiously, Darcy considered how to prove those suspicions but could think of nothing.

Lydia maintained a steady stream of chatter and, fortunately, did not expect a response. "Oh, look at what Emma Smith is wearing! That is not becoming to her at all, poor thing! There are ever so many officers here. Don't they look heavenly in their regimentals? Perhaps you could get a set of regimentals to wear about Pembleham. It would make you look that much more handsome and responsible."

Darcy reminded himself that he could not strike a lady. "I most certainly will not."

Lydia pouted prettily for a minute but soon forgot her disappointment in favor of another observation about someone's wardrobe choices. Her dancing suffered as she constantly surveyed the ballroom and commented on others. "Peter DuLac is dancing with Emily Mathers. Her parents will not be happy! La! Denny finally convinced Anne Mason to be his partner. They look so well together."

During the next dance, they were required to stand up next to Wickham and Miss Lucas. Wickham smirked at Darcy, who endeavored to ignore the other man. Lydia regarded the two with a furrowed brow. Then the dancing commenced. When Darcy and Lydia came together, she whispered to him, "Why is Wickham dancing with Charlotte? She is the dullest, plainest girl in the neighborhood!"

"I believe they are betrothed," Darcy answered absently, distracted by his need to watch Elizabeth with Bingley.

Lydia stumbled and nearly tripped the man next to her. "Betrothed?" She gasped. Taking her hand, Darcy encouraged her to return to the rhythm of the dance. "No, it is not possible!" Lydia protested. "She is such a nasty, plain little thing. He cannot possibly—"

Lydia was only confirming Darcy's suspicions. "I believe her father is offering a generous dowry."

"I cannot believe he would agree to such a thing!"

I can easily believe it if money is involved. The scoundrel would be acquiring a respectable wife and far more money than he deserved. Darcy was concerned for poor Miss Lucas, tethered to Wickham for the rest of her life. Perhaps he should discuss the situation with Sir William.

Lydia's steps faltered again. "Married to Charlotte Lucas! It is so unfair." Her lips twisted into a grimace. "He is so—" Her voice broke.

Unreliable, conniving, mendacious, Darcy thought.

"Charming!" Lydia said. "And Charlotte is so dull!" Darcy realized the shine in her eyes was caused by tears. *Good Lord, could the girl possibly care for Wickham that much?* Lydia exhibited even worse judgment than he had thought.

His suspicions about Wickham's identity grew stronger. If only he had proof! "Mr. Wickham is by no means a respectable man," Darcy cautioned her.

"Of course *you* would say that!" Lydia cried. "You have been horrid to him for his entire life!"

Darcy's entire body tightened. "I do not know what Wickham has told you, but—"

She tossed her head. "No! You shan't turn me against him! You shan't!" she cried so loudly that heads all over the ballroom turned in their direction. Darcy ground his teeth together. Elizabeth had been similarly persuaded by Wickham's lies, but at least she had listened to his side of the story.

The dance called for them to turn in a circle, back to back. When Darcy faced her again, he must chastise her for this behavior; he could not allow her to defend such a scoundrel. But when he turned toward her again, she was gone. He saw her fleeing the dance floor, her hand over her mouth. Darcy did not even consider going after her.

Another day he might have been more disturbed at her abandonment, but what was one more mortification today? Darcy walked away from the dancing couples with as much dignity as he could muster, ignoring the stares as he strode through the crowd.

Finally, Darcy found an isolated corner of the room from which he could observe the other dancers finishing the set. They provided a distraction from wondering what the revelers were whispering about him behind their fans.

Not surprisingly, his eyes were drawn to Elizabeth where she was dancing with Bingley at the head of the line. Darcy was forced to admit they were well matched; they danced elegantly together. His blond hair complemented her dark hair. Her gown even matched the colors in his suit. Damnation! Why did she accept Bingley's offer? Why could she not have accepted a proposal from Collins or some other fool? Then Darcy could have easily fought for her.

Darcy felt muffled as if engulfed in a dark shroud. Around him everyone was happy, laughing and talking, but he was surrounded by silent misery. He was more determined than ever to extricate himself from the engagement to Lydia, but Elizabeth would still be promised to Bingley. He would not—should not—interfere with his friend's happiness.

Once my engagement is broken, I must leave Hertfordshire immediately lest I be tempted to kiss Elizabeth once more. Perhaps he could return to the neighborhood eventually, when he had overcome this obsession. *In five years.* Darcy watched as Elizabeth laughed at something Bingley had said. *Maybe ten years.*

Darcy felt his fists clench at his sides. When would this torturous ball be over? This final dance was lasting an eternity.

***

This dance was taking forever. Jane was a charitable soul, but even she could not bring herself to describe Mr. Collins as a good dancer under the best of circumstances, and these were hardly the best. He was still red-faced from having imbibed excessively and frequently staggered—perhaps as a result of the injury he had suffered at Mr. Bingley's hands. In addition, his cravat and the front of his suit were stained by copious quantities of punch. However, he was determined to demonstrate his good health and would not hear of quitting the dance floor.

During this set alone, he had gone in the wrong direction twice and trodden on her toes three times. Other dancers stared and whispered. Jane endeavored to ignore it but could not help wondering if they were noticing the egregious dancing or gossiping about the fight. She apportioned blame for that awkwardness equally between Mr. Collins and Mr. Bingley. Indeed, Mr. Collins was irritating and insulting, but why must

Mr. Bingley cause such embarrassment by punching the man?

Her mood was not improved by Mr. Collins's insistence on maintaining a constant stream of commentary, even though the exertion was putting him quite out of breath.

"This ballroom"—pant—"this ballroom puts me in mind of the one at Rosings Park"—pant—"home of my esteemed patroness, Lady Catherine de Bourgh." Such explanation was entirely unnecessary at this point. Jane was intimately familiar with everything connected to Lady Catherine—and had even been forced to admit privately to herself that she was not looking forward to making the lady's acquaintance.

"Of course"—pant, pant—"Rosings's ballroom is much larger and has"—pant—"—the most exquisite gold ornamentation. Lady Catherine said"—pant—"—it took the craftsmen nearly a year to complete it." The couples formed into lines once more, and Mr. Collins blotted his forehead with his handkerchief. "You will have the opportunity to experience it for yourself as her ladyship will surely invite us to a ball."

A response seemed to be expected, so Jane murmured, "How lovely."

Mr. Collins gave her the oily smile that Jane had difficulty returning; truth be told, she had difficulty looking at it. "I do believe that your delicacy of spirits and natural modesty will be quite acceptable to her," he assured her. "She is very condescending to those of lower rank."

Jane struggled to think of something pleasant— or at least innocuous—to say. "Thank you for reassuring me."

They had come together again and were turning in a slow circle. "You are very welcome, my delicate English rose." He regarded her intently and smiled.

This passionate gaze gave Jane the sensation of insects crawling all over her body.

As they finished the maneuver, Mr. Collins released her hand too soon, and she stumbled. Fortunately, she was able to prevent a fall and returned to the steps of the dance. She gritted her teeth. *I can do this. I must do this. I can marry Mr. Collins. The feeling in my stomach is not nausea.*

As the dance brought them together again, he was frowning slightly. "However, you may wish to dress more modestly in Lady Catherine's presence."

Jane glanced involuntarily down at her gown. No one would call it immodest, surely! The neckline was not too low, and it was not too tight nor transparent.

Mr. Collins blathered on, oblivious. "Lady Catherine prefers to have the distinction of rank preserved." Did he feel her dress was too elegant for her station in life? How absurd! "You would do better to dress like Miss Lucas."

Jane stole a look at Charlotte Lucas, who wore a very plain, unornamented blue gown with a neckline far higher than was currently fashionable. Indeed, it was a bit too informal for a gathering of this sort. Jane could not help but notice that Mr. Collins gazed on Charlotte admiringly as if beholding a beautiful statue. *How odd!* Charlotte was universally declared to be the plainest woman in Meryton.

Mr. Collins directed his eyes and ingratiating smile back to Jane. "After all, my rose blossom, we must please Lady Catherine above all things."

No one would ever have described Jane as quick to anger, yet she experienced an uncharacteristic desire to take the punch bowl and empty its contents onto Mr. Collins's head.

Or perhaps, as they danced, she could move her foot just so…and he would trip and fall.

Oh, heavens! What am I thinking? I would never do such a thing. I am quite losing my mind.

If Mr. Collins could bring her to this state in the short time of their acquaintance, how would he affect her disposition after years of marriage? Best not to think on it. Despairing, she cast a glance at the musicians. How much longer must they play? She felt as if she had been dancing forever.

Chapter Thirteen

Wickham had been dancing forever.

Dancing with Charlotte now was no more satisfactory than the initial proposal had been. She remained pleasant and reserved, apparently unaware of the very great honor their marriage would bestow upon her. Women all over Meryton—all over Hertfordshire—were sighing his name while his fiancée did not appear to even remember it!

Now Charlotte was sneaking admiring glances at that damned oily-haired parson. If Wickham did not know better, he would suspect her of wishing to increase his ardor by stoking his jealousy. But Wickham was an expert at that game, and Charlotte never glanced at him to note the effectiveness of her ploy. That made him even angrier; he was jealous, and she did not care!

What did that fat parson have to offer that Wickham did not? He was not half again as handsome, and he did not wear regimentals. In fact, his garb was drab even by clerical standards. He was a horrid dancer; Wickham almost felt sorry for Jane Bennet. Granted, Collins probably had no debts, and—given Miss Bennet's pitiful dowry—he was not marrying her for mercenary reasons. Also, the parson was honest and held a steady job. But what were such superficial considerations when compared to the figure Wickham cut in his regimentals?

Clearly Charlotte was running mad if she preferred the parson to him. *Hmm. After we are wed, perhaps I could stow her in an asylum. Then I would not need to manage her tiresome demands for children and a home—and, most likely, marital fidelity. But I could keep the money.* The matter deserved further consideration.

While Charlotte made calf's eyes at the foolish parson, Wickham carefully averted his gaze from Lydia Bennet except when the dance steps necessitated it. Charlotte was too little interested in Wickham, but Lydia was too much. She wished to catch his eye and flirt at every opportunity, even in Darcy's presence.

Lydia was undeniably a toothsome wench and knew how to dress to best display her assets—a skill which Charlotte sadly lacked. It was such a shame that Lydia did not possess Charlotte's dowry! Then Wickham remembered the irritating sound of Lydia's laughter and some of the silly words she had uttered. No, being shackled to Lydia would be no treat.

Nevertheless, when Lydia smiled at him, Wickham fantasized about taking her for a roll in the hay. She had caused him quite a lot of bother, and all he had to show for his pains were a few kisses and some gropes. She owed him more, much more. The problem—as was so often true in Wickham's life—was Darcy.

Darcy did not appear to suspect Wickham's relationship with Lydia. However, the more Lydia flirted, the more suspicious Darcy would become—and the more likely Wickham would face a situation more unpleasant than just a punch from Darcy.

Even now, as Lydia and Wickham stood in opposite lines waiting for the next dance to commence, she gave him a coy little wave. Wickham ignored her. Now the wave was getting bigger and faster; soon Darcy or the other dancers would notice. Damn the girl! She was as pretty as a rose and about as clever as one, too. Wickham gave her a half smile and a nod of his head; she smirked back, apparently satisfied.

Then Wickham noticed Darcy's frown. Hell! Wickham hastily took a great deal of interest in Charlotte's unfortunately flat bodice, which allowed him to watch her make eyes at the parson. How long until the dancing was finished? This final set seemed interminable.

***

How long could one set of dances last? wondered Bingley. He liked Elizabeth and enjoyed dancing with her, but nothing could prevent his eyes from seeking out Jane.

All evening, whenever she was near, he would experience that thrilling awareness that his place was beside her. She was his lodestone, pulling him inexorably closer. Elizabeth understood the circumstances, but Bingley still felt like a traitor.

Jane closed her eyes and pursed her lips as Mr. Collins once again bumped into another dancer. She must be very unhappy to even allow that much disapproval to show. When their eyes met, Bingley gave her a sympathetic smile, but her mouth did not so much as twitch in response, and she hastily looked away.

What was I thinking when I struck Collins? Well, clearly I had not been thinking. The whole incident was mortifying. He was doubly shamed that he had come to blows over an insult to Jane, who was not his fiancée, while Darcy had been left to defend Elizabeth's honor. Although Darcy's reaction undoubtedly had more to do with his dislike of Wickham. After all, Darcy did not care for Elizabeth or anyone in her family.

Past Jane's figure, Bingley glimpsed his mother, watching him dance from her position near the wall. Had she learned he had brawled at his own ball like a common ruffian? Perhaps not. She was smiling broadly, and the tears shining in her eyes reminded Bingley why he had undertaken this charade. His engagement to Elizabeth brought his mother such joy.

Although his mother's first introduction to Elizabeth had not been…auspicious, their later conversations had been quite pleasant, and his mother had warmed to his fiancée. Mrs. Bingley's color was better, her voice was stronger, and she walked with greater vigor. Indeed, despite the confusion, the engagement had been worth any sacrifice.

As they twirled, Bingley took Elizabeth's rather stiff hand. She did not seem as furious about the brawl as Jane had been, but Bingley still felt a twinge of guilt over his behavior. Here was yet another injustice he had heaped on the heads of the blameless Bennet sisters. By agreeing to the engagement, Elizabeth was doing Bingley a great service, but so far it had only given her misery.

They separated and returned to opposite lines. *Huh, how odd!* Elizabeth seemed to be observing Darcy, who was lurking in a corner of the room. *I wonder why?* Darcy had been a bit rude to Elizabeth early in their first visit to Hertfordshire, but Bingley thought the situation had improved. Perhaps she was still angry over his earlier treatment of her, although the expression on her face was not resentful.

A thought struck Bingley. *That is one good office I may perform for Elizabeth to repay her for her kind assistance. She has been so good in helping me with my mother and endeavoring to reunite me with Jane. Perhaps I may speak with Darcy and improve his opinion of her—maybe even make peace between the two. That would benefit both of them.*

Elizabeth made an effort to smile as they came together again. "Your ball is very well attended."

He nodded. "Yes, and the weather is as fine as one could hope for this time of year."

"Your sister hired some excellent musicians."

"I enjoyed them at the last ball and requested them specifically."

She nodded and fell silent as they danced. Finally, she said, "It is nice that so many of the militia were able to join us."

"Yes, I extended an invitation to them specifically."

"That was very good of you."

He shrugged, a little disconcerted by the banality of the conversation. It was never thus with Jane. Conversation flowed effortlessly between them with no hesitations or awkwardness. Elizabeth was known for being clever and witty, but Bingley did not seem to draw out these qualities.

Elizabeth's eyes darted once more to Darcy, who frowned as he observed the dancers. Did Darcy's opinion indeed trouble her so? Perhaps she was concerned about being connected by marriage to a man who showed her such disdain.

Bingley must talk to Darcy.

If only this blasted ball would end!

***

Darcy was quite ready for this blasted ball to be over. He massaged his neck with one hand; the throbbing headache had undoubtedly been provoked by a wrongheaded action, but which one? Somehow he had almost managed to kiss a woman who was not only not his fiancée but also was engaged to his best friend. Then he had engaged in a practical brawl. And had been abandoned mid-dance by his actual fiancée.

Idly, he wondered which of his actions was the most offensive to Elizabeth and realized that his life must be truly out of control if he had so many from which to select. He watched her dance with Bingley, laughing at something he said. She did not appear to be offended.

What he really needed was a glass of brandy…or two…or three.

Immediately.

But he forced himself to remain in the ballroom until the final dance was finished. He need not add to the evening's mortifications by disappearing prematurely. However, once the last musical notes died away, Darcy could suffer the company no longer. Taking advantage of his long legs, he strode toward the exit.

"Darcy, a moment, if you please." Bingley took his elbow. Darcy sighed and allowed himself to be maneuvered to one side of the room where the sound of the departing guests was nothing more than a dull murmur.

"I apologize for my inappropriate behavior at your ball," Darcy said in a clipped voice.

"That is not—well, thank you." Bingley ran a hand absently through his blond hair. "I might as well apologize to you for the same offense. But I wished to speak on a different subject."

From Bingley's demeanor, it was obviously a subject of some delicacy. Darcy's heart sank, but he nodded for his friend to continue.

Bingley was already red in the face, and his hands fidgeted unceasingly. "Before I was en-engaged to E-Elizabeth, your manner toward her bothered me, but I felt it was not my place to say anything."

My manner? Had Bingley somehow learned of the interlude behind the draperies? Had Elizabeth told him? Darcy was suddenly dizzy. Losing Bingley's friendship, no matter how richly deserved, would certainly be the pinnacle of an already awful day.

Bingley took a deep breath. "Y-you have been quite rude and cold to Elizabeth, s-saying disparaging things and ridiculing her family. I know my sisters have instigated much of it, and I will speak with them as well. But I know this conduct bothers Elizabeth, and I w-wish you would be more civil to her." Bingley's shoulders sagged now that he had said his piece; they were probably the harshest words he had ever uttered.

Darcy gaped at his friend. *How could he believe...? Why would he think...?* Then the irony struck him forcefully. If only Bingley had seen Darcy with Elizabeth in the alcove, then Bingley would see how "civil" he could be!

Laughter started in Darcy's stomach. *Bingley does not believe I like Elizabeth!* Chuckles clogged his throat. *Bingley thought the issue which disturbs Elizabeth is my* coldness? The laughs erupted, unchecked, from his mouth. He could not prevent them.

"Darcy?" Bingley asked uncertainly as his friend shook with uncontrollable laughter. No doubt Bingley found the sight somewhat alarming; he had once complained that Darcy did not smile enough.

Darcy could not stem the laughter. It was as if somehow the day's tension was being exorcised through gales of mirth. "You believe—" Darcy gasped out another laugh. "—I do not like—" another gasp. "—her." This provoked more laughter. The irony was simply too delicious. The situation was too absurd.

He was in love with his best friend's fiancée and engaged to a fifteen-year-old flirt who disdained him. It would make an excellent plot for a comic opera.

"How much punch did you consume?" Bingley asked in a whisper.

Darcy braced himself with a hand on Bingley's shoulder, still nearly doubled over with laughter.

Bingley surveyed the nearby environs for someone to assist him. "Darcy, perhaps some brandy and a chance to lie down—"

I must bring myself under control before Bingley believes recent events have driven me mad. "I will be all right," Darcy wheezed as the laughter died down. "I simply—it has been a difficult day." Bingley nodded sympathetically, although he still appeared mystified. "I will endeavor to show abundant kindness to Miss Elizabeth in the future," Darcy promised. Bingley gave him a bemused smile.

However, Darcy was not interested in answering additional questions to clarify his feelings toward Elizabeth. "I think you have it right. I need a brandy and a good night's sleep." Darcy clapped Bingley briefly on the shoulder and then hurriedly strode for the exit. He knew Bingley's anxious eyes followed him. His friend undoubtedly thought Darcy drunk or insane—or both—but it was better than if he suspected the truth.

***

Lydia had observed Charlotte Lucas dancing with Wickham—and seethed the whole time. *How dare Charlotte presume? Wickham belongs to me!* Yes, at first Lydia had only perceived him as one of *her* militia officers, but at some point—perhaps the adventure in the library—that had changed. Now Lydia knew Wickham was the prince she had been seeking. In addition, he had sort of quasi-promised to rescue her from Darcy and marry her. It was almost as good as an engagement!

He loves me, not Charlotte. He would never tell Charlotte that she was charming after a few cups of wine punch or how her smile reminded him of a baby squirrel. Or that her beauty made him lose control of his hands. The very thought of anyone addressing such remarks to Charlotte made Lydia snort with laughter.

And as for Mr. High-and-Mighty Darcy, Lydia had decided to forego her plans to make his life more fun. After his behavior during the dance—not to mention punching Wickham—he did not deserve her efforts. Let him be boring!

Kitty wandered over and stood next to Lydia. "La! I am pleased the night is almost over. I am so weary." Kitty fanned herself slowly.

Lydia grunted a response, not taking her eyes from Charlotte and Wickham, who had finished dancing and were now talking rather familiarly.

At first Charlotte had not seemed pleased to be dancing with her fiancé—indeed she had appeared quite distracted. But when Wickham had said something to her as they promenaded, she had smiled at him. And she was *still* smiling. "Do you see?" Lydia hissed to her sister. "She smiles at him!"

Kitty blinked and turned her attention to the guests leaving the dance floor. "Charlotte?" she finally asked. "Is she not permitted to smile?" Kitty's brow creased.

"She smiles as if Wickham is hers."

"They are engaged. He *is* hers."

"As if that gives her the right!" Lydia spat out.

"Well, actually it does."

Lydia ignored Kitty's logic, her gaze fixed on the couple. Charlotte's eyes traveled over Lydia briefly. "Oh, she is gloating!" Lydia muttered.

Kitty's brow furrowed. "Charlotte? Gloating?"

"She is so pleased to have bested me. She has ever been jealous of me."

"Charlotte?"

"Honestly, is that all you can say?" Lydia grumbled. "Yes, Charlotte! Can you not see? She is so smug that she has him and I do not!" Lydia bit her lip. "And he looks so fine in his regimentals. While Charlotte is so plain and dull."

"She is very plain," Kitty said dubiously. "But—"

"Do you think he has kissed her?" Lydia interrupted. "How could he ever bear it? It would be like kissing a horse. No, he only cares about her money."

"I suppose," Kitty replied. "But why do you care? Mr. Darcy is worth ten times Wickham."

The thought of Mr. Darcy made Lydia's stomach churn unpleasantly. "But Darcy is so stiff and formal. He only talks about duty and responsibility— and he never, ever laughs. *He* should marry Charlotte. What a pair they would be!" Lydia laughed at her own joke.

But then she sobered. *It was so unfair! Why couldn't I have that money? I would look so much better on Wickham's arm! All the officers would admire him and tell him what a pretty, charming wife he has!*

Charlotte Lucas was ruining all of Lydia's plans—at the very moment when it became clear: "Wickham is meant to be mine."

Kitty's brow furrowed again. "But you have Mr. Darcy. Why—?"

Lydia rolled her eyes and tossed her head. "You just do not understand love!" She stalked away from Kitty and toward the dance floor.

The few remaining dancers were leaving, many walking right past Lydia. Charlotte, her face flushed from the exertion, ambled by with her arm in Wickham's. She gave Lydia a broad smile.

That was the last straw! Lydia could bear no more. Charlotte's smug attitude, her superiority, her claim over Wickham—it was all too much.

And that was when Lydia slapped Charlotte.

Chapter Fourteen

Darcy had almost made good his escape when someone, recognizing him as Lydia's fiancé, had raced after him to relay news of a fight. When Darcy arrived, Lydia was pulling Miss Lucas's hair out of her coiffure. Darcy took a second to absorb the fact that yes indeed that was *his* fiancée pulling another woman's hair on the floor of the Netherfield ballroom. In that moment he vowed he would find a way out of the betrothal, even if it required that he give her Pemberley. *Nothing* would be worse than being married to this woman!

A crowd had formed around the two women, watching with a combination of amusement and disgust. However, there were no faces Darcy recognized; he would need to resolve this disaster alone.

Lydia had both hands in Miss Lucas's hair, yanking strands with abandon. *At least Miss Lucas was not a shrieker.* The poor woman attempted to maintain her dignity despite the circumstances. Her lips were white, pressed together in a tight line as she endeavored not to cry out. She had one hand in her hair, trying to prevent further damage to her coiffure—plain though it was. With the other hand, she was attempting, in vain, to push Lydia away.

In contrast, Lydia was shrieking nearly incoherently, her face red and contorted with rage. Darcy considered for a moment what could have possibly led to such a virulent disagreement but then decided it hardly mattered. His only objective was stopping Lydia and rescuing Miss Lucas. He took a deep breath and waded into the fray.

"Lydia! Lydia, stop at once!" he commanded, not really expecting to be obeyed. Lydia continued to fight like a hellcat, giving no indication that she had heard him. Darcy stooped down and grabbed one of her arms; this caused her to strike out blindly with the other hand, landing a fist quite neatly in his right eye. As Darcy reeled backward, he heard laughter from the surrounding crowd. He did not, however, release his hold on Lydia's arm and used it to haul her to her feet.

Fortuitously, Sir William arrived at that moment and helped his distraught daughter stagger to a standing position. With as much dignity as she could muster, Miss Lucas straightened her bodice, smoothed out her skirts, and endeavored to repair the damage to her hair.

Lydia continued to struggle in Darcy's hold, straining to reach Miss Lucas and muttering nearly incoherent threats, which provoked laughter from the watching guests. She never once glanced at Darcy, and it was uncertain she even knew who restrained her. He held her firmly by the upper arms to avoid touching more inappropriate parts of her anatomy.

"She is no better than me!" Lydia shrieked. "Why should she get all the benefits?"

"Lydia, stop this at once!" he hissed at her. "This is unseemly behavior. Leave off!"

But Lydia shook her head violently. "Not after what she did!" Lydia cried. Again Darcy wondered what plain, unassuming Miss Lucas could have possibly done to incur Lydia's wrath.

Finally, Sir William led a sobbing Miss Lucas away. Darcy said a silent prayer of thanks when her departure coincided with Elizabeth's arrival. No doubt Elizabeth could handle Lydia better than anyone. After assessing the situation with a quick sweep of her eyes, Elizabeth immediately marched over to Darcy and her sister.

"What has happened?" she inquired through clenched teeth.

"Apparently Miss Lydia struck Miss Lucas and then attempted to deprive her of some of her hair—from the roots," Darcy replied.

"Oh, Good Lord!" Elizabeth closed her eyes as if begging for patience.

Lydia still struggled as if she hoped to chase after Miss Lucas. Elizabeth grabbed her sister by the shoulders and shook her. "Lydia! Cease this embarrassing behavior. Stop this instant!" Lydia made no sign that she had heard. "Do you want Papa to cut off your hat and glove allowance?" Miraculously, Lydia fell limp, gaping at her sister. Darcy tentatively released her, prepared to grab her once more if necessary.

Lydia gave her sister a very contrite look. "Do not tell Papa. I need a new bonnet!"

Darcy rubbed the back of his neck. This girl's impudence knew no bounds!

Despite shaking with anger, Elizabeth kept a calm voice. "The ball is over, Lydia. We must return home." Darcy admired Elizabeth's strategy. Although Lydia certainly deserved a tongue-lashing, Elizabeth's patience allowed for the quickest escape from the public eye.

Drawing herself up to her full height, Lydia blinked at Elizabeth. "Very well, let us go home. I want no more of this ball!"

A corner of Elizabeth's mouth quirked upward at this declaration, but she nodded solemnly at her sister. "The carriage is this way." Placing her arm around Lydia's shoulder, Elizabeth guided her toward the doorway. Over her shoulder, she threw Darcy an apologetic smile, which cheered him despite the circumstances.

It was one more confirmation that he was engaged to the wrong Bennet sister.

***

"You should not be capable of doing much damage in here." Elizabeth led Lydia to a small, unoccupied sitting room adjacent to Netherfield's front hallway. "Stay right here. Do not move!" Elizabeth instructed Lydia, pointing to a particular stone floor tile near the back of the room. "I shall find Papa, and he will have the coach brought round." She took a step away and then turned back. "Do not move at all!" she growled.

Lydia said nothing but stuck out her tongue at her sister, who rolled her eyes and finally departed in a rustle of silk, closing the door behind her.

"Oh, Lordy!" Lydia collapsed onto a settee, noting that it was the most ghastly shade of pink. *Why is Elizabeth so unhappy? I had a little disagreement with Charlotte! Why must everyone else become involved?*

Mr. Darcy had turned red with rage. It was actually quite amusing; he looked sunburned. Then Elizabeth chastised her so angrily, for no good reason. She was liable to tell Papa everything, and he would then give Lydia a very dull lecture and might even reduce her hat budget. All because of a little squabble with Charlotte Lucas! *Charlotte was not even hurt. She looked quite well afterward. Yes, her hair was a mess, but it is not as if I punched her or did something really vulgar!*

And why did everyone assume I started the fight? I did, of course, but Mr. Darcy and Elizabeth did not know that. It could have begun with Charlotte striking me! They always listen to others; nobody ever takes my side! Elizabeth had not requested Lydia's recounting of the incident before lecturing her. It was all so tiresome!

Lydia had been so excited to attend real balls once she came out, but all her amusements were circumscribed by these stupid rules. They stole all the fun out of being an adult!

Lydia idly played with one of her curls. *If only Mama were here! She would understand that I just want to have some laughs and would not take a simple disagreement with Charlotte so seriously.* After all, Charlotte thought she had some claim on Wickham; Lydia needed to demonstrate otherwise. *Yes, I will go in search of Mama at once.* But before Lydia stood, her attention was caught by a scuff on her right slipper.

"My new slippers!" She removed the offending article to examine the smudge more closely. As she was rubbing at the spot, the door opened, and Wickham slipped into the room.

"Wicky!" she cried. "What has brought you here?"

Wickham peered out through the crack in the door. Whatever he saw caused his shoulders to relax; he turned to her. "Oh, hello, Lydia. I just want to avoid Darcy. He's a madman!" Wickham pointed to his black eye. "Do you see what he did?"

"Poor Wicky!" Lydia gave him a sympathetic look, finally exerting the effort to climb off the settee. "I am so pleased Mr. Darcy did not kill you!" She kissed his cheek very prettily. "It was very clever of you to find where Elizabeth had hidden me away! Did you look for me very long?"

Wickham blinked several times. "Er, no, not long at all."

Lydia crossed her arms and pouted. "I am very put out with you."

"Oh?" Wickham gave her that rakish grin that always made her knees weak.

"You did not dance with me once. Denny danced with me twice, as did Carter. Even Colonel Forster danced with me once. And of course, I suffered through *two* dances with Mr. Darcy. He was a good dancer to be sure, but talking with him was about as interesting as conversing with one of Papa's pigs. He knows nothing of fashions or anything happening in Meryton. He said he doesn't listen to gossip and would rather read the paper!" She grimaced at Wickham's shocked reaction. "As if anyone would prefer the paper! And when I talk, he does not even have the decency to pretend to be interested!" Lydia paused to take a breath and noticed that Wickham was smirking.

"I did plan to dance a set with you, but then Darcy punched me." Gingerly, Wickham felt his jaw.

She slipped her arm through his. "You would have provided much more interesting conversation than that old bore."

"I daresay." Wickham glanced at the door, which was firmly closed. "But keep your voice down!" he hissed. "We don't want people getting suspicious!"

"About what?" Lydia asked coyly, playing with the trim on his uniform.

He gave her a conspiratorial grin. "We don't want anyone knowing how…close we are. You and I are both engaged now. We both have good situations; let's not spoil it."

Lydia punched him lightly on the arm. "Ow!" He rubbed the spot. "Why did you do that?"

She rolled her eyes. As if she had struck him hard! "You got engaged to Charlotte Lucas and did not tell me!"

He scowled. "Why would I tell you?"

This response would have hurt if Lydia thought he was sincere, but she knew he was just teasing. "She has a face like a fish, and I think she dresses in old dish towels!"

Wickham chuckled. "You are so pretty when you are jealous!"

Lydia snorted. "Jealous? Her family may have money, but I have seen prettier scarecrows." She stamped her foot. "I simply wanted you to rescue me from Dullard Darcy! And I know you will be happier with me than Charlotte!"

Wickham appeared almost embarrassed, tugging at the collar of his uniform. "Charlotte is fine. She will let me be."

"You will actually marry her?" Lydia's stomach contracted. "I-I thought—you said you would rescue me from Darcy, and we would run off and be wed."

Wickham frowned as he pressed around his black eye. "I never promised you any such thing. We had some laughs. You're quite a pretty girl."

He had never planned—? But I thought—? Lydia felt tears threaten. He would actually marry Charlotte Lucas, just for her money! But then Lydia straightened her spine. *I will not surrender that easily. I must simply remember what he loves about me.*

Lydia stepped a little closer to him. "But don't you want to have a little fun? It was fun, was it not? What we did in the library here and then behind the pub last week." Both times they had been interrupted before they could reach what Wickham called "the best part."

Lydia was eager to learn how the best part happened; all she knew was it involved removing clothing—which was so daring! She had liked everything that Wickham had done to her so far—well, almost all of it. His kisses could use some improvement. Once they reached the best part, Wickham would certainly declare his love for her. Then she would not be forced to marry fussy old Mr. Darcy, and Wickham would forsake these silly ideas about Charlotte Lucas. She would be sad to lose Mr. Darcy's fortune, but what was money compared to fun?

Wickham regarded her with half-lidded eyes. "It was more than fun." He gave her a lazy smile. "It *would* please me to do it again, but we cannot get caught. It would ruin all my plans."

Lydia nodded eagerly. Ruining his plans was what she had in mind. And she would do anything to earn that look of naked desire. "We can meet somewhere." She clapped her hands and squealed. "Oh, I know! There is an abandoned hunter's cottage on my family's estate. I shall direct you where to find it."

Wickham licked his lips. "Perfect. Would it be possible for you to slip away from Longbourn tomorrow?"

Lydia grinned. "Without a doubt."

Chapter Fifteen

Darcy guided his horse along the road to Longbourn, wondering what he would do when he arrived at the Bennets' house. His avowed intention was to speak with Lydia, but his mind continuously slipped away to thoughts of seeking out Elizabeth and kissing—no, *talking* with her—he chastised his wayward heart. *I am visiting Longbourn to persuade Lydia against the betrothal.*

He had brought a necklace—recently purchased in London—as an inducement. And he was prepared to offer more gems and money, although he feared his largesse might stiffen her resolve to become his wife. Argh, the situation was a tangle!

He took a deep breath of cool, late-morning air, hoping it would clear his head. Although he had not overindulged the night before, it hardly signified; his emotions were in such a state that he might as well be foxed.

In the distance he saw a figure, a woman, walking in his direction. It was difficult to distinguish her features, but he recognized dark hair, and she was about the right height... His heart quickened. There were any number of women that size with dark hair, but his hopes were excited. Perhaps it *was* Elizabeth.

He kicked the horse into a trot, and soon the woman came into focus. "Elizabeth." He breathed her name out like a prayer. Now that he had confirmed her identity, an odd reluctance warred with his excitement. *Will she even speak with me after my disgraceful behavior at the ball?*

When she identified him, she tilted her head to the side slightly, but her expression remained carefully neutral. Was she pleased to see him, or was she gleefully imagining him falling from his horse? At least she did not whirl around and march away in the other direction! As she grew closer, he noticed she was fiddling with a twig dotted with bright green spring leaves. He dismounted and tied his horse's reins to a nearby sapling.

"Mr. Darcy." She curtsied quite correctly but directed her eyes to the road.

"Miss Bennet." He bowed.

During the ensuing silence, Darcy dared to search her eyes, but her cool neutrality unnerved him, and he quickly averted his gaze. Still she said nothing. The silence built pressure within him. *I must say something!* "Bingley believes I was discourteous to you," Darcy blurted out.

Devil take it! It was all Darcy could do not to clamp his hand over his mouth. That was not at all what he intended to say. In fact, that was the very last thing he had wished to say, but somehow it had roared from his mouth the moment he opened his lips.

Her eyebrows rose. "He does?"

There was no choice now but to brazen it out. Darcy rushed on. "I apologize if I have created the impression I dislike you. It does not reflect my true feelings. Indeed, I hold you in quite high esteem. I—"

She silenced him by raising her hand. For a moment he thought she might touch her fingers to his lips.

He hoped she would.

"At one time I did believe you disliked me," she admitted. "But you have suggested the opposite opinion…rather convincingly of late." One corner of her mouth quirked up.

She was teasing him about the almost-kiss! Teasing him! If she teased him about it, she could not be angry over his inappropriate behavior. Could she?

Nevertheless, it *had* been inappropriate. "I must apologize for..." Darcy broke off. What would he apologize for? He had not actually kissed her. "For..."

"Appearing as if you were about to kiss me?" she asked with an arch smile.

She is smiling about it! She is smiling at me! Her eyes are so fine when she smiles in just that way... What are we discussing again? Darcy rubbed his chin, recalling the immediate conversation. "I do not believe one can properly apologize for the way one *appears*..."

He was becoming lost in her smile again. It was intoxicating to bring that expression to life on her face—and know that she smiled because of him. Her eyes sparkled, and she gave a throaty laugh that sent shivers down his spine. "No apology is necessary in any event."

Oh, Good Lord, how long have I been staring at her?

He knew there was some reason he should not stare, should not kiss her...

Then reality came crashing back into his memory. Lydia. Bingley.

Darcy ducked his head and averted his eyes. "Forgive me, I know our situation is impossible." Even if he could free himself from Lydia, he could never steal Bingley's fiancée. He backed away from her, edging toward his horse.

"I am not offended. You need not leave," she said, taking a few steps toward him.

Darcy's heart warmed at her words even as he shook his head. "We should...I should not..." Heavens, it was difficult to even form coherent sentences in her presence! "I must leave." He stumbled away from her, focusing his gaze on his horse.

"I will not marry Mr. Bingley!" she said abruptly and immediately colored, biting her lip.

Darcy froze, uncertain he had heard her correctly. Slowly, he turned in her direction. Hope and trepidation warred within his breast. What did she mean? "Why not? He is eligible in every way. A good man. Very amiable. With a good income."

A line appeared between Elizabeth's brows. "Do you *wish* me to marry him?"

"No!" *Oh, Good Lord, what am I saying?* "Yes! I mean—" He clamped his lips shut and took a deep breath. Had he somehow come between Bingley and Elizabeth? The thought of ruining his friend's happiness was intolerable. "You should do as your heart dictates." *Yes, that was a fair answer. But what did her heart want?* Darcy's stomach clenched at the thought. "But there must be a reason you accepted Bingley's offer…"

"Mr. Bingley did not tell you about his mother?"

"His mother?" Darcy felt his eyebrows shoot upward. "What is his mother's role in all of this?"

"I thought—surely you and Mr. Bingley spoke of our engagement? You are his dearest friend. For heaven's sake, you abide in the same house!" She threw her arms in the air and rolled her eyes.

Darcy blinked several times, searching for the right words. "No, I felt…we…uh…never discussed it."

She exhaled a harsh breath. "I believe Mr. Bingley would understand if I relate everything to you. He arrived in Hertfordshire intending to request Jane's hand, but she was already betrothed to Mr. Collins." She fixed her gaze on the early spring leaf she held in her hands.

Darcy nodded, a bit mystified about where this story was heading.

"He was…most unhappy when I relayed the news. He had told his mother, who is in failing health, that he was engaged to a Miss Bennet. So he asked me if I would play the part of his fiancée."

Darcy's jaw dropped open. She had never seriously considered marrying Bingley? She did not harbor fond feelings for him?

"So you are not-not in love with Bingley?"

Elizabeth's hand covered her mouth. Was she distressed? No, she was laughing, he realized. He ordinarily disliked being the object of merriment but found he did not care today as long as she was not heartbroken over Bingley. Finally, she brought herself under control. "I accepted in part because I hoped that his continued presence in Hertfordshire would encourage Jane to break off her betrothal with Mr. Collins."

"Oh!" A knot in Darcy's chest—of which he had previously been unaware—suddenly loosened, and it became easier to breathe. Abruptly, the whole situation struck him as humorous. If Darcy had only spoken with Bingley over lunch at Netherfield… Laughter bubbled up from Darcy's throat and emerged as an undignified chuckle.

Darcy rubbed a hand over his face. "I nearly kissed a woman at her own engagement ball…I was ashamed of myself."

Elizabeth was still laughing. "I thought Bingley had explained to you about the engagement!"

Darcy rubbed his face with both hands. Many small puzzle pieces now fitted together. Elizabeth and Bingley behaved more like friends than lovers. Bingley always attached himself to Jane Bennet's side, and Elizabeth did not appear to mind. Miss Bennet always seemed unhappy, *except* when she was with Bingley.

"Is you sister aware of this…scheme?" he asked.

"Yes, but she has refused to contemplate breaking off her engagement with Mr. Collins. She believes she cannot break her promise. I believe he will make her miserable for the rest of her life!" Elizabeth's lips twisted with bitterness.

Darcy's thoughts could not help returning to what this meant for his own marital hopes. "So you are not to marry Bingley?"

She uttered that tantalizing laugh again. "No. But hopefully we need not reveal this to his mother until Jane is prepared to take my place."

Darcy's knees were weak, and for a moment he worried he would fall. "Oh, thank God!" *I must be closer to her!* Once his legs were steady, he covered the distance between them in a few short strides. "Miss Bennet—Elizabeth—you must allow me to tell you how ardently I admire and love you."

She appears more alarmed than excited. What is the difficulty?

"Sir, you are still engaged to Lydia."

Blast and damnation! In his excitement, Darcy had completely forgotten this most critical fact. Elizabeth might be free, but *he* was not. His chest was so constricted that he found it difficult to breathe.

"I had hoped…" How could he articulate his thoughts?

"You had hoped to persuade Lydia against the engagement." She did not ask; she stated it as a fact.

Darcy nodded. "I thought to find the scoundrel who was with her in the library and persuade him to undertake his responsibilities toward her."

Elizabeth rubbed her chin thoughtfully. "Although I do not know how we may accomplish that unless Lydia cooperates—when so far she has resisted."

Darcy was heartened by her use of the word "we." It suggested she might accept his suit if he were free to pursue her. He cleared his throat. "I hired a man to conduct some investigations—mostly discreet inquiries among the officers—to see if anyone knew, or suspected, the man's identity."

Her eyes clouded as she surveyed the field near the road. Was she distressed that Darcy sought evidence of her sister's loose morality?

"I am sorry," he said softly. "I do not wish to damage her reputation. If the stakes were not so high—"

She blinked, and he noticed a soft sheen of tears in her eyes, but she gave him a level gaze. "If her…behavior is so widely known among the officers, then her reputation was already compromised." Elizabeth sighed heavily. "She must marry someone— better an officer she knows and likes." Ah yes, she must be aware of how Lydia regarded Darcy.

Elizabeth massaged the back of her neck. "I should have kept a closer watch over her."

Darcy scowled. "Surely that is your parents' responsibility, not yours."

She shook her head. "I could have prevented—"

"If you had followed her around all day perhaps, but she would not have allowed that. And surely you had other pressing business."

She smiled ruefully. "You are determined to absolve me of blame."

Darcy considered his words carefully. "I wish events had not come to this pass, but Lydia must take responsibility for her own decisions."

Elizabeth opened her mouth to reply but then suddenly stiffened, squinting past Darcy to see something in the distance. Darcy followed her gaze and discerned a female figure walking along one of Longbourn's fields, apparently following a path.

"Why is Lydia walking *there* at this time of day?" Elizabeth wondered.

"She is not fond of walking?" Darcy asked.

Elizabeth shrugged. "She walks sometimes but always with others since she likes to talk, and always into town. She finds my solitary nature rambles boring."

"What could her destination possibly be?" Darcy asked.

Elizabeth frowned, watching her sister's figure move along the field. "Hmm... I do not believe there is anything in that direction, save fields and a small bridge over the stream. Oh! There is an old hunter's cottage built by my grandfather. My father does not hunt, so it has fallen into disrepair."

"A cottage?" Darcy exchanged a look with Elizabeth. Her expression was not so much alarmed as resigned.

Elizabeth sighed. "Perhaps we should follow her."

***

As they trudged along a dirt path running between the two fields, Elizabeth tried to quell her misgivings. She disliked following her sister like a spy in a cheap novel; however, Mr. Darcy should not be forced to marry Lydia since he was not responsible for her lost reputation and should not suffer for it. If they found her with another man, at least they would know who was responsible.

But did her own feelings about Mr. Darcy color her judgment? She attempted to view the situation dispassionately, as if the participants were strangers to her, and believed she would behave in the same way. But she was forced to admit that when Mr. Darcy was about, her thoughts would tangle in her emotions, and she might not possess the best judgment.

She shook her head sharply as if it would clear the fog of confusion. If Lydia were out for a stroll, then nothing would come of it; she would never learn of their suspicions. However, if Lydia did meet a man in the cottage, then that man was taking advantage of her virtue and had a responsibility to her.

Yes, that was the way of it. And Elizabeth's feelings about Mr. Darcy were not relevant to the circumstances.

She quickened her step to avoid losing sight of Lydia's small figure. They followed at a discreet distance, but Lydia appeared to have no concerns about being observed. The ramshackle cottage, set on the edge of Longbourn's wooded area, was in view. Elizabeth found herself praying that Lydia would pass it by; otherwise her too-young sister had shown the bad judgment to have planned an assignation with a man.

Elizabeth's heart sank as she watched Lydia rush toward the cottage and slip through the door. She gave Mr. Darcy a sidelong glance; his expression was grim. "Well," he said, "let us see whom she is meeting." Elizabeth held onto a small shard of hope that Lydia would be alone in the cottage but knew it was not likely.

Mr. Darcy put his hand under her elbow as he lengthened his stride, and she quickened her pace to keep up with him. Now that Lydia could not glimpse them, they could move with more alacrity.

As they approached the cottage, Elizabeth heard the distinctive sound of Lydia's giggles—and then her voice. "Don't touch me there! I am too ticklish." Then a small shriek and more giggles. Elizabeth and Mr. Darcy positioned themselves near the door.

The cottage had a broken windowpane, so the sounds easily carried outside. "Are you certain no one will find us?" a male voice asked.

Darcy started. Did he recognize the voice?

Lydia snorted. "Yes, silly! No one comes all the way out here."

Oh, Lydia, Elizabeth thought despairingly. *Poor, foolish Lydia*. There was the rustling of clothing and a few murmured words Elizabeth could not understand. Then some sounds of what might have been kissing.

Elizabeth looked up at Darcy. What a terrible situation! She had no desire to enter the cottage, but the alternative was allowing this unknown man to take further advantage of her sister's virtue.

He grimaced and put his hand to the cottage's doorknob. When he looked to her for approval, she nodded. As Mr. Darcy turned the knob, he simultaneously shoved the door open with his shoulder.

Chapter Sixteen

The interior was dimly lit after the bright sunshine outside, and Elizabeth's eyes required a few seconds to adjust. The cottage was one room, furnished with only a bed, table, and two chairs. Bright sunshine from the broken pane carved a path through the otherwise murky interior. The other window was covered with burlap to serve as an improvised curtain.

The two figures in the room sprang apart, Lydia shrieking at the top of her lungs. Backing away from the man, she tripped over a bucket behind her and fell inelegantly on her bottom. From her position on the roughhewn floor, Lydia yanked up her untied bodice. Elizabeth rushed to Lydia's side, helping her tuck herself back into her clothes. Finally, she cast a glance over at the man who had been embracing Lydia. Elizabeth supposed she should not have been surprised to discover his identity.

"Darcy!" Mr. Wickham snarled as he fastened up his trousers. "What the hell are you doing here?"

Mr. Darcy folded his arms over his chest and shook his head. "I thought it might be you."

"This isn't what— You don't know— We were simply having a friendly conversation!" Elizabeth was impressed with Mr. Wickham's thespian skills. He acted the wounded innocent very well. Unfortunately for him, the state of his clothing and Lydia's gave lie to his words.

Lydia scrambled to her feet. "He was— teaching me whist!"

Mr. Darcy blinked. "With two people? And no cards?"

"You already know whist," Elizabeth observed.

Apparently Mr. Wickham had time to recover his wits. "I was telling her about new crop rotation ideas." He looked at Elizabeth. "Your father should consider them."

"How altruistic of you, sir," Elizabeth said.

He gave her a little bow. "My father was a steward."

"So I heard," Mr. Darcy said dryly.

Mr. Wickham was committed to his lie. "So, you see, it was completely innocent."

Mr. Darcy looked pointedly at the disheveled bed and raised an eyebrow. "Completely." Then he turned a glower on Mr. Wickham. "Wickham, you have compromised this young lady's virtue; you have an obligation to marry her."

Mr. Wickham sneered. "I believe you have a prior claim."

"When word of this assignation gets out, no one will fault me for relinquishing my claim in your favor." Mr. Darcy's voice was calm and level.

Mr. Wickham straightened his shoulders. "You cannot force me, Darcy. I am betrothed to Charlotte Lucas. Her father is very pleased with the arrangement." Mr. Darcy started to object, but the other man continued. "And Sir William already knows of my…meetings with Lydia, so it is useless to tell him."

The muscles in Mr. Darcy's jaw clenched. "You seem to prefer Miss Lydia's company to your fiancée's."

The other man snorted. "I do not want this chit; she has no dowry to speak of."

Elizabeth gasped at this cold-hearted assessment, but it was drowned out by Lydia's shriek. "But Wicky, you said you loved me!"

"Be quiet, wench!" Mr. Wickham hissed at her, causing Lydia to recoil. But the man was so preoccupied with grimacing at her that he was quite unprepared when Mr. Darcy's punch caught him under his chin. Mr. Wickham flew back into the wall, hitting his head on the rough planks.

"Do not speak so to a lady," Mr. Darcy warned.

Mr. Wickham laughed balefully from where he was slumped on the floor. "She's not a lady," he jeered. "Not anymore."

"That's not true!" Lydia cried.

Mr. Darcy advanced on Wickham implacably, provoking the other man to scramble to his feet. "Her virtue or lack thereof is your responsibility. Her reputation is ruined because of you."

Mr. Wickham sneered and would not meet the other man's eyes.

"I wish I could find her a more worthy husband, but you must suffice," Mr. Darcy said.

"I shan't marry her." Mr. Wickham's mouth twisted in a snarl.

Lydia gasped. "Don't you love me?"

Mr. Wickham did not even look toward her. "Of course I do, my pet." The flatness of his voice belied his words. "But a man must have something to live on."

Elizabeth did not immediately grasp all the implications, but Mr. Darcy was quicker. "How much is Sir William paying you to marry his daughter?"

Mr. Wickham laughed. "Enough so that I know the Bennet girl is a bad bargain." Behind Elizabeth, Lydia let out a wail.

"You have seduced her and made it difficult, if not impossible, for her to find a husband! It is your responsibility." Mr. Darcy held himself very still as if restraining an impulse to strike the other man once again.

"That's where you come in, Fitz." Mr. Wickham clapped Mr. Darcy on the shoulder. "I cannot." He shrugged. "I am engaged to Miss Lucas."

"I will not marry her," Mr. Darcy said through gritted teeth.

Mr. Wickham smirked. "I think you will. You are too honorable to allow a girl to be ruined in such a way. And of course, everyone believes *you* did the ruining. If you fail to follow through on the engagement, it will be a *great* scandal." The man's smile was quite unpleasant.

Mr. Darcy ground his teeth together but said nothing.

"It is so good of you to rise to the occasion." Mr. Wickham tipped his hat to the other man and stuck his hands in his pockets as he strolled out of the door.

For a moment no one moved. Then Lydia shrieked, "Wicky, you can't simply leave me with them! They will give me the most tiresome lecture!" She raced out of the cabin after her erstwhile lover.

Elizabeth made to follow, but Darcy shook his head. "Let them go. Wickham shall not take your sister anywhere, and she might persuade him to change his mind."

Elizabeth shook her head wearily as she sat on the rickety cot. "Clearly he would be pleased to abandon my sister to her fate rather than accept any responsibility. How is such a man to be worked on? How can we convince him of something so wholly against his nature and self-interest?"

I should never have imagined a different result. For a moment she had thought perhaps there would be a happier outcome for Mr. Darcy—and possible even for herself. But she could never be happy at the expense of her sister's reputation. How awful that her happiness depended on the whims of someone as untrustworthy as Mr. Wickham!

Mr. Darcy seated himself on the cot beside her, making it creak and groan. He took her hand in his, interlacing their fingers. Elizabeth should have objected to the liberty; the others might return at any moment. But Mr. Darcy's hand felt so warm in hers, so reassuring…

"Do not abandon hope yet, dear heart." The endearment warmed her despite her anxiety. "I have one idea." She turned her head toward him, hope in her eyes.

Mr. Darcy's lips were a thin, white line. "But it depends on cooperation from Sir William Lucas."

***

The day after the Netherfield ball, Charlotte Lucas walked in the garden at Lucas Lodge. The house was one of the older dwellings in the neighborhood, and part of the garden was actually surrounded by a tall brick wall. Few others visited the secluded garden, but Charlotte found the silence and solitude restful.

As she wandered along the paths she could not help remembering Mr. Collins. He had such a pleasant…fleshy countenance. And he was easily the most amiable man of her acquaintance, always so concerned about her delicate sensibilities and the proper way to do things. If Charlotte was honest with herself, she was also impressed by his association with the noble family of de Bourgh. Why, their chimney piece alone cost one hundred pounds! It was hard to conceive of so much money. And he was so easy to talk to, with his open, wholesome conversation. He was altogether admirable.

A sigh escaped her lips. *What a shame I am engaged to Mr. Wickham; the brilliancy of his features paled in comparison to Mr. Collins's.*

Charlotte reached the end of the walk, marked by some bushes before a high brick wall. *Perhaps it is time to return to the house.* Before she could turn, however, her attention was drawn by a scuffling sound from the other side of the wall. Then came the noises of someone panting as if from some great exertion. Curious, Charlotte drew closer. Suddenly, a hand appeared at the top of the wall.

Charlotte stiffened in horror. Brigands were assaulting her garden! *I should scream. I should flee.* Yet she could only remain frozen in place.

Then she glimpsed a head, surmounted by a black hat, cresting the wall. The hat fell and tumbled onto Charlotte's side of the wall, revealing a man's brown hair. The hat landed at Charlotte's feet, black and wide-brimmed, almost like a clergyman's hat. *Could it be?*

Charlotte's eyes darted to the top of the wall. *It was!* Mr. Collins was now throwing a leg over the wall and grunting. *Oh dear! What if he hurt himself?* "Mr. Collins!" she exclaimed in shock.

He made no sign that he had heard her but brought his other leg up to the top of the wall. This caused his weight to shift dangerously, and slowly, inexorably, Mr. Collins slid down into the garden, collapsing in a heap on a holly bush.

Charlotte rushed over. Fortunately, the parson appeared unharmed but was struggling to extricate himself from the nest of holly leaves. One of the berries had smashed against his cheek, leaving a red streak.

"Mr. Collins!" she exclaimed again.

He noticed her for the first time, giving her a sunny grin and reaching out his hands. "Miss Lucas, some assistance, if you please?"

She took both of his hands in hers and pulled. Most of Mr. Collins came free at once, but the holly bush threatened to keep his trousers. Charlotte gave a mighty yank, and the garment ripped free from the foliage. However, the force pulled Mr. Collins right into Charlotte's arms, and he fell against her. She staggered, but fortunately she was sturdy enough to prevent them from falling.

Charlotte looked into the man's eyes, which were conveniently at eye level.

Their faces were inches apart.

Their *lips* were inches apart.

Charlotte had never been romantic, but for the first time in her life she wondered what it would be like to be kissed. Mr. Collins must have been thinking along similar lines because his eyes dropped to her lips. Then they darted back up again, looking rather panicked.

He hastily pulled out of her embrace and staggered into a standing position.

"Please forgive me, my dear Miss Lucas!" He waved his arms about in great distress. "I-I did not—I would not—I did not intend any insult!" Charlotte started to respond, but the parson continued. "I would offer recompense for thus compromising your virtue…" The gaze he gave her was frankly desirous. "But I am, unfortunately, already betrothed."

Charlotte nodded dumbly, attempting to make sense of his appearance in her garden. But she failed.

It did not make sense.

"W-why are you here, Mr. Collins?"

He stood straighter and put his hand to his heart. "I simply had to see you again, my dear Miss Lucas—if you will forgive the liberty in naming you thus. I heard from Miss Elizabeth that you often strolled in the walled garden alone. So I bethought myself to visit it and wait until you passed by."

Charlotte was speechless for a moment. He had climbed the wall to see her? "B-but…there is a gate!" She waved to the far wall.

Mr. Collins's gaze followed her gesture, and he eyed the wrought iron gate with narrowed eyes. "I do not have a key."

Charlotte's brows knit together. "It is unlocked."

"Oh." Mr. Collins blinked rapidly. "I shall keep that in mind if I should be called upon to visit the garden again."

She had embarrassed him! That would not do. "Nevertheless, I am pleased to see you again. Our time at the ball was far too short."

He gave her a most gratifying smile. "Indeed! I thought so as well. And I did not have an opportunity to finish telling you about the stonework at Rosings or to recommend appropriate passages from Fordyce for your enlightenment."

A thrill ran down Charlotte's spine. He wanted to speak with her! "I would love to continue our discourse," she said.

He boldly took hold of one of her ungloved hands. "I must confess, however, that such discourse is merely a pretext. The truth is…a greater force drew me hither. I simply *had* to see you once more. Never before have I beheld such a beauty as I did last night." Charlotte felt her cheeks warming; no one had ever spoken of her in such a way. It was highly inappropriate, of course, but she would not have stopped him for the world. "Of all the precious love blossoms in the world, you are surely the…loveliest and, er, most precious."

Charlotte gazed down shyly in the way of all maidens who were given extravagant compliments. "You are too kind."

He shook his head. "Not at all. I have never had such amiable conversation as I did last night."

Charlotte felt faint. She could have spoken the same words herself. Some sense of destiny *had* passed between them the previous night. But she could not allow herself to be carried away on waves of desire. She sighed deeply.

"Sir, I am betrothed. As are you. This—" she gestured between them. "—cannot be."

Mr. Collins's shoulders sagged, and he shook his head sadly. "So true! We are a pair of star-crossed lovers. Fate has been cruel!"

"But you love Jane, do you not?" Charlotte asked.

He regarded her very seriously. "I thought I knew what love was…until I met you. But fate has brought us together too late! Far too late!" He put a hand to his forehead, and Charlotte feared for a moment that he might faint.

I must alleviate his distress somehow! "No! It is not so."

He regarded her with shining eyes. "Do you see a ray of hope?"

Charlotte bit her lip. "Truth be told, I have had some misgivings about Mr. Wickham's character, and I know he does not care for me."

Mr. Collins gasped. "How could anyone not care for you? You are perfection itself!"

Unsure how to respond to such a compliment, Charlotte said nothing. They were lost in each other's eyes for a long moment. "I have been considering breaking off my engagement to Mr. Wickham," she finally confessed. Her eyes did not waver from his. "It would be easier to do so if I had hope that I would not be alone after…"

"You would not be alone," he said, squeezing her hand gently.

Charlotte could not prevent a little sigh from escaping her lips. "You are so romantic!"

He was pulling her closer, she realized suddenly. And they were slowly, inexorably, drawing nearer to each other—their lips destined to meet.

"Charlotte! Charlotte?"

Her father's voice interrupted her reverie. She straightened her spine and dropped Mr. Collins's hand instantly. "My father!" she exclaimed, eyes wide. "He will be here in a trice!"

Mr. Collins hastily kissed the back of her hand. "I will never forget you, my precious one!"

"You must go!" she urged.

Mr. Collins whirled around, seeking handholds in the brick wall behind him.

"The gate!" she whispered.

"Oh! Yes, of course!" Mr. Collins stumbled over to the gate and was through it before Charlotte heard the crunching sounds of her father's footsteps on the gravel.

Sir William found his daughter staring at the brick wall enclosing the garden. He regarded her with a curious frown. "Is something troubling you, my dear?"

Charlotte drew a deep breath. "Papa, would you be very angry if I broke off my engagement?"

***

Wickham was suspicious. He had been summoned to Sir William's office, and he did not know the reason. It could not possibly be Darcy's doing, could it? Wickham had not heard from the man since yesterday, but he could not possibly compel Wickham to marry a girl he did not want.

And Wickham wanted Charlotte Lucas. Their plans were all set, and the date for the wedding was fixed for a fortnight from now. Wickham had assured his debtors they would be paid by then. What could the problem possibly be?

He sat himself once again in the leather armchair across from Sir William's desk. The bewhiskered man looked very grave. "George Wickham, we have a problem."

Gnawing anxiety churned his stomach. "Sir?"

"I heard a very interesting report about you from Mr. Darcy."

Wickham's veins suddenly boiled with rage. Damn Darcy for interfering once again! Why could he not simply stay out of his life? "Sir, with all due respect, you knew I had…kept company with Lydia Bennet when you suggested I propose to your daughter."

Sir William's face was stormy. "Yes, but I expected such behavior to cease."

"It will! It will! Once we are married." Devil take it! This was the worst possible time to encounter such obstacles. He needed the money from the dowry as soon as he could lay his hands on it.

Sir William drummed his fingers on the table pensively. "Hmm. I am not certain I find your assertions credible, young man. After all, you are the one responsible for ruining Lydia Bennet's reputation and leaving Mr. Darcy to take the blame. He appears to be a man of good character and should not be responsible for your misbehavior." *Yes, he should!*

Wickham wanted to cry out. *That is why these circumstances are so perfect.*

The study suddenly felt quite warm; Wickham tugged his cravat away from his neck. "Darcy has held a grudge against me since childhood. Any word he speaks about me should be regarded with suspicion."

Sir William stroked his whiskers as he regarded Wickham. "Yes, I have heard your story of ill use at Mr. Darcy's hands. But your encounter with Lydia Bennet was witnessed by her own sister. I find that particular tale entirely credible."

Wickham was out on a tree limb, with the tree being chopped out from underneath him. He breathed more rapidly, considering how he could turn this situation to his advantage. "Think of your daughter, sir." Wickham hated the whiny quality that had leeched into his voice. "She will become an old maid with a broken engagement. Surely she does not deserve such a life."

Sir William chuckled. "That is the most amusing part, actually. Charlotte recently informed me that her affections have been bestowed elsewhere."

Wickham gaped. What? Charlotte the Spinster loved someone else? Such a possibility had never occurred to Wickham; he had not even bothered to expend the energy to woo her. "S-sir?" He shifted in his seat. "How can you be certain the other man will make her an offer?"

Sir William folded his hands over his capacious stomach. "I have no doubt we can come to an agreement."

Damn it all! No. That is my dowry! Sir William cannot simply offer it up to another man. Wickham had no doubt the other man would take it. Charlotte was plain, but the dowry was a powerful inducement. Now Wickham would need to find another rich family to fleece. Perhaps Mary King was still available...

Wickham was careful not to reveal his anger as he shrugged and stood. "I see you cannot be moved..."

But Sir William gestured for him to sit once more. "Our business is not yet concluded, young man."

This does not bode well. Wickham sank back into his chair.

"Now, I had planned to pay your debts as we discussed. However, I had actually not started the process. Although a few of the creditors I spoke with were...extremely eager to be paid. *Extremely.*"

Wickham buried his head in his hands. Without the promise of Charlotte's dowry, there would be no reason for his creditors to delay collections. They might be waiting at his lodgings even now! Then when his fellow soldiers learned he had not paid the merchants, they would demand payment for his gambling debts. Wickham did not have one-tenth of the money required. Furthermore, once news of his debts became widely known, Mary King would be less easily persuaded in favor of Gretna Green. The prospect of debtors' prison had never loomed so large before.

Wickham took a deep breath, hoping to slow his frantic heartbeat. He would need to flee the area at once. No other choice was left to him. Perhaps he could delay until nightfall, but no later. This time he would journey north to some small town where they had never heard of George Wickham.

"I see you fully grasp your situation," Sir William intoned with a hint of mirth. Did he enjoy Wickham's discomfiture? "However, there is another option. Mr. Darcy has very generously offered to pay your debts. *All* of your debts."

Wickham remained wary. *Darcy would never help me without some reason.*

"If," Sir William continued, "you will marry Lydia Bennet."

Oh. Wickham should have guessed. *Damnation! The choices were equally bad.* He glanced about the room, feeling a little like the dazed victim of a carriage accident. He could escape prison, but he would be shackled to *that girl* for the rest of his life. Worse, he would be shackled to her braying laughter. And her constant complaining. Wickham shuddered at the thought.

Lydia was pretty enough, aye, and fun to have around—for a while. But before long, her conversation became tiresome. She would demand constant avowals of love and praise for her beauty. Wickham only said such things to coax a woman into bed; there was no point if the woman was *already* in his bed. How tiresome! At least Charlotte had promised to leave him in peace, and she would not have minded if he sought out...other companions. Lydia would no doubt become a screaming harpy if she smelled another woman's perfume on his clothes.

Wickham scrubbed his hands over his face as he slouched into the chair.

Lydia...prison....Lydia...prison...

Which to choose? Surely there was another alternative. Wickham considered the situation, attempting to poke holes in the net Darcy and Lucas had cast over him.

Ah yes, that was the solution! He would board the carriage with Lydia, but he need not stay until Gretna Green. Wickham could ensure the driver was someone he knew. Once they were on the road, Wickham would pay the man to divert for London or some other big town. Then he could leave Lydia with a little money; he was not heartless, after all. She would find her way back to Hertfordshire eventually. In the meantime, Darcy would have paid Wickham's debts, and he could reunite with the militia as a free man. Wickham had to suppress a smile. The scheme was perfect. He was only sorry he would not witness Darcy's face when he discovered Wickham had slipped through his fingers again. Darcy would never outsmart him!

Sighing heavily to disguise his elation, Wickham glared at Sir William. "Very well, I suppose I will marry Lydia Bennet."

"Capital!" Sir William stood. "She is in the carriage right outside the door."

What? Leave now? I have plans to put in place! He shot to his feet. "I cannot leave now! I have duties...and I do not have clothing with me!"

Sir William stood as well and clapped Wickham on the back. "No cause for alarm! Darcy wrote Denny, who acquired some leave for you from Colonel Forster and packed your trunk. Your whole regiment thinks it is terribly romantic—running off to Gretna Green to marry so suddenly. Colonel Forster does expect you back by Monday."

Darcy informed the entire regiment? Wickham could have cheerfully strangled the other man at that moment. "How very thoughtful," Wickham said through gritted teeth. *It does not matter,* he reminded himself. *I will still escape somehow. They cannot force me to Gretna Green.* Even without having made plans in advance, Wickham could still abandon Lydia at the first opportunity.

Sir William grinned. "Indeed, Darcy considers every detail!"

"How kind of him to take interest in my humble affairs," Wickham ground out.

Sir William walked Wickham out of the study, down the hallway, and through the front door. His hand remained firmly on Wickham's elbow as if he feared the other man might flee at any minute.

A carriage did indeed await Wickham on the gravel drive before Lucas Lodge. The driver and footman both wore Sir William's livery. *It will be a little more difficult than I originally planned, but I can still give them the slip.*

The carriage door opened, and the doorway was filled by the sight of Lydia in a light blue travel dress and bright blue feather protruding from her hair. "My darling Wicky! Isn't this simply thrilling? I knew you really wanted to marry me, not that dried up old Charlotte Lucas." Lydia then noticed Sir William scowling at her. She giggled and covered her mouth with both hands. "Oops!"

Lydia babbled as Wickham drew closer to the carriage. "It is such a long trip to Gretna Green, but I am sure we will find ways to stay occupied." Now that was a cheery thought. Wickham leered at her; at least he could have some fun before he abandoned her. She giggled wildly. "I know, we can sing! I love to sing; Lizzy and Mary say my voice needs training, but it sounds perfectly good to me. We shall sing and be merry all the way to Gretna Green!"

I will escape the first time the carriage stops, Wickham vowed as he placed his foot on the bottom step and climbed into the carriage. It cannot be too soon. He focused his thoughts on those plans so he would not give in to the impulse to strangle Lydia with her bonnet ribbons.

Wickham settled into the seat next to Lydia, and Sir William closed the door, signaling the driver to start the journey. The carriage lurched into a steady movement. Wickham stared rather disbelievingly out of the window. How had this come about? Then he noticed Darcy's figure leaning against a tree, watching the carriage pass. *I should have known it was his scheme. Well, I shall have the last laugh today!*

Only when Wickham turned to peer into the carriage did he realize that he and Lydia were not alone. There was a brown-haired, rather nondescript man sitting across from them. He was observing Wickham carefully, but his expression was blank. His clothing suggested he was in trade of some kind, maybe a doctor or shopkeeper. But why was he in Sir William's carriage?

The man nodded pleasantly.

"Who the devil are you?" Wickham asked.

When the man did not answer immediately, Wickham looked at Lydia, who shrugged. "I don't know. He appeared a few minutes ago."

The man sat up straighter. "My name is Lionel Figg. Sir William hired me to ensure your trip to Gretna Green proceeds…smoothly."

Wickham narrowed his eyes at the man. In other words, Figg's job was to make sure Wickham actually married Lydia. Wickham wanted to laugh; he could give old Lionel the slip when they stopped to change horses. "I understand." Wickham smiled disarmingly at the other man.

"Good." Figg's smile was all teeth. He settled back against the coach's velvet squabs; however, in the process, his coat fell open, revealing not one but two revolvers.

Damn it to hell! Wickham thought. *This will be more difficult than I expected.*

Chapter Seventeen

Chaos had descended upon Longbourn. Lydia had left a note in her room explaining that she was traveling to Gretna Green to marry Mr. Wickham. Since the family had believed Lydia was visiting Maria Lucas, the note was not discovered until the morning after her departure—too late for any hope of retrieving her. In the note she described how she had come to realize her love for Mr. Wickham. She declared that she could not marry Mr. Darcy in good conscience under the circumstances and freed him of any obligation to her. She also warned Kitty not to borrow her yellow dress.

Although Elizabeth had not been aware of Lydia's impending elopement, she had known it was a possibility and had done nothing to prevent it. None of Lydia's choices were good, but visiting Gretna Green with Wickham was the least bad one.

Elizabeth and Jane had spent the morning calming their mother, listening to her complaints, and fetching her vinaigrette. Mrs. Bennet shrieked and fluttered about the house, blaming everyone for the disaster, including Mr. Wickham, Mr. Darcy, Mr. Bennet, Mr. Bingley, Miss Bingley, Kitty, Hill, and Elizabeth. The only people, in fact, who were *not* culpable were Mrs. Bennet herself and Lydia.

Punctuating nearly every one of Mrs. Bennet's sentences was an expression of concern about Mr. Darcy's reaction to the news. Elizabeth suspected he would be less shocked than her mother anticipated but could not say so. Mr. Bennet—who was considerably calmer than his wife but still quite anxious—had sent a note to Netherfield requesting Mr. Darcy's presence. Mrs. Bennet expressed concern that Mr. Darcy might fly into a rage, sink into melancholy, throw valuable objects (she had Hill lock some away), challenge Wickham to a duel, or threaten to sue the Bennets for breach of contract—although the marriage articles had never been signed.

Was her mother more concerned about Lydia or the prospect of losing the ten thousand a year? Elizabeth could not be sure.

Finally, when Mr. Darcy, accompanied by Mr. Bingley, did arrive at Longbourn, Mrs. Bennet could not wait for him to reach the drawing room. She rushed into the front hallway to deliver the dire news at once. "Mr. Darcy! Mr. Darcy! I am so sorry. My apologies! We are not accustomed to behavior such as this from our daughters. It is all that Mr. Wickham's fault! She would not do such a thing if it were not for his influence!"

Mr. Darcy stopped and stared, momentarily stunned by this maternal onslaught. Finally, he said, "I do not have the pleasure of understanding you, ma'am. What has occurred?"

A straightforward recitation of events was beyond Mrs. Bennet; she could only collapse into Jane's arms, shrieking, "Ruined! We are all ruined!"

Fortunately, the commotion had drawn Elizabeth's father from his study. Mr. Bennet cleared his throat and addressed Mr. Darcy. "We found a note this morning in Lydia's room informing us she has departed for Gretna Green…with Mr. Wickham."

Elizabeth thought Mr. Darcy did a rather good job of feigning surprise, although he did not attempt anything approximating regret. Mr. Bingley, however, appeared truly shocked. "I see," Mr. Darcy said. "When did they leave?"

"Yesterday evening," Mr. Bennet replied.

"Then they cannot be brought back," Mr. Darcy concluded. "Has this news been conveyed to Lucas Lodge?"

"My understanding is that they received a similar missive from Mr. Wickham breaking off his engagement with Charlotte Lucas. It seems he had a great many unpaid debts and was fleeing creditors," Mr. Bennet said with a grimace.

"Ah."

Jane was encouraging their mother to return upstairs, but Mrs. Bennet was immobile. Her brows drew together as she regarded Mr. Darcy. "You will not sue us for breach of contract? Or challenge Mr. Bennet to a duel?"

Elizabeth clapped a hand over her mouth to stifle her laughter. If only her mother understood how pleased Mr. Darcy was to be freed from his engagement.

Mr. Darcy stared at her as if she had spoken Russian. After a long moment, he responded, "No, of course not. I do not hold this incident against your family."

"You are too good to us!" Mrs. Bennet cried. She might have thrown herself into his arms if Jane had not been holding her. "What a shame you will not be spending the rest of your days with our dearest Lydia. She is a jewel."

Mr. Darcy coughed but did not reply to this assertion.

Then a thought occurred to Mrs. Bennet. "Of course, we have other daughters. Jane and Elizabeth are spoken for, but perhaps you would consider Kitty or Mary? They are both pretty, accomplished girls as well. Either one would be an excellent mistress of Pemberley. Kitty is very popular with all the officers.

And Mary plays and sings—and she reads Fordyce's sermons every day."

Mr. Darcy merely blinked at her; perhaps he did not believe he was actually having this conversation.

"Mama, I believe you should give your nerves a rest upstairs," Jane said hastily before her mother's monologue resumed.

"But I have not told Mr. Darcy about Kitty's needlework or…" Mrs. Bennet's soliloquy continued even as Jane turned their mother around and guided her toward the stairs. Before setting foot to the first step, however, Mrs. Bennet glanced over her shoulder at Mr. Darcy. "Be sure to stay for dinner! You are our friend as well, you know!" With that last word, she suffered herself to be led upstairs.

Elizabeth stole a glance at Mr. Darcy and saw that his lips were twitching. Their eyes met for a moment of shared amusement.

"Mr. Darcy, Mr. Bingley. Would you join us in the drawing room?" Elizabeth asked. "I will have Hill bring in some tea."

Both men agreed with pleasure, and so they all repaired to the drawing room. The discourse focused on inconsequential matters as they sipped tea and ate biscuits. Elizabeth felt Mr. Darcy's eyes on her more than once, and it was difficult not to stare at him. If only Jane would come down! Then they might walk out and enjoy some private conversation.

However, Mr. Collins arrived before Jane did. He had departed for a conference with the Meryton cleric earlier in the morning in order to discuss the other parson's improper pouring of wine during communion. Thus, Mr. Collins remained ignorant of Lydia's letter. He seated himself on the far side of the drawing room from Mr. Bingley, regarding the other man warily. For his part, Mr. Bingley said nothing but glared daggers at the parson.

After Elizabeth informed Mr. Collins of the particulars from the letter, he was predictably surprised. "How very shocking! What lamentable behavior! And she was promised to Mr. Darcy!" He put his hand to his lips. "Perhaps I should have spoken earlier, but I wondered if perhaps your parents practiced too great a degree of indulgence with Miss Lydia." *Oh, the man's arrogance knew no bounds!* "Although I am inclined to believe her disposition is naturally bad."

Mr. Darcy's face had turned an alarming shade of red at these insults, but Elizabeth had glimpsed an opportunity to free Jane from Mr. Collins's clutches. She shook her head sadly. "These circumstances will be the hardest on poor Charlotte. She had happily anticipated a household of her own."

Mr. Collins sat up straighter and spoke with great warmth. "That is so! Miss Lucas is no longer engaged." Then he added as an afterthought, "Poor girl." He cleared his throat. "She will be all alone."

Charlotte had confided how she admired Mr. Collins, and now the eagerness in his expression confirmed that he returned the admiration. *But how may I encourage him to forsake Jane and court Charlotte?*

"Do you think Wickham must love Lydia?" Mr. Bingley asked. Elizabeth made no response. Mr. Darcy's eyes met hers briefly. Were they thinking the same thing?

"Now that I think on it…perhaps it was Wickham who was in the Netherfield library with Lydia before I arrived," Mr. Darcy said.

Elizabeth saw realization dawn on Mr. Bingley's face, and even more slowly on Mr. Collins's.

"They must have been in love even then!" Mr. Bingley said with great excitement.

Elizabeth tended to believe this was a generous interpretation of the evidence—given the characters of the participants.

Mr. Darcy's head was lowered, but he was surreptitiously observing Mr. Collins. "Wickham must have been quite enamored of Miss Lydia to surrender such a generous dowry," he said.

Mr. Collins hastily set down his teacup. "Generous?" His voice squeaked, and he cleared his throat. "Miss Lucas has a generous dowry?"

Darcy nodded. "Wickham bragged about it. Certainly it was the only reason he was marrying her. There was no love lost between them."

Elizabeth suppressed the urge to smile as she joined in the conversation. "Indeed. They barely knew each other, and I do not believe he would have made her happy. She likes sober, steady men and wants a comfortable home and children. Mr. Wickham seemed a little too…wild for her."

"Yes. Yes, indeed….And now Miss Lucas is all alone…when she had hoped for a husband and children." Mr. Collins raised a completely empty teacup to his lips and then lowered it abruptly. "Perhaps I should visit Lucas Lodge to give them my condolences over this unhappy turn of events. The presence of a clergyman at such times can often bring comfort."

"So true," Elizabeth murmured. "That is very good of you."

Mr. Collins placed his hat on his head. "We all must do our Christian duty."

"Indeed," Elizabeth agreed blandly.

"Oh, Cousin Elizabeth?" He turned from the open door. "Do you happen to know where your sister, Jane, may be?"

"I believe she is upstairs with our mother," Elizabeth replied, managing to conceal her grin.

Mr. Collins nodded, bowed his way out of the drawing room, and closed the door behind him. Elizabeth wished she and Mr. Darcy had wine with which they could toast their success. However, she could not prevent a laugh from escaping. Even Mr. Darcy's lips were twitching, although his eyes were fixed on Elizabeth with a look of…apprehension? What worried him now?

Mr. Bingley, who seemed shaken from Mr. Collins's visit, looked from one to the other in bewilderment. "I do not have the pleasure of understanding what is so amusing."

"Miss Lucas finds Mr. Collins…appealing," Darcy said. "They danced twice at the ball."

"But Mr. Collins is betrothed to Jane, so I fail to understand how he—" Mr. Bingley's eyes opened wide. "Oh." Then he frowned. "But then Jane, er, Miss Bennet, will be thrown over for Miss Lucas! The whole neighborhood will hear of it. Would not Jane find that distressing?" He frowned at Elizabeth while Mr. Darcy watched her with a disconcerting intensity.

Elizabeth shifted in her seat. Never before had she received such scrutiny from two eligible, wealthy men, one of whom was ostensibly her fiancé. She was acutely aware of their eyes on her and chose her words carefully. "Jane does dislike scandal, naturally, but I do not believe she would regret losing Mr. Collins as her betrothed."

Mr. Bingley considered these implications for a moment, and then a smile crept over his face, which he quickly concealed behind his hand. Was he worried he would hurt Elizabeth's feelings if he displayed his partiality to Jane? Surely he knew her sentiments by now!

Mr. Darcy's eyes were darting between Elizabeth and his friend, his expression unusually somber and anxious, even for him. The atmosphere in the drawing room was now so highly charged that Elizabeth expected to see lightning bolts at any moment.

After a long silence Mr. Bingley stood rather abruptly. "T-this is a busy day at Longbourn, and I am sure you have long been desiring my absence." A denial was on the tip of Elizabeth's tongue, but Mr. Bingley continued. "I will return to Netherfield, but perhaps I might visit tomorrow?"

He raised his eyebrows quizzically as if asking her permission, but she had not the slightest idea why. "We will be pleased to see you whenever you may visit," she replied.

Mr. Darcy could hardly remain if Mr. Bingley left, but he stood slowly, almost reluctantly. He placed his hat on his head. "Yes…we shall call at Longbourn tomorrow…when circumstances are less…chaotic."

Elizabeth nodded, still mystified at Mr. Darcy's odd scrutiny. "I wish you good day." He nodded to Elizabeth with a smile that more closely resembled a grimace.

She watched the two men file out through the doorway, feeling as if she had missed some undercurrent in the conversation. Some days she felt she simply did not understand men!

***

Mr. Collins stood trembling on the threshold of the Lucas's parlor, watching Miss Charlotte darn stockings. Darning was an activity of which Mr. Collins particularly approved; it demonstrated a pleasing sense of a woman's domestic economy.

And Miss Charlotte presented a particularly lovely picture as she sat by the window, with her plain blue gown and her mousy brown hair. She was not a great beauty like Jane Bennet, but she compensated with other charms. Her father had been most agreeable to the suggestion that Mr. Collins might make his daughter an offer and was pleased to pass along the dowry which would have been Mr. Wickham's. The dowry was…most…attractive. One might even say…alluring. Fate had been kind to Collins after all his suffering.

There had been the difficult matter of informing Jane Bennet of his change in affections. On the whole she had taken it well. Although she had frequently ducked her head—possibly to wipe away tears—while he had detailed the canon law on broken engagements. But she had borne up with admirable stoicism and grace.

Collins did experience a twinge of guilt about the circumstances; he *had* hoped to marry one of the Bennet girls. But Miss Charlotte Lucas had a…quality he could not ignore. Something that drew him to her like a siren call…a bee to a flower. *Well, flowers made no noise.* Like a duck to water. *Not quite.* Like a male duck to a female duck. Collins smiled in satisfaction at having found such an accurate metaphor.

He had endeavored to forget Miss Charlotte when she had been engaged to that Wickham scoundrel, but now that she was free…his passion could not be denied.

She glanced up and gave a beautiful smile when she noticed him. "Mr. Collins! So good to see you." She set her darning aside and curtsied. He bowed.

"Please have a seat." She gestured to the chair next to hers. *That is an auspicious sign.*

He seated himself, attempting to quell his nervous stomach. This would be his third proposal, and he flattered himself that he had improved with each one. He took a deep breath. "I was very sorry to hear the news about your fiancé."

Charlotte shrugged. "I must confess I do not miss the man very much. Quite ill-favored."

Collins blinked. His younger Bennet cousins had spoken of Mr. Wickham's handsome features quite often. "Ill-favored?" he echoed.

"Yes." As she spoke, her eyes were focused on the hands clasped in her lap. "Many girls, including my sister, Maria, are enamored of regimentals." Now she looked at him through the veil of her lashes. "But as I told you, I find a more somber garb to be far more becoming."

Be still my heart! Collins gulped, suddenly feeling quite warm—and a bit wild. "I have broken my engagement to Jane Bennet." Miss Lucas's eyebrows rose. "I felt we would not suit."

"I am sorry to hear that," she murmured.

He cleared his throat. "However, you were correct when you said I should not give up hope. I spoke with your most excellent father just now, and he assured me of his support for my suit."

"Your suit?" Her brow furrowed becomingly.

Women delight in grand, romantic gestures, he reminded himself. Collins threw himself to the floor at Charlotte's feet. She started in surprise. *Indeed, my proposals have improved in quality.*

He considered detailing why he wished to marry; he had become very good at reciting the list. But, no, he could raise the subject once they were married. Instead, he allowed his feelings to carry him away.

He rested one hand boldly on her knee. "I…Miss Lucas…am…Miss Lucas, you are uniformly charming… I promised you would not be alone…and…I am now seeking a wife. Would you be that woman? And…I…perhaps I should have mentioned this first: I love you passionately, ardently, beyond reason. Please say you will marry me and make me the happiest man in England, or at least Hertfordshire—well, certainly Meryton."

Charlotte's brows quirked up at this declaration but then she smiled. "Yes, I will marry you."

Collins staggered to his feet, intending to kiss Charlotte's hand. But before he could move, the entire length of her body was pressed against his, and her tongue was in his mouth. *Oh my! What is happening?*

Collins had the very distinct sense that he was not in charge of this marriage proposal. That should have troubled him. *But merciful heavens! The feeling of her tongue… I probably should not enjoy it so much… It is probably quite wicked… Would Lady Catherine approve?* Charlotte twined her arms around his neck and drew him closer. And her tongue moved… *Well, we simply will not perform such acts near Lady Catherine.*

Finally, she released his mouth. They were both panting. "I do find clerical garb *extremely* flattering," Charlotte gasped before she pulled him close and kissed him again.

No, Collins was forced to acknowledge, *I am not in control*. But at the moment he did not care.

***

Bingley had sent a maid to Longbourn the day before on the pretext of obtaining a recipe for the Netherfield kitchen from the Bennets' cook. The maid had learned that yes indeed Mr. Collins had broken off his engagement with Miss Jane Bennet. Reportedly, Miss Bennet did not appear heartbroken at this development, although her mother was very vocal on the matter. The maid had further learned that Mr. Collins had traveled straight from Longbourn to Lucas Lodge, where he had proposed to Charlotte Lucas! Hopefully, Jane was not too mortified at being so quickly replaced.

Although Bingley had experienced relief at the news, he found himself delaying his departure for Longbourn. His nerves were in tatters. As eager as he was to ask Jane to marry him, Bingley was not happy about the necessity of breaking off his engagement to Elizabeth—which, naturally, must happen beforehand.

When he had first asked Elizabeth to consent to an engagement for his mother's sake, he had assumed they would somehow end it once his mother left Hertfordshire. She was just pleased to see her son engaged and less concerned about *when* the marriage would be.

But as he had passed more time in Elizabeth's presence over the past weeks, Bingley had come to appreciate her finer qualities. She had a quick wit and was fast to discern problems and offer solutions. She was very caring—particularly toward her sisters and her friend, Charlotte. She seemed to have an endless store of patience for people like Caroline, without tolerating insults. She was, in short, a delightful woman, and Bingley harbored a deep sense of guilt over the thought of jilting her.

She was nothing like Jane, who was far better suited to be Bingley's wife and whom he loved deeply.

He knew Elizabeth would understand his choice and would be happy for Jane. In fact, she would expect this decision now that Jane was free.

However, her tender understanding would not prevent malicious talk, particularly since the Bennets were already objects of gossip after Lydia's elopement. Once Mr. Collins's defection to the Lucas family was widely known, there would be even more talk. Now Bingley was about to add fuel to the fire. The neighbors would be all too happy to discuss Elizabeth's failure to keep her fiancé happy, and they would blame Jane for stealing him away. Jane and Elizabeth might know the truth, but that would hardly prevent sidelong glances and whispers behind fans at the assembly hall.

As Bingley had considered it the night before, his initial elation over the prospect of proposing to Jane had given way to anxiety about how it would appear and what the consequences would be for Elizabeth. He had even thought about delaying his proposal; however, becoming engaged to Bingley would help Jane by ameliorating some gossip over Mr. Collins's abandonment. And Bingley could not endure the thought of exposing his beloved to such malice when it was within his power to prevent it.

So he had resolved to go through with the proposal…but he still worried about Elizabeth. He even considered speaking with Darcy about it, but then he recalled Darcy's dislike for the Bennets—and Elizabeth in particular—and decided silence was the better course.

Bingley guided his horse to the front of Longbourn and dismounted, handing the reins to a waiting groom. He steeled himself to enter the house. Elizabeth was not prone to dramatics; she would be gracious and understanding. However, that almost made it worse. Bingley almost wished someone would yell at him; he deserved it. *Perhaps I could arrange it with Mrs. Bennet.*

Bingley was fortunate that Elizabeth was alone in the drawing room when he arrived. When he entered she gave him a warm smile and set her needlework aside. Sitting beside her on the sofa, he took her hand in his.

There is no use in waiting, he thought. *Best get it over with.* "Elizabeth, you have been very good to me in helping to make my mother happy. Far better than I deserve."

She shook her head. "Being your fiancée is not a chore; it is certainly preferable to being engaged to Mr. Collins or Mr. Wickham." She gifted him with such a sweet smile that he felt his guilt even more acutely.

He swallowed hard. "But you know that my first love was always your sister, Jane." He could not look her in the eye, focusing instead on their intertwined hands.

"And now that she is no longer betrothed, you would like to be free to propose to her." Elizabeth's tone was matter of fact. "I understand. Of course, I release you from any promises you have made to me."

Did she look a little sad? Bingley thought there was a wistful edge to her smile. Perhaps she had come to care for him a little. And it was by no means certain that another man might ever make her another offer of marriage. With a pang he realized he could be dooming her to a life of spinsterhood.

Bingley closed his eyes and conjured up the image of Jane's face. *This is the right thing to do*, he reminded himself.

Elizabeth patted his hand. "Do not be uneasy. I know you love Jane. You will make a very lovely couple. I could not be more delighted for you both."

He appreciated that she was showing a brave front for his sake, but guilt still weighed heavily on his shoulders. He caught and held her gaze. "If you ever have need of assistance or anything that might be within my power to grant, please do not hesitate to call on me."

She laughed. "Do not give such promises, Mr. Bingley! I might subject you to hearing me practice the pianoforte at Netherfield."

How good of her to laugh under these circumstances. "You will always be welcome at Netherfield—for any reason," he said.

"Thank you." She squeezed his hand briefly and released it. "Jane walked to Meryton this morning, but you might meet her on the road if you would like to speak with her."

Bingley had jumped up before he realized it; he did not wish to appear too eager to rid himself of Elizabeth. He gazed sheepishly down at Elizabeth. "I should go…and…"

She laughed indulgently. "Yes, go!" She waved him out of the room. "Go propose. Make her the happiest creature on earth!"

She is so brave, Bingley thought as he exited the room.

Chapter Eighteen

It is enough, Jane told herself. Usually she undertook the walk to Meryton in the company of her sisters, but today no one had been free to accompany her, and she had relished the idea of a solitary ramble, leaving her alone with her thoughts. That, more than any search for bonnet ribbons, had driven her journey. Which was fortunate since the trip had not yielded any satisfactory ribbons or even the right color thread to finish her embroidery.

It is enough that I am free from Mr. Collins. Deep within, her secret heart yearned for another, but she dared not articulate the thought, let alone hope that it would be fulfilled. No, it was enough to be free of any obligation toward Mr. Collins.

When she had first pledged herself to him, Jane had believed he possessed a kind and generous heart and an unexpressed cleverness concealed behind his unfortunate awkwardness. However, she had soon discovered that the awkwardness and an accompanying conceit and disregard for others' feelings were in fact his true character.

And she had almost tied herself to the man for life! Jane shuddered at the memory. When Mr. Collins had given her the "unfortunate" news that he must break off the engagement, Jane had suppressed an urge to dance a jig right there in her mother's sitting room. It was, truth be told, what she had been praying for every night. God was good.

It was enough; I should not be greedy for more.

It was likely she might never marry, and she was content with that thought. Now Lydia would not marry Mr. Darcy either. Fortunately, Mr. Bingley was still engaged to Lizzy, so her parents would have one daughter with connections who might help in case of financial difficulties. Yes, weeks ago Mr. Bingley had expressed an interest in Jane herself, but she would not allow herself to believe that such devotion persisted. *Who would choose me over Lizzy?* It was too much to hope. And she could not steal a fiancé away from Lizzy, who was by far more deserving than Jane.

No, it was enough that she was free from Mr. Collins. Jane's vision was suspiciously blurry; she increased her pace so that she would arrive at Longbourn a little sooner. Perhaps she would rest a little before lunch.

Jane rounded a bend in the road and discerned a figure in the distance: a man on a horse. She could not make out his face, but he had a tall, fine form and an excellent seat. If only it was… No, she must be happy with what she had. *It was enough.*

As the man drew closer, Jane could indeed see that it *was* Mr. Bingley. She fought an irrational desire to dive off the side of the road and hide in the bushes. He had noticed her; she could not conceal her presence. Very well. They would stop and have a brief, amiable conversation before they went their separate ways.

Jane blinked rapidly, not daring to wipe her eyes. She must present a calm, serene face to Mr. Bingley.

As he drew close, Mr. Bingley reined in his horse and slid from the saddle. *Oh, merciful heavens!* Jane thought. He must intend a long conversation. She prayed for the strength to endure it. She gave him an amiable smile and a curtsey. "Mr. Bingley."

"Miss Bennet." He bowed and beamed at her. *At least one of us is pleased.* "Are you for Longbourn?"

"Yes. I did some shopping in Meryton."

"If you would allow me, I would be pleased to escort you home."

Jane's eyebrows rose. "I assumed you had some business in the town."

"No." Heaven help her, he was still smiling! "I have some business with you."

What could he possibly mean? Jane's heart beat faster as she set a brisk pace for Longbourn—as if she could somehow escape her confusion. Mr. Bingley fell into step beside her, with one hand pulling the reins of his horse.

"First, I wish to apologize for my disgraceful behavior the night of the Netherfield ball."

Oh, this was awkward! "No apologies are necessary, sir," she murmured.

"I believe they are. I should not have—but Collins provoked my anger with the way he spoke to you…and I admit to some…jealousy. I was wrong to strike him."

"Speak of it no more, I pray you." She hated the pain in his voice. "All is forgiven and forgotten."

"You are too good," he said.

They walked in a companionable silence for a little while. Then Mr. Bingley cleared his throat. "I just paid a visit to Longbourn," he said conversationally. "Elizabeth and I agreed that we would not suit, so we have ended our engagement."

Jane's hand flew to her mouth. Her worst fears had come true! She was to be the instrument of Lizzy's misery. Yes, Lizzy had insisted she did not love Mr. Bingley and had encouraged Jane to consider his suit, but Jane knew he was a good man and would make Lizzy a good husband. Jane had been content at the thought that they would build a life together.

Mr. Bingley must have noticed her expression. "Elizabeth is not distressed. Her feelings were not deeply engaged in our betrothal—nor were mine. She spoke of this to you?"

Jane nodded, keeping her eyes fixed on the road ahead despite the blurring of her vision. She knew what Lizzy had claimed, but how could any woman not be in love with Mr. Bingley? He was perfection itself.

"Elizabeth did not love me, and I do not love her. She did me a favor to help with my mother," Mr. Bingley said.

Jane nodded again, not trusting herself to speak.

He cleared his throat and abruptly stopped walking, dropping the reins of his horse, who was well trained enough to simply stand in the road. He took her hand in his and gently kissed it. "I was and will always remain deeply in love with you. Jane, will you consent to be my wife?"

Jane was filled with conflicting emotions; her conscience demanded that she return him to Lizzy so her sister might have a happy life. But Lizzy had already made the sacrifice; she was unlikely to change her mind once again. And Jane yearned—oh, how she yearned—to accept. Marrying Mr. Bingley would be a dream come true. Did she dare allow herself so much happiness? Was it right?

"Jane?" Mr. Bingley regarded her with concern. *I must have been silent too long.*

Jane swallowed. Yes, she *would* grasp at happiness when it was offered. "Yes, Mr. Bingley, I will be your wife."

The next thing Jane knew, Mr. Bingley's arms were around her, and he was kissing her—passionately. In the middle of the road where anyone might notice! It was most inappropriate, but, oh, it felt heavenly!

He released her lips and regarded her with concern. Was he anxious about her reception to his kisses? *We should not be so...intimate here. In public!* But all Jane could say was, "More!"

Mr. Bingley grinned and took possession of her lips once again.

***

Darcy was about to knock on the door to Longbourn when it opened, and Kitty Bennet stepped out. "Oh! Mr. Darcy, you startled me," she managed to say with only a few giggles.

"I beg your pardon."

She fluttered her hands. "I am visiting Maria Lucas, but you can go into the drawing room. I believe Mama and Elizabeth are about. Jane is...somewhere..."

With that useful information conveyed, Miss Kitty skipped off down the road.

Darcy let himself into Longbourn despite feeling a bit like an intruder. He scanned the hallway for a servant who could announce his presence to the family, but even the ubiquitous Hill seemed to have vanished. Well, he knew the location of the drawing room and was already impatient at the delay. Darcy strode toward the drawing room door. Miss Kitty had not mentioned Bingley. His friend had been here nearly two hours; hopefully, Darcy had given him time enough to break off the engagement with Elizabeth and initiate an offer to Jane Bennet.

No doubt Darcy's presence at Longbourn, and his intended purpose, would appear bizarrely rushed, perhaps even opportunistic, to others. But once he knew Elizabeth was free, Darcy could not persuade himself to wait a minute longer than necessary.

The drawing room door was ajar, and voices emanated from within. Darcy did not intend to eavesdrop, but the sound of Mrs. Bennet's shrill tones stopped him cold. It would be awkward to interrupt a familial dispute.

"He has broken off your engagement?" Mrs. Bennet asked.

"Yes, Mama." Elizabeth's voice was so soft that Darcy strained to hear it.

"Well, I cannot say I am surprised!" Mrs. Bennet cried. "You are far too opinionated and outspoken for a young lady. And you should have smiled at him more frequently."

"I smiled," Elizabeth protested.

"A woman cannot smile enough at her fiancé," her mother retorted.

Elizabeth sighed. "Mr. Bingley broke off our engagement because he wished to propose to Jane."

"So you said," Mrs. Bennet sniffed. "And I am happy for Jane. But she will never want for suitors. She is the most beautiful of my daughters."

Hearing this, Darcy clenched his hands involuntarily into fists. Not only was Mrs. Bennet wrong—since Elizabeth was clearly the most beautiful sister—but also she should not say such harmful things about her own daughter!

"Mr. Bingley might have been your last chance to marry. Yet you could not be troubled to keep your opinions to yourself."

How could she be so cruel? The back of his neck grew hot. Mrs. Bennet criticized those aspects of Elizabeth's personality that Darcy most treasured. He loved her *because* of her opinions, not in spite of them.

"My opinions—whatever they are—do not matter if Mr. Bingley is in love with Jane!"

"And what will the neighbors say? Oh, the talk! Directly after Lydia's elopement, Mr. Bingley breaks off your engagement to marry Jane? They will be recalling it for years! They will say you are unmarriageable."

Darcy grasped the doorframe to suppress his impulse to rush into the drawing room.

"I hardly think I am unmarriageable," Elizabeth said.

"What would you know? You will be a spinster, and now that Mr. Collins is not to marry Jane, he will throw us into the hedgerows as soon as your father is cold in his grave!"

Darcy had heard enough. He should not have been eavesdropping, but a man could tolerate the woman he loved being abused for only so long.

"If only you had danced with him more or worn his favorite color—"

Darcy pushed the door wide and hastened into the room. "Mrs. Bennet—"

Mrs. Bennet was glowering over Elizabeth, who was hunched miserably in a loveseat wedged in a corner. She barely glanced in his direction. "Not now, Mr. Darcy. I am discussing a sensitive matter with my daughter."

Darcy blinked. He was not accustomed to being thus addressed. "But I—"

"In a minute Mr. Darcy," Mrs. Bennet said with a touch of exasperation. Then she turned her attention to Elizabeth. "Now you will die an old maid!" Elizabeth rolled her eyes but did not respond. Her mother's voice climbed higher and higher as she spoke. "And you will most likely die an early death as well. Like that lady in the poem…what is it called? Pining away because no man wants her—"

"I want her!" Darcy thundered.

"And aged before her time—" Mrs. Bennet's mouth snapped shut as she apprehended Darcy's words.

She whirled around to face him. "I b-beg your pardon? Y-you what?"

Darcy pinched the bridge of his nose. This was certainly not the way in which he had intended to reveal his feelings to Elizabeth. "I want Elizabeth" he repeated more softly. "I wish her to be my wife. I arrived at Longbourn for the express object of proposing marriage to her." His eyes sought out Elizabeth, who seemed stunned. *Is she merely surprised, or is she appalled?*

"But—" Mrs. Bennet's mouth was hanging open again. "Are you certain?

Darcy straightened to his full height. "Please do me the courtesy of believing I know my own mind."

"But Mr. Bingley did not want her," Mrs. Bennet said faintly.

"I am not Mr. Bingley; he is in love with your eldest daughter."

Darcy had spent quite enough time talking to Mrs. Bennet. Ignoring her, he crossed the room to sit beside Elizabeth on the loveseat.

He clasped her hand in both of his. She did not object but continued to regard him with wide eyes that revealed nothing of her thoughts. *What if she is angry I broached the subject of marriage in this way? This is hardly an auspicious start. What if I have already lost my chance with her?* He endeavored to push such doubts aside and focus on finding the right words to express his feelings. Perhaps simple was the best approach.

"Elizabeth, you must allow me to tell you how ardently I admire and love you. Will you do me the honor of being my wife?"

Darcy realized he was holding his breath.

Her smile reassured him before her words. "Yes, I will marry you."

Love and relief flooded Darcy's body in equal measure. She had consented! She would be his wife!

He longed to kiss her but not before her mother, so he gently lifted her hand and laid a loving kiss on her palm. Elizabeth shivered exquisitely.

Simultaneously, both Darcy and Elizabeth turned their heads toward Mrs. Bennet, who was not only struck dumb by this unanticipated event but immobilized. Their scrutiny, however, apparently spurred her to action.

"Mr. Bennet! Mr. Bennet!" she shrieked at a volume that would no doubt convince the entire household the French had invaded the drawing room. "Come quick!"

Elizabeth sighed. "Mama—"

Mr. Bennet rushed into the room, leaving the door ajar. Mary Bennet and assorted servants crowded around the open doorway.

"What is it, my dear?" Mr. Bennet's eyes surveyed his wife—apparently uninjured—and Darcy sitting beside Elizabeth on the sofa. His agitation faded to puzzlement.

Mrs. Bennet, however, was still in a frenzy. "Mr. Darcy has proposed to Lizzy!"

"I...see." The man's forehead was creased with lines. "This is indeed cause for alarm. Has Lizzy accepted him?"

"Yes!" Mrs. Bennet cried in a tone that suggested more outrage than pleasure.

Mr. Bennet blinked at his wife. "Then what do you hope I can accomplish?"

Mrs. Bennet twitched and fluttered her hands but did not actually reply.

"Should I deny him my permission? Granted, he is no Mr. Wickham, but he does seem like a decent enough fellow. Perhaps he can rise to Wickham's standards with time." Mr. Bennet gave his daughter a wink and a smile.

Then he turned a grave countenance on his wife. "Or should I ask him to describe how he intends to support a wife and children?"

Now his wife knew she was being teased. "Oh, Mr. Bennet!" She waved dismissively. "He has ten thousand a year!"

"So you believe I should give him permission?"

"Oh, Mr. Bennet!" Now her protestation was more affectionate.

Mr. Bennet did peer over his glasses at Darcy. "I *would* like to discuss the particulars with you in my study, Mr. Darcy—in good time."

Darcy nodded, grateful that he apparently had Mr. Bennet's approbation.

"But in the meantime, my dear—" he took his wife's arm, "the two lovebirds might prefer to be alone for a little while."

"Oh!" Mrs. Bennet looked stunned. "But there is so much to do! We must find the best warehouses for the dress. And select a wedding date. And—"

"There will be time enough for that, my dear." Mr. Bennet slowly guided his chattering wife from the room.

***

Darcy met Elizabeth's eyes, feeling suddenly apprehensive. Was Elizabeth angry he had proposed in front of her mother? Her disparagement of Elizabeth had provoked such disgust that his only thought had been to demonstrate her worth. Darcy had never been so impulsive in his life; would he regret it?

Darcy's blood still sang through his veins with the thrilling knowledge that she had accepted his proposal. But had she agreed because her mother expected it? Had she taken him for the right reasons? Would she change her mind before—or even worse, after—the wedding? Were his, admittedly intense, feelings for her reciprocated?

Abruptly, he dropped Elizabeth's hand, provoking a startled look from her. He ran both hands through his hair, averting his gaze as he attempted to organize his disordered thoughts.

"Mr. Darcy?" Despite the anxiety in her voice, her low alto sound sent shivers through his body.

"Please call me William."

He heard a little intake of breath. "W-William, is there—are you—?" Elizabeth made a little self-conscious laugh. "I must apologize for my mother's…excessive enthusiasm."

Aghast at this misinterpretation of his silence, Darcy hurried to reassure her. "You need not apologize. I admit to some…anger at your mother on your behalf. It is not your fault Mr. Bingley—" He faltered; how to phrase this?

"Prefers my sister?"

He took her hands in his, rubbing his thumbs gently over the backs—and appreciating the lack of gloves. "Were you—did you—that is, were you very distressed when Mr. Bingley broke it off?"

Elizabeth laughed. "No, I am not the victim of a broken heart. Although I shall be extremely vexed with Mr. Bingley if he has not already proposed to Jane!" This provoked a laugh from Darcy.

Finally, they both sobered, and silence fell over the drawing room. He steeled himself to ask the question he least wanted her to answer. "Elizabeth, I apologize that my proposal was not more…romantic." She waved this concern away. "I hope—that is, I do not want—you should not accept because I proposed

before your mother—or because you felt pressure—"
He held his breath. *What if she says yes?*

Her laughter was like silvery bells. "When have
I ever allowed myself to be pressured into anything?"
Darcy laughed in rueful recognition of this truth.
"After all, I rejected Mr. Collins's proposal."

"He made you an offer?" Darcy frowned, not
liking the thought at all.

She nodded. "Before he proposed to Jane."

*Collins might be a fool, but he was quite a good
match for someone in Elizabeth's situation. Perhaps
she did accept me because she cares for me.*

Elizabeth reached out to take Darcy's hand, and
he experienced a secret thrill at her boldness. "Mr. Dar-
William, I—" She bit her lip, obviously having
difficulty expressing herself. "You should not doubt
for one moment that I care deeply for you...I-I love
you."

She is so brave to be so honest with me. Darcy
saw tears shimmering in her eyes and was suddenly
overwhelmed by the cascade of emotions he felt for her.
Admiration, gratitude, awe, hope...and, of course, love.
"I love you as well, Elizabeth. Very much." He had
intended the words as a bold statement, but they
emerged as a hoarse whisper.

He leaned toward her, and she made no attempt
to evade him. His lips brushed hers softly, tentatively,
so as not to frighten her. But she responded with bold
passion as she immediately deepened the kiss and
embraced Darcy, drawing his body closer to hers.
Could a man could die from too much happiness?
Darcy wondered.

Responding eagerly to her enthusiasm, he ran
his tongue along the seam of her lips. Her mouth
opened instantly, and then his tongue was exploring her
mouth, their tongues intertwining in a sort of mating

dance. Elizabeth moaned deep in her throat. There was no better sound in the world. *She enjoys this! She likes my kisses.* His tongue delved deeper into her mouth.

He allowed his hands more freedom; one stroked her back while the other found its way to her hair. It was every bit as silky as he had expected. He tenderly stroked one of the glossy curls.

Finally, reluctantly, Darcy drew away, allowing himself to catch his breath and permitting his heartbeat to return to normal. He pressed his forehead to Elizabeth's as they recovered their breath.

"I hope," Elizabeth said finally, "that you no longer have concerns about my feelings for you."

He chuckled. "You have indeed laid to rest any doubts. However, I-I must apologize…again for making inappropriate advances."

She laughed a throaty laugh that made him want to kiss her again. "Please do not apologize, William. Just tell me when you will make inappropriate advances again. I cannot wait."

The last of his anxiety melted away. "Nor can I. But perhaps your family's drawing room is not the best location.

She laughed again. "Perhaps a different venue would be appropriate…I do like to take long walks."

That offered a host of intriguing possibilities. "Perhaps I might meet you for a walk tomorrow?"

"I would be pleased to have some company."

Their fond smile stretched for a long moment. But ultimately Darcy stood. "I must speak with your father before he investigates the cause of my delay. Do you have a preference about wedding dates when I discuss the plans with him?"

She shook her head. "Only that I do not want an overly long engagement." Darcy sighed in relief; in this they were in agreement. The look she turned on him was frankly desirous; his heart beat faster. "I would like it to be short."

Darcy smiled. "I believe that can be arranged."

Epilogue

Mr. Bennet raised his glass. "To Mr. and Mrs. Bingley and Mr. and Mrs. Darcy. Many years of happiness!" Everyone around Wickham raised their glasses and drank, but—although he held a glass of champagne—Wickham did not. Petty, he knew, but he was in a petty mood. The two couples, radiant and hopeful, were standing near Mr. Bennet *Well, they shall learn soon enough how miserable married life truly i*s, Wickham thought with some glee.

He had only received an invitation to this wedding breakfast after Lydia had begged Elizabeth to include him. Apparently Darcy still held some sort of grudge for some imagined slight. It could not possibly be the incident with Georgiana; that was so long ago, and she had not suffered any harm, after all.

If anyone should harbor a grudge, it should be Wickham. Darcy had given him such a pittance when he had married Lydia; Wickham had already spent more than half of it. When it was all gone, he might be forced to drastic measures, even purchasing a commission in the regulars. The whole situation made him sick to his stomach. It was all Darcy's doing; if he had not colluded with Sir William to force Wickham into marrying Lydia, none of this would have happened.

Despite his despicable treatment of Wickham, Darcy was celebrated at a lavish wedding breakfast, where family and friends congratulated him and pretended he was such fine gentleman. It made Wickham want to vomit. Wickham's Gretna Green wedding to Lydia had not even taken place in a church; it had been a filthy blacksmith shop, with no one to celebrate it except the smith's sour-faced wife. Life was unfair.

"Mr. Wickham?"

Wickham looked about to see who had addressed him and noticed the pale, pudgy face of the parson who had married Charlotte Lucas. What was his name?

"Mr...Collins?" Wickham had never spoken with the man.

The man smiled widely; apparently Wickham had recollected the name properly. "Yes, yes!" Wickham did not know this fool. Why was the man so pleased to see him? "I wanted, most humbly, to convey my thanks, sir, for having the perspicacity to recognize that you and Charlotte were not suited and for making the courageous decision to step aside."

That was not quite how circumstances had unfolded, but Wickham nodded anyway; this poor soul had been saddled with Charlotte Lucas's face. Although Wickham would give a great deal to have that dowry now.

The man put his hand to his heart with an expression of rapture. "Charlotte and I are in perfect harmony. It is as if we were formed for each other."

Wickham was unsure how to respond to such a remarkable statement. "How fortunate for you."

"Yes, yes..." Mr. Collins's voice trailed off, and his face sobered as he stared into space. "Although I must say, I never realized how...*taxing* marital life could be."

What is this idiot blathering on about now? Wickham wondered. But he did not care enough to inquire.

"I mean...the—" Collins lowered his voice. "—'marital duties' alone are...exhausting." The man nudged Wickham in the ribs with his elbow as if they shared a secret. What marital duties? Like helping your wife across mud puddles or opening doors for her

and that sort of rot? Wickham did not find it
particularly tiring, when he thought to do it.

Collins yammered on without apparently noting
Wickham's puzzlement. "But of course, you were
engaged to Charlotte. You well know how...*ardent* she
can be."

Ardent? *Oh! Those sort of marital duties.*
Wickham happened to catch a glimpse of mousy-
haired, buttoned-up Charlotte Collins across the room.
"Ardent" was surely the last word he would use to
describe her.

Wickham took a gulp of champagne. "Indeed."
He kept his tone neutral.

Mr. Collins's voice dropped to a whisper. "Yes.
Just between you and me, some nights I would prefer
to...just sleep...if you understand my meaning. A man
needs...rest. But Charlotte—quite rightly—stresses the
importance of my marital duties."

Wickham took another gulp, not wishing to
imagine Mr. and Mrs. Collins engaged in "marital
duties." However, the alternative appeared to be
recollecting his own marital bed, which was not
something he did willingly.

Lydia was pretty enough, but the truth was, she
was *fifteen*...And she talked...a lot....all the time. She
would rattle on about whatever occurred to her at the
moment...even when they were performing
their...marital duties. Lace was a particular favorite
subject—where to buy it, how to discern its quality,
how to find it inexpensively. Another preferred topic
was hair—coiffures, pins, curls, textures, colors.
Wickham might explode if he heard one more word on
either subject.

"As a newlywed yourself, you must be well
acquainted with the rigors of married life." Mr. Collins
gave him a conspiratorial grin. Wickham shrugged. He

was not about to reveal the state of his marital bed to anyone, let alone this pompous fool.

From across the room, Mrs. Collins gave her husband a fond little wave and a stupid smile. "Ah, my precious honeysuckle rose has need of me!" He grinned foolishly at her. "Is she not a true rose of loveliness?"

Collins apparently did not require a reply, fortunately, since Wickham had choked on his champagne. The next moment, Collins was gone, having hurried across the room to his beloved.

It was a relief to be free of the other man, but Wickham actually envied the idiot. Collins had a wife who obvious enjoyed "marital duties," and who undoubtedly ceased talking at least occasionally. *I really should have taken her mother's temperament into consideration*, he thought ruefully. *Perhaps Mr. Bennet could supply me with ideas about encouraging a woman to be silent.* He glanced over at Lydia's parents. Mrs. Bennet was talking loudly and gesticulating with a glass of champagne that threatened to spill at any moment while Mr. Bennet rolled his eyes. *Perhaps not.*

If only Mrs. Collins could give Lydia some hints about "marital duties!" *Most likely it would not help anyway*, he thought gloomily.

Wickham finished his champagne and went in search of more…or perhaps something stronger.

***

Charlotte was unsure how this had occurred, but somehow she had fallen into conversation with Lydia Wickham and the new Elizabeth Darcy. Lydia had ever been wayward and self-centered, and marriage had not improved the girl.

Lydia giggled when she first encountered Charlotte. "La! I hope you bear me no ill will for stealing your fiancé."

Charlotte ground her teeth together. Naturally, Lydia would lead with the subject most of polite society would avoid. "Not at all. I believe everything was resolved for the best."

"My Wickham is so dashing in his regimentals, is he not?" Lydia then demanded of the other women. Elizabeth nodded, and Charlotte made a noncommittal noise. "Nothing becomes a man so much as regimentals."

Elizabeth said nothing, but Charlotte would not allow such a statement to stand unchallenged. "For my part, I have always believed that the uniform of a clergyman was much more... alluring."

Elizabeth coughed, and Lydia blinked in disbelief. "Clerical garb?"

"Yes, I believe black...enhances a man's figure, rendering him uncommonly pleasing." Charlotte smiled sweetly at Lydia, gesturing toward her husband. "There is my Collins. Is he not the essence of everything a gentleman should be?" She blew a kiss to her husband, and he bestowed on her a little wave.

Elizabeth experienced a coughing fit, which she covered with a handkerchief.

Charlotte waxed on; she could sing her husband's praises for hours. "There is a certain something in his air that I cannot define...perhaps it is the sobriety of the clergy. The comfort of knowing he will never indulge in drinking or whoring or gambling. Of course, his finances are sound, and he has a particularly bright future." Charlotte smiled at Lydia. "Such attributes may render a man uncommonly attractive."

The coughing was causing Elizabeth's eyes to water.

Lydia regarded the other woman blankly for a minute. Charlotte continued to smile. Lydia's face fell just a fraction. Then she turned her attention away from Charlotte toward her sister. "La! Lizzy, now that you are married, I may explain all you must know about the wedding night." Lydia gave her sister a sly smile.

Elizabeth regarded her with tolerant amusement. "I know everything necessary, thank you, Lydia."

Lydia waved her hand dismissively. "You have had it all from Mama! She would never tell you the most important parts." Elizabeth rolled her eyes, but Lydia paid her no heed. She lowered her voice. "There are ways to make it go faster—so it is over more quickly." She gave Charlotte a conspiratorial wink.

That was enough! Lydia's air of superiority was hard to take, but now she was conveying a false impression of the marriage bed. Charlotte lowered her head and smiled shyly. "I find that I do not wish it to be over more quickly. It is one of the greatest pleasures of marriage, in my opinion."

Lydia looked at Charlotte as if she had three heads. "Pleasures of—really? Better than having your husband buy you gowns or attending balls with the militia?" She made a grand, sweeping gesture with her arms. "It is just delightful when people call me, 'Mrs. Wickham.' And when I walk out on a handsome man's arm and all the heads turn! But the actual marriage bed is so…messy."

Charlotte did not understand the girl at all. "Perhaps your enjoyment of it will increase with time," she suggested.

Lydia narrowed her eyes. "Perhaps you speak on a subject about which you know nothing," she hissed.

Charlotte maintained a carefully calm façade. "Or perhaps I am simply married to the right man."

Lydia laughed disbelievingly.

Charlotte continued, "It could be that Mr. Wickham does not quite understand how to make such events pleasurable for you. I could have Mr. Collins provide a few suggestions to him."

By now Lydia was quite red in the face. "I do not—! Wickham does not—! Oh, I cannot believe—! You—!" Finally, she could only emit an inarticulate squeal as she stalked away. Behind her retreating back, Elizabeth and Charlotte exchanged looks—and then burst into laughter.

***

Elizabeth experienced a twinge of guilt over enjoying Lydia's discomfort. But her youngest sister had been insufferable all morning, hinting about their need for money and boasting about her husband's attractiveness and "prospects" for the future.

Jane joined their party, giving Charlotte an enthusiastic hug. They were both extremely pleased Charlotte had made the trip from Kent for the occasion. Their friend moved a bit closer to the other women and spoke in a low voice. "Tell me, has there been a great deal of talk over the…um…"

"Swapping of fiancés?" Elizabeth finished for her.

Charlotte shrugged uncomfortably.

"I believe most of the gossip has died down," Jane said. "That is why we waited two months for the ceremony, although William was most impatient to be wed."

"You were concerned about rumors that Jane had 'stolen' your fiancé…" Charlotte's eyes darted uneasily to Jane.

Elizabeth smiled. "William was particularly effective at dispelling that particular misconception. He confided in Mrs. Long how he was heartbroken after Lydia's defection and how I comforted him. When he formed an attachment to me, Charles graciously offered to step aside to clear the way for William. Then Charles set about comforting Jane since she was now abandoned."

Charlotte tittered. "And she believed this tale?"

"I suppose. It had spread throughout Meryton within a week."

"Mrs. Carter told Charles how admirable he was to sacrifice for his friend who might have done himself harm," Jane added. They all laughed at this.

"Mama heard a version that Jane was the despondent one, and William took me off Charles's hands so he could comfort her," Elizabeth said.

"Oh my!" Charlotte laughed heartily.

When they had sobered, Jane admitted, "There are some who are scandalized and make cutting remarks."

Elizabeth nodded. "But we do our best to ignore them."

Her friend took and squeezed both women's hands. "I am so happy for you!"

"And I for you," Elizabeth replied. "Your description of life at Hunsford Parsonage sounds idyllic."

"It is very good. Lady Catherine is a bit tiresome at times. However, Collins mostly visits without me now."

"Oh?" Elizabeth raised an eyebrow.

A corner of Charlotte's mouth curled upward. "Whenever I was at Rosings Park, I insisted on playing the pianoforte for everyone's enjoyment."

"I did not know you played the pianoforte," Jane said with a slight frown.

"I do not."

Elizabeth and Jane laughed heartily. Charlotte grinned. "After two 'performances,' Lady Catherine suggested my husband might visit Rosings without me. Now I only go for an occasional dinner."

"Has the parish been welcoming to you?" Jane inquired.

"Oh yes, they were very pleased when I arrived. I enjoy being the parson's wife; there is so much good I may do. The parsonage is quite lovely. And…" Her voice lowered to a whisper. "I believe…I may be with child."

Elizabeth barely refrained from a squeal of happiness. "Oh, Charlotte!"

Charlotte's eyes were shining. "It is all I ever wanted. A comfortable home, a good husband, and children to love."

Impulsively, Elizabeth hugged her friend. "I am so pleased for you!" She released Charlotte but still clasped her hands. "And you must visit Pemberley before your confinement."

"When will you return from your wedding trip?" Charlotte asked.

"We will be away for a month. William is taking me to Scotland. I am very excited."

"How wonderful!" Charlotte turned to Jane with an inquiring look.

"We will go to the Lake District and then to Scarborough so I may meet some of Charles's relatives," Jane said.

Charlotte frowned with concern. "How is his mother's health?" They all glanced to the other side of the room where Mrs. Bingley was conducting an animated conversation with her son.

"Much improved actually." Jane gave a wide, serene smile. "Her new London doctor believes the situation is not as dire as was previously believed. She will come to live with us once we are settled at Netherfield."

A hand descended on Elizabeth's shoulder, and she looked up to see William standing behind her. "My love, Lydia prevailed upon Mary to play a dance tune, and they are forming couples."

Elizabeth laughed. "Dancing at a wedding breakfast?"

He shrugged. "Our courtship was anything but traditional. Why should our wedding celebration be any different?"

Elizabeth shrugged to concede the point.

"Would you care to dance with me?"

The intensity in his eyes demonstrated that her response was of more than passing interest to him. "Yes, of course, I would love to."

"I shall fetch Charles," Jane said. "He would dearly love to dance." She hurried off.

"And I shall fetch my husband," Charlotte said. "And we shall…observe." Her lips quirked in a smile as she took leave of the others.

"Hmm," William remarked. "She appears to have made a realistic assessment of her husband's strengths…and weaknesses."

"Indeed."

"Shall we?" William took his wife's hand so they could join the other dancers, although the music had not yet commenced. However, rather than join the rows of dancers, William pulled Elizabeth into an embrace and whispered in her ear.

"Three months ago I sought to deny my attraction to you and fled the Netherfield ballroom lest I ask you to dance." Elizabeth's eyebrows rose. She had not heard that story. "As you well know, that decision led to many other disasters. However, I believe my greatest error that night was not dancing with you. For if I had, we would have enjoyed three more months of this…"

He bent his head and pressed his lips against hers. The kiss soon turned passionate, more passionate than was appropriate in a public setting. Elizabeth heard murmurs and titters of laughter from the other guests. Finally, she pulled away, out of breath and red in the face.

Onlookers were watching, but she ignored them. She pressed her cheek to his and whispered in his ear. "Your decision did bring chaos to Longbourn, but it all worked out for the best. I love you."

"I love you, too, my Elizabeth."

The End

Thank you for purchasing this book.

Your support makes it possible for authors like me to continue writing.

Please consider leaving a review where you purchased the book.

Learn more about me and my upcoming releases:

Website: www.victoriakincaid.com

Twitter: VictoriaKincaid@kincaidvic

Blog: https://kincaidvictoria.wordpress.com/

Facebook: https://www.facebook.com/kincaidvictoria

About Victoria Kincaid

The author of numerous best-selling *Pride and Prejudice* variations, historical romance writer Victoria Kincaid has a Ph.D. in English literature and runs a small business, er, household with two children, a hyperactive dog, an overly affectionate cat, and a husband who is not threatened by Mr. Darcy. They live near Washington DC, where the inhabitants occasionally stop talking about politics long enough to complain about the traffic.

On weekdays she is a freelance writer/editor who now specializes in IT marketing (it's more interesting than it sounds). In the past, some of her more…unusual writing subjects have included space toilets, taxi services, laser gynecology, bidets, orthopedic shoes, generating energy from onions, Ferrari rental car services, and vampire face lifts (she swears she is not making any of this up). A lifelong Austen fan, Victoria has read more Jane Austen variations and sequels than she can count – and confesses to an extreme partiality for the Colin Firth version of *Pride and Prejudice*.

Please enjoy this sample from *The Gentleman's Impertinent Daughter* by Rose Fairbanks

When Fitzwilliam Darcy and Elizabeth Bennet meet in Hyde Park, Darcy immediately finds his opinions of the world challenged by the lady. Their attraction grows at the next meeting as Elizabeth finds she has at last met a man who accepts her wit and intelligence. The budding romance may be killed, however, upon their arrival in Hertfordshire. Darcy must meet Elizabeth's family while Elizabeth grapples with the jealous Caroline Bingley, all the while a man in uniform watches and plots. Fate brought them together, but only love can overcome their obstacles. Short and sweet, The Gentleman's Impertinent Daughter *is an uncomplicated romance for all who love Jane Austen Fan Fiction.*

Chapter 1
September 30, 1811

"Come, Brother, let us rest ourselves for a moment," Georgiana Darcy beseeched her elder brother. The two settled on a nearby bench.

"I am sorry Sweetling. It is very warm, and I should be more attentive to you. Would you like to go home?" Fitzwilliam Darcy looked at his sister with concern. The sun was shining unseasonably hot for late September.

"No, I am well."

"I do wish you would come with me to Hertfordshire, or allow me to stay behind with you. I do not like leaving you after your ordeal just yet."

They had arrived in London only two days before, after celebrating the customary Michaelmas feast at Pemberley, their country estate. After the betrayal of the summer and the hustle of the harvest, Darcy was looking forward to enjoying a holiday but hated to leave his dear sister behind.

"Really, William, it was not an illness. I have simply had low spirits because of my foolishness."

Georgiana lowered her voice. "I would enjoy the countryside, but I will take the cowardly way out and avoid Mr. Bingley's sisters since you offered. You know how difficult it is for me to make new friends and I do not trust my judgment in regards to their sincerity anymore. Therefore, I would be trapped with the ladies all day and make you feel guilty for any enjoyment you experience. No, you go. You work so hard. Mrs. Annesley and I shall see you at Christmas."

After a short pause she added, "Now, I think I shall watch the ducks just down there."

Mr. Darcy watched his baby sister leave. She had grown into a beautiful young lady while he was unawares. Early in the summer, she had been taken advantage of, her heart broken asunder, by his childhood best friend and very own father's godson. Swept away by romance she believed herself in love and consented to an elopement.

Learning the man in question only desired her stout dowry of thirty thousand pounds and revenge on her brother made her feelings of guilt even worse than when she understood the gravity of the scandal her actions would have caused. She had not recovered her spirits and was still filled with shame and melancholy.

I was charged to protect her, and I have failed her.

Nearby he heard something wholly unexpected, a full, hearty laugh from a woman. It had been years since he heard a woman laugh so openly, not since his mother's death. And the tone of this particular laugh was delightful and enchanting. Women of his circle rarely laughed unless they were belittling someone. It was a sad way to live, to be so bitter and angry.

His eyes sought out the owner of the musical laughter and saw a young woman surrounded by four children under the age of ten.

Surely she is much too young to be their mother but dressed too fine to be a governess. Though clearly she takes little care of her wardrobe, given the way she romps with the little mites. Refreshing, a young lady not interested in fashion.

He had never seen a woman with such obvious zest for life before. This lady had an inner happiness and was unafraid for the world to see it.

Now available on Amazon, Nook, Barnes and Noble, Createspace, Kobo & iBooks.

Follow Rose on:
Facebook: https://www.facebook.com/Rose-Fairbanks-Author-538834066185913/
Twitter: https://twitter.com/Rose_Fairbanks
Mailing list: http://rosefairbanks.us10.list-manage.com/subscribe?u=77328865bcdb5c238d88b7a25&id=eb0103b944
Blog: https://rosefairbanks.com/

Please enjoy this excerpt from *The Abominable Mr. Darcy* by J. Dawn King

Mr. Darcy was an enigma... until he spoke. Then, he was the enemy.

Miss Elizabeth Bennet's eyes are instantly drawn towards a handsome, mysterious guest who arrives at the Meryton Assembly with the Bingley party. The gentleman destroys her illusions by delivering an insult that turns him from Mr. Divinely Attractive to the Abominable Mr. Darcy.

While Elizabeth sets in motion her strategy for retaliation, Darcy plans to win the campaign being waged in the genteel drawing rooms of Hertfordshire. As more players from Jane Austen's beloved cast of characters enter the fray, complications arise--some with irreversible consequences. Can a truce be called before their hearts become casualties as well? How many times can two people go from enemies to friends and back again before it's too late?

A Regency romance from best-selling author, J. Dawn King, inspired by Pride and Prejudice.

From Chapter 11

"Who is Miss Clark, Brother?" The reactions of both men raised the curiosity in both ladies. "How did you come to know her?"

"Yes, Cousin, I would deeply appreciate being reminded of how you came to know her." The colonel rocked back on his heels, grinning from ear to ear.

Before he could stop himself, Darcy ran his hands through his hair. He wanted to ring his cousin's neck—a feeling he suffered quite regularly of late. Darcy noted the anticipation on Georgiana's face and closed his eyes, sighing.

Seeing he had the attention of the whole room, he released his breath and began his tale. Richard would pay later.

"It was summer, twenty years past, when Richard and his older brother were visiting Pemberley. Derbyshire summers are normally not as warm as they are in Hertfordshire. That August the sun was blistering hot. Whilst our parents relaxed in the coolness of the pavilion in the shade of the trees on the south lawn, the three of us boys, along with a childhood companion, decided to swim in the river to cool off."

"Of the four of us, I was the youngest and the smallest. I was desperate to prove I was as strong as the others. In addition, I longed to be as honourable as my father." He paused. "We came upon your aunt, a young woman of eight and ten in some distress." Darcy considered how much to mention in mixed company. Miss Clark's clothes had been torn, and it was his first sight of a woman's bare feet. "Apparently she had tripped over an obstacle on the trail and twisted her ankle. All of us young boys thought Miss Clark the most beautiful woman and felt incumbent on being of service."

Elizabeth smiled in delight. "It was you? You were the boy who offered to carry her home?"

Darcy blushed. "I was."

"But, Brother, it is five miles from Pemberley Woods to Lambton, and you were but eight years old!"

"Yes, Georgiana, I am aware." Everyone laughed. The tops of his ears turned bright red. "I had hoped your aunt would keep the tale to herself."

Elizabeth was touched by the thought of this chivalrous little boy. "Rest assured, Mr. Darcy, that my aunt took your offer most seriously. She told us that story as one of her most cherished memories."

Even Mrs. Bennet had been impressed with the story when she first heard it from Madeline.

"Mr. Darcy, is it true you brought a white horse to carry her home?" Mrs. Bennet may have been the fiercest of matchmakers for her daughters for her own interest, but she was also a romantic at heart. "Imagine that!"

Elizabeth continued. "My aunt called you her knight, sir."

The colonel added, "We called Darcy 'Sir Knight' until he grew into his height. Now, we only call him that out of his hearing."

"Thank you for that, Richard." Darcy could not recall when his chagrin was so acute. He wished the tale unshared, until he looked at the faces of the women. Even Miss Bingley had a bemused expression on her face.

Elizabeth's eyes were wistful and bright. Had he known the story would have had this effect, he would have told her the first night they had met. *If only he had instead of the insult.*

Facebook: J Dawn King
Twitter: @Jdawnking
Web: jdawnking.com

Victoria Kincaid's other books:

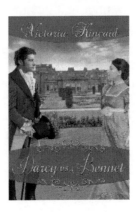

Darcy vs. Bennet

Elizabeth Bennet is drawn to a handsome, mysterious man she meets at a masquerade ball. However, she gives up all hope for a future with him when she learns he is the son of George Darcy, the man who ruined her father's life. Despite her father's demand that she avoid the younger Darcy, when he appears in Hertfordshire Elizabeth cannot stop thinking about him, or seeking him out, or welcoming his kisses....

Fitzwilliam Darcy has struggled to carve out a life independent from his father's vindictive temperament and domineering ways, although the elder Darcy still controls the purse strings. After meeting Elizabeth Bennet, Darcy cannot imagine marrying anyone else, even though his father despises her family. More than anything he wants to make her his wife, but doing so would mean sacrificing everything else....

When Mary Met the Colonel

Without the beauty and wit of the older Bennet sisters or the liveliness of the younger, Mary is the Bennet sister most often overlooked. She has resigned herself to a life of loneliness, alleviated only by music and the occasional book of military history.

Colonel Fitzwilliam finds himself envying his friends who are marrying wonderful women while he only attracts empty-headed flirts. He longs for a caring, well-informed woman who will see the man beneath the uniform.

A chance meeting in Longbourn's garden during Darcy and Elizabeth's wedding breakfast kindles an attraction between Mary and the Colonel. However, the Colonel cannot act on these feelings since he must wed an heiress. He returns to war, although Mary finds she cannot easily forget him.

Is happily ever after possible after Mary meets the Colonel?

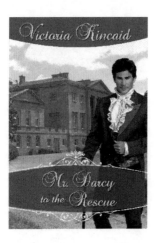

Mr. Darcy to the Rescue

When the irritating Mr. Collins proposes marriage,
Elizabeth Bennet is prepared to refuse him, but then she
learns that her father is ill. If Mr. Bennet dies, Collins
will inherit Longbourn and her family will have
nowhere to go. Elizabeth accepts the proposal, telling
herself she can be content as long as her family is
secure. If only she weren't dreading the approaching
wedding day…

Ever since leaving Hertfordshire, Mr. Darcy has been
trying to forget his inconvenient attraction to Elizabeth.
News of her betrothal forces him to realize how
devastating it would be to lose her. He arrives at
Longbourn intending to prevent the marriage, but
discovers Elizabeth's real opinion about his character.
Then Darcy recognizes his true dilemma…

How can he rescue her when she doesn't want him to?

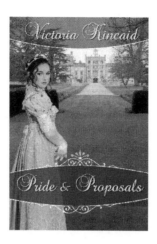

Pride and Proposals

What if Mr. Darcy's proposal was too late?

Darcy has been bewitched by Elizabeth Bennet since he met her in Hertfordshire. He can no longer fight this overwhelming attraction and must admit he is hopelessly in love. During Elizabeth's visit to Kent she has been forced to endure the company of the difficult and disapproving Mr. Darcy, but she has enjoyed making the acquaintance of his affable cousin, Colonel Fitzwilliam.

Finally resolved, Darcy arrives at Hunsford Parsonage prepared to propose—only to discover that Elizabeth has just accepted a proposal from the Colonel, Darcy's dearest friend in the world. As he watches the couple prepare for a lifetime together, Darcy vows never to speak of what is in his heart. Elizabeth has reason to dislike Darcy, but finds that he haunts her thoughts and stirs her emotions in strange ways.

Can Darcy and Elizabeth find their happily ever after?

The Secrets of Darcy and Elizabeth

In this *Pride and Prejudice* variation, a despondent Darcy travels to Paris in the hopes of forgetting the disastrous proposal at Hunsford. Paris is teeming with English visitors during a brief moment of peace in the Napoleonic Wars, but Darcy's spirits don't lift until he attends a ball and unexpectedly encounters…Elizabeth Bennet! Darcy seizes the opportunity to correct misunderstandings and initiate a courtship.

Their moment of peace is interrupted by the news that England has again declared war on France, and hundreds of English travelers must flee Paris immediately. Circumstances force Darcy and Elizabeth to escape on their own, despite the risk to her reputation. Even as they face dangers from street gangs and French soldiers, romantic feelings blossom during their flight to the coast. But then Elizabeth falls ill, and the French are arresting all the English men they can find….

When Elizabeth and Darcy finally return to England,
their relationship has changed, and they face new crises.
However, they have secrets they must conceal—even
from their own families.